Melissa Green's Status: Single

April Gutierrez

This is a fictional work. The names, characters, incidents, places, and locations are solely the concept and products of the author's imagination or are used to create a fictitious story and should not be construed as real.

Author Website:
www.aprilgutierrez.com

Editing by: Karen Venancio of Brooksville, FL
Contact: KVee014@gmail.com

Cover and Author Photograph:

Ailyn La Torre
PHOTOGRAPHY
www.ailynlatorrephotography.com

ISBN: 0692236244
ISBN-13: 978-0692236246

DEDICATION

To my mother, Ana,
whom I love so much.

ACKNOWLEDGMENTS

I would like to first thank Karen Venancio for all of your continued support and help in getting each of these blog posts up and out.

I would also like to thank the readers who made each week exciting. Your comments were wonderful and an encouragement to keep writing.

April Gutierrez

CONTENTS

April Gutierrez

SEASON 1

Monday, April 8, 2013
Melodramatic Much?

I will start by saying that in the pit of my alcohol-filled stomach I know tomorrow is another day and that tonight's events will not hinder the sun from rising. Melodramatic much? Maybe just a little, but a girl can only cause herself so much embarrassment before her single status becomes a permanent label.

Tonight was thanks to one of my bffs, Ivy (Thanks if you read this). She invited us girls (Amy, Dana, and myself) to one of the events she had been planning with her P.R. company, Sparkles. As per usual, the promotions company sent over 3 incredible gowns to show off in front of as many reporters and cameras as we could get our face centered in. I was honored with a backless royal blue knee-length Marc-Jacobs while Amy lucked out in a red De La Renta. To my surprise, it was Dana that had me watching quietly as I found her awe-struck at her reflection, while she softly handled the crisp edges of her conservative white Vera Wang suit. My mind wondered in those few seconds what she could possibly be thinking of herself, but then again I am always left wondering what

1

Dana is thinking being that she only really comments and passes judgments on others. Never herself ;)

When she caught me staring she smiled and deflected the attention by complimenting how Pilates must be working for me. I didn't have the heart to tell her that I quit Pilates when I realized how much work actually went in to exercise. Yes, you will find that out of all things - sweating for anything other than, well...you know... isn't really my thing.

Ready to leave, Amy rushed into my kitchen and resurfaced with a bottle of champagne in hand for the limo ride. First thought: Glasses? Then again, who needs glasses when in a limo with your best friends in the fit of fun, at least not when your intentions are to wash down any reminiscence of a horrible relationship-less week. Needless to say, between traffic and big city chaos we finished the champagne before we got to the Red-Carpet. Amy (my Model bff) thrived for the mayhem of flashing cameras and nosy reporters. She also doesn't have a bad side to any photograph taken of her. Dana and I locked arms and followed Amy sheepishly, only occasionally stumbling over our own stilettos. Luckily the crowd was so loud walking in; no one was really focused on our giggling and carefree laughter.

Once inside the event, we immediately paused in amazement and welled up with pride for our best friend. Ivy had busted her (arse) tush to get this event lime lighted and it was obvious by the star-studded attendance that she pulled it off. She ran over to where we stood and hugged us all in excitement. Her suggestions and expected rounds flew out of her mouth a mile a minute. Sadly the bubbly from the earlier limo ride had me at her screeching, 'Hello'. The moment she got called away, we laughed it off and made it to an empty table near the front of the room.

Amy refused to hide and decided that she would make a round, find some guys and bring them back to the table with her -YES-girls do this too...I am just not interested in Amy's taste in men anymore. Dana looked fidgety until a handsome suit sat next to her. His ruse was that he was being followed, and while that would typically offend most women, lucky for the suit was that she's one of a kind. She even laughed at his charm, not that I thought him charming a bit.

The more I waited for a walking server to come by, the less likely it felt I was getting any more bubbly for the night. Amy came back, both arms adorned with pretty guys and Ivy appeared on stage and started to welcome everyone to the event. She had my full attention for as long as it took her to introduce the new music group for which the event was being held. The moment the music started blaring from the speakers I excused myself from the group with a feeling of needing to escape.

Sadly it was and always will be my lack of patience that has me stumbling into the arms of Gods. Only a few steps away from the back bar and I miss-stepped, fumbling like a clumsy fool. His arms reached out and saved me from mass embarrassment.

HOWEVER! This is all depending on if you have a hierarchy of embarrassment. If you are like me, there are many levels in which things can be embarrassing and their severity. Wretchedly, this particular man MAXed me out in levels of embarrassment only little puny high-school boys have ever sunk to. Steadying my legs, with his arms firmly around my waist I lifted my cobalt blue eyes to see it was none other than Brent Bishop - New York's most eligible bachelor socialite, grinning in amusement.

He could have said anything, anything indeed, to put the nail in my coffin but no, he smiled as no man should ever be allowed to smile at a woman and quoted poetry, "The night was washed in desire, as she fell into my arms." The words by poet-Dee faded as he said them and all I could focus on for those brief moments were his incredible hazel green eyes peering into mine. Mind you his voice has a sexual drive dripping in liquid gold. If only men could market his appeal. Finally he let go of my waist, which was right about when I found the words to say thank you. See this is right about the time I would shove my foot firmly in my mouth and ruin any chance of getting to know this charming man, and I would have done so had Ivy not come prancing to my rescue. Surely she knew I'd need saving from utterly devastating embarrassment but in this case she only made things worse. And of course, in my case that is always possible. After a proper introduction where he now knows me as copy-editor Melissa, they had a boisterous laugh about my long standing clumsiness.

What is it about Humor that makes a man more handsome? Is it because his face becomes less seductive and wanting and more readable and soft? I can't say for certain but I could swear that before he and Ivy started laughing it up, his expression was easily comparable to that of a hungry lion hunting his prey. In this case I was that cunning fragile prey. Within moments I felt forgotten enough to split from them and high tail it back to Dana and Amy. Hiding out to watch the rest of the show felt safe enough. Amy saw to it that the champagne kept coming and Dana never once gave me a scowling glare as to why I had almost altogether shut my mouth.

And as a cold breeze sweeps in to say goodbye, Brent Bishop appeared out of nowhere and sat next to me for as brief a moment as it took for him to hand me a folded napkin and kiss me softly on the cheek. In shock we all watched as his mischievous looking self got lost in the crowd as he left our table.

Why is it that we can so easily let someone walk away from us when all we really want to do is 'talk' the night away with them?

Reader comments:

Anonymous   April 10, 2013   Fear stops us from getting up. A coward is very rarely the one to be with who they wanted to be with... they settle. Sorry sista, grow some!

Anonymous   April 10, 2013
Just because you don't follow someone doesn't make you a coward and definitely doesn't mean you settle for another. Some people move at a slower more modest pace!

Anonymous April 10, 2013

I believe people are afraid to be rejected. If we let them walk away, that rejection won't happen. Maybe if we meet again....

Friday, April 12, 2013
Coward be Damned!

Sweaty palms, knotted stomach, but most of all – over analytical brain! This is what being handed a folded little white napkin with THE MOST valuable phone number scribbled on it does to a single female. The night of Ivy's event ended up in a drunken blur. Dana, my more responsible friend, made it a point to call at the crack of dawn the following morning; Just to wake me up. (And Piss my Hung-over self off)

"You slurred nonsense about being a klutz all over Mr. NY. Not when the music was playing Melissa, you broke silence in the crowd!" she scolded on and on about how red she turned while all I could do was giggle in the corner.

I can't recall the event, or even the morning after without cringing in shame. Not only because I have a loud mouth when I'm tipsy, no - more so because even in that silly frame of mind I managed to get the number of the one guy all the girls were crushing on all over in New York City.

So there I sat 2 days later, still staring at the napkin contemplating the action I would take. And don't start with all this 'Coward' crap that I'd heard earlier this week. I didn't run after him the night of the event because quite frankly I was wearing the type of shoes No woman should try sprinting in. Not to mention my track record for walking in a straight line while under the influence of yummy bubbly. It just aint going to happen, Sista. While earlier this week I was wondering why it is we find ourselves 'wanting' to follow that particular interest, honestly, had I followed him – wouldn't that action itself make me look desperate??? I mean, I don't know him from Adam. He may be in the public eye and all, but having money means you can avoid certain things from coming out to the public. Fine, maybe I'm being paranoid; but who is to say that he isn't some sort of creep that has been out to silence all the women he's been with, hmmmm, by signing confidentiality agreements. It's not far-fetched and you know it!

Anyhow, so there I was waiting for the answer to bite me in the arse when Amy called for a lunch distraction. A.D.D. at its best! Of course, all she really wanted was a sounding board for her newest issue of over-share with Fernando- her Wednesday-Buddy. Apparently, he hasn't gotten use to the idea that there are some women on this planet that don't want, nor need a conventional relationship. Amy is such the type-she likes having one here, one there- it's all the same to her. She also has this horrible habit of over-sharing Everything!

 "He had the nerve to make a face at me like a nerdy little child when I told him he had to leave because I had to take a dump.", yet another thing poor Fernando isn't accustomed to. Beautiful face with very little couth! Sadly it's looking like her odd lifestyle will end another potential warm body on her weekly calendar. ~shakes head~

Later that afternoon Dana stopped by to drop off a purse she had borrowed a few weeks ago. I love it when she's around but mostly because I get to be the Amy in the relationship. Dana listens to my madness and while I know she has her own opinions, she only tells me what I really need to hear. She doesn't agree with the comment from the other day about my being a coward…

"You may be slow to start, but I'm sure eventually you will find the, *achem*, Balls needed to call Brent. He is just another man, sweetie."

She was right about 'Growing Some', I always do! Sweaty palms and shaky voice and all, I called our Mr. NY. Incredibly my nerves ironed themselves out within moments of his saying hello. I didn't take offense to his kidding around about my klutzy nature. Ivy had made it a point to divulge more information than necessary, which I still need to repay in some excruciating way.

"So why did it take you so long to call me back?" he asked, the evident smile on his face beaming through the phone.   *He doesn't realize what he's getting himself into* – a voice in my head seems to mock.

"I had to remember which face it was that came and went so quickly by that point in the evening." I countered, with an equally extended smile on my face.

The laugh that followed seemed like an unlocking of a new secret compartment of the conversation, as if saying, 'Well done little lady, let's get on to round 2 why don't we.' What kept me on my toes was how he would ask a question and clearly bounce back to it when he realized I never answered the question to begin with. My natural instinct to deflect personal questions apparently pushes a few of his buttons....FUN! What sent me over the limit was the one question you always get asked in those first 20 queries us single folk work through to weed out the hooligans...

"So why are you still single?" he asked, but this time I couldn't tell if he was being lighthearted about it or if this was the make-it or break-it answer he was working on.

In that fraction of a lifetime, where my cheeks burst into flaming shades of red and the miniscule hairs on my upper lip beaded with a fine line of moisture from a stress I had neither conjured nor provoked, the response was already firing out of my rose colored lips before my adult brain could yell, 'Wait!'.

"I haven't met a man worthy enough yet to fight with everyday." Once the words were out, my eyes shut firmly and the heart in my chest pounded in mortification. Lord only knows I am not the arguing type, and so much more like the 'whatever you want, just shush up already' type.

It was his heavy chuckle that prevented me from seeing red and wanting to change my name.

Not being the type of girl to play games, I jumped.....COWARD BE DAMNED!!! I asked him out for coffee this coming Sunday, which would seem weird to a lot of people, but actually it's the best time of week to meet up for coffee if you know where to go.

It didn't feel awkward after that, and when his voice went down a few octaves as he almost whispered the words, 'goodbye' the giddy school girl inside me jumped for joy. Staring at the phone receiver, I did have a moment of imaginative fun, daydreaming about how our run in would occur, but let's keep this clean shall we ;)

Now the only problem I have to worry about is my deflection issue. It's not that I want to remain a mystery to every man I meet. I just don't know what is actually necessary to disclose all at once. It should be written in a handbook somewhere...1. If you want to go into a relationship honestly you must disclose this, this, this.... Please be advised that if you do not share x, y, and z but he later finds out- Shame on you, you deserve to be single!

What is it men Don't want to hear about when working through the 20 questions part of getting to know one another? And what is completely necessary?

Reader Comments:

Anonymous   April 13, 2013
They dont want to hear about your last boyfriend, what a dick he was, or why you are no longer with him.

Anonymous   April 13, 2013
I don't think they want to hear about your ex-boyfriends and how crappy they treated you, or that they cheated on you, etc. Also, they really don't want to hear about all your problems either. That's a good way to say bye bye to a guy real fast. He'll think "WOW" what a complainer, I'll never be able to make her happy. I think they like to hear light-hearted stuff like what you do as a career, do you have/like animals, favorite colors. Easy stuff like that! Maybe just keep answers simple and not too detailed. Leave a little mystery in the relationship. It could be a good thing to keep them wondering a little....

~ALF~

Anonymous   April 14, 2013

Depends on what type of "getting to know you" he is looking for. If he's looking for a long term relationship, he would want to know about your likes and dislikes, your family, where you grew up and anything to make it more personal. BUT, if he's only looking for a "hi there" kind of relationship, then he really only wants to know your name, if your single/available, if your "into" him (if you know what I mean) and are you ready, willing and able? ;)

Tuesday, April 16, 2013
Kryptonite!

'A woman of immediate action', that would be a phrase I would use to describe myself at any given moment. Now in the silence of my own room- I can think, contemplate a logical response to a question as simple as, "In a few words, how would you describe yourself?" and within seconds, the answer is shooting off and I am filled with an undeniable confidence by what I truly mean.

Go Figure! A 5 word statement that expresses not only my impatience but also my ability to think and make decisions in a short matter of time, while still keeping my well paid educated mind intact. BUT, the one new kryptonite to this assertive statement has merely been discovered. Insert Brent Bishop into the scenario and you inadvertently change the way my brain makes connections. I become oblivious that I can know mundane things and it's as if I am living in Los Angeles spending most of my days interested in the color of my tan. Seriously, around him I've lost my IQ.

I took the time to read your comments from the other day and let me say, THANKS!! For some reason I hadn't really thought about the whole date process as a system, it's always been a, 'Fly by the seat of your pants kinda thing'. Which is fine, except for the fact my success rate has never shot past zero!

Being that Ivy had been the one and Only to stack my insecurities high to the ceiling in regards to Brent, I made sure she and I would spend some time together Saturday so she could give me the 'low down' on our Mr. NY. To be utterly honest, she still owes me for adding to my embarrassment all together from that night at the event.

"I don't see why you are all upset. His reputation for being flaky is what I've been trying to spare you from." She started innocently. It was the way she avoided eye contact with me while talking about him that concerned me. Made me feel like high school. It's not like I'm trying to steal the guy she is interested in away from her.

The tug of war on information had me wondering if maybe she didn't want me to get to know Brent better because she secretly had a thing for him herself. So when I flat out asked her, she denied it saying I was being absurd. Brent was not her type.

Tread on thin Ice with that confession! –a voice in my head seemed to warn.

'He is old money, Melissa, and doesn't really go into family matters with the public. He has been working for his Uncle, Clive for about 10 years now... Of all the girls he has been linked to, only 1 has actually struck a chord and that is Megan Moore. While the name sounded familiar, I wasn't sure where I knew it from. NY Hazard I suppose!

Anyhow, Saturday night felt endless. I kept playing absurd scenarios in my head, over and over until finally one of them must have put me to sleep. Sadly, I am not an alarm type of gal...Yes, as you can imagine I woke up in Shock to see the sun blaring brightly on my face. What are the chances of being late to a first date when one of your Biggest annoyances in Life is Late people? Who believes that on a first date anyway? No One! Not me at least.

I rushed, and in doing so realized that Brent would meet the real person behind all the paZam. I've always been one to describe myself as medium pretty. That is unless I have a makeup artist on hand, and then I am Gorgeous ;) But in this case, on a Sunday morning after a night of hardly any sleep at all, I would say that he was lucky to find me with lip gloss on my lips. Honestly, I know about men and their visual needs...First impressions are purely based on the visual aspect which peek a man's interest. Sunday morning was not a first impression in my mind. No, that was the night of the event when I stumbled into his arms and apparently won the lottery in the intrigue department. All I really had to do was to watch that my mouth didn't match the typical action my feet take. I had to make damn certain I didn't have a 'diarrhea of the mouth' moment.

Arriving a few minutes late, I found him sitting in the back of Starbucks reading a book. By the time the door shut behind me, he was looking up, smiling and standing to meet me as I walked over. Slowly the steps my feet made felt heavier than normal. Was my body telling me something I couldn't figure out on my own? Was he someone I shouldn't sit too close to? Surely my Brain would think logically in the event my heart was struck with a bout of unmentionable…Nope! Brain turned to shit.

Hind sight is 20/20, isn't that what they say when you have an 'Ah-ha' moment much after going through something out of the ordinary. Yes, I dare say that I should have known better, Damn-it! Kryptonite Indeed!

At any rate, he immediately proved to be a gentleman, asking me what my caffeine intake of choice was so that he could stand in line to grab it for me. Hmmm. Occasionally he would look over and muse with an adorable soft smile. I took that particular moment to size him up…he looked tired, as did I. He was dressed comfortable, like he too just woke up and rushed over. He had to be over 6 foot, being that he was taller than my 5'9'' build. He seemed the type to exercise, but I would only say that because he isn't carrying any extra weight around his waist. While checking him out, the oddest sensation came over me. He almost seemed noticeably giddy.

Do Men Get Giddy?!?! The longer I watched him in that line, the more I noticed the way his body moved, specifically shifting from left to right but with an almost invisible bounce.
HA! It was great! Men do get Giddy…and for Me no less.

The moment he sat down and we leveled the playing field, none of the baggage in my imaginary meeting fit. Our conversation was very much like a tennis match, the points Only going to those who successfully answered a question at hand or managed to change the topic of questioning all together. It never once felt forced. By the time we got to the 'nitty-gritty', we had begun to laugh at the 20-question version about getting to know one another. He challenged me to ask something out of the ordinary. *Like asking a mouse to 'Lick' the cheese and not Bite!*

"What is your biggest pet peeve?" I asked, wanting to know more than anything else really. It was not a typical question you get all the time, but still something easy enough for him to fire back quickly.

"I can't stand negative people." He said firmly. I was glad it wasn't something absurd, or something I was a guiltier of. Oddly enough, the response changed his demeanor but he bounced back with an equally interesting question.

'Worst bad habit? My brain shut down...not because I was embarrassed, but probably because I wouldn't want to admit anything wrong with myself. My silence prompted a chuckle which in turn had me shaking my head. ...Blank...The worst of all my bad habits, goodness, what could that be?

'I don't know... I bite my bottom lip when I'm nervous... I don't know what the worst is." I stammered still thinking of something worth admitting.

'Come on, there has to be something more than a little cute lip-biting.' He urged.

Shaking my head I said the one thing I probably shouldn't have. "Sometimes I waste time imagining how a situation should have gone.''

The instant it was out, I hid my face in the palms of my hands and laughed. He tried to make me feel better by saying that he too spent time doing the same exact thing, but I highly doubt his imagination is as keen as my own. I mean, seriously, I had us in all different positions by the time our cups were empty. O_o

Out of all the questions he asked me, the oddest was one of his last ones. 'What is your favorite novel of all time?" It didn't seem like a bullshit question either, but if you know me at all, I tend to call out bullshit when I hear it. There is a Bad Habit for Ya!

"Why would you want to know my favorite novel?" This was when, had I been standing, the wicked grin he produced would have weakened my knees. I'd been staring at him for at least an hour by that point and felt almost immune to the charm he'd created with merely the gleam in his eye, but add this particular smile into the mix and KABOOM- I was done for!

"Just play along." He urged

"Fine" I shout out playfully, "Pride and Prejudice, by Jane Austin." I never had to think about that one, I'd always known it was my favorite above all others since the age of 17 when Mandy Hollacer gave it to me for my birthday.

His grin became a wild smile and his head began to nod as if agreeing that he got the right answer. Only issue was, he hadn't been asked a question, I had. Asking him what I had missed produced the 1 reply that still has me wondering.

"You can tell what type of relationship a woman wants by knowing the title of her favorite novel."

Really?!?! Is that so! Men Actually Contemplate This Sort of Thing! *Where the hell have I been?!?!*

So there I sat, thinking, awe-struck by his comment when in walked a buddy of his. (Probably prescheduled) The guy intruded in on our coffee time and the annoyance pushed me to a high I hadn't expected. *It wasn't like we planned on spending the rest of the day with each other.

Not that I wouldn't have had he asked.

There is an Idea for ya!

I didn't think. I excused myself, saying that it was **okay** he catch up with his buddy, 'Phil from Brooklyn'. So a mixture of his buddy, and that last question, alongside with being easily annoyed by the interruption, I left a perfectly good date.

YES! The damn Pride and Prejudice connection wobbled my confidence. Does it matter that a woman wants Romance? I mean, that crazy awe-inspiring love that only happens once in a lifetime…Don't men Ever want that? I'm just as horny as the next guy, Believe Me, but I've waited all this time to give my forever to someone, shouldn't I want that? To have my very own Mr. Darcy-Diamond in the rough type of guy only I would be able to understand?

Readers Comments:

Anonymous   April 17, 2013
Sure you should want to have a man like that, but dont expect prince charming to live up to every expectation. He is bound to ruin it somehow with how their brains work.

Anonymous   April 17, 2013
First of all, let me say, that I don't believe men think of Romance the same way as us women. But I think there is a difference between being romantic and romance. Secondly, there is nothing wrong with waiting to give your forever to that someone special or wanting the awe-inspiring love that only happens once in a life time, as long as your image of that is realistic. You can't believe in complete "happily ever after" as in the Disney fairytales because that is fantasy. In real life, even the truest love has its ups and downs but it can also be awe-inspiring if it's with the right person.
~ALF~

Anonymous   April 18, 2013
You can want whatever, but The fact is men are only interested in F.B.B. Face Boobs, and Butt. It's all wa wa wa until you agree to get nekked, then they do anything for you to stop talking altogether. Good luck with that though.

Anonymous   April 18, 2013

Not ALL men are only interested in F.B.B. as you say. I'm not saying looks don't play a big role in dating but some men actually do care about the woman inside. And as for getting Nekked, who doesn't want that but we don't stay "pretty" forever so there better be more to your relationship than FBB's and nekkedness!

Anonymous   April 18, 2013

I say take a poll on the F.B.B. You'll be surprised at what you find!

Friday, April 19, 2013
Meaningful Silence

Often, times in the life of a single person is as repetitive as a record stuck on replay. The same song and dance becomes a day-in and day-out routine. Even our spontaneity tends to be predictable. While I'm not saying life in general is boring or uneventful, I'm admitting that in the grander scheme of things it takes two to dance. Pairs make the world spin in a fashion, finding ways to create moments that at the end of the day take our breath away.

My status on social media sites has been, 'Single' for 4 years, 6 months, and 28 days. In this (alone) time I have gotten to know the real Melissa Green. Not the me that had once given *Everything* up to be with a douche-baggery type of man. See the /Face, Boobs, and Butt/ theory applied to him- I'm not sure a poll would make any difference- while there is always an exception to the male gene pool, fact is I agree with that reader's comment to some extent. Men Are Visual- they are going to be attracted first to what they SEE before they ask you anything at all.

Now, now- don't get your panties in a bunch –I'm not going to rant about shit men and why I broke up with my ex. I won't even go into what a horrible person he turned out to be. I will however, admit that back then I didn't know any better. I thought I was in **Love**, and that phrase we use to excuse our actions, 'love blinds us', well in my case – it was true. Being young and in love is worse than being Old and naïve. At least when you're older, you have seen and experienced much more- you tend to see all signs more clearly.

One of the first things I learned in this span of <u>Single Reality</u> was who my REAL friends are. Have you ever noticed that when you are in a relationship, most of your friends or the people you hang out with are Also in relationships? Couples are like magnets for other couples, the 'Oooohhhh, Lets double date.' phrase constantly getting thrown around like hot-potatoes. Once a break-up occurs it's like banishment from a secret cult, you never see or hear from them again. Single friends are always around, even if they are secretly cursing you for your happiness behind your back.

Dana, Amy, and Ivy have been my rocks all these years. They have helped me make the 'almost' relationships seems like seasons that are meant to change. But who are we kidding, eventually I will be IN a season, and while I want to be in a relationship- it is which Particular season in question I don't want to feel (Stuck) in.

When I hadn't heard from my 'Mr. NY- Brent after a few days, I wondered if Sunday was the last time I would ever see him again. With the news blaring about the 'Boston Marathon' tragedy, I used it as an excuse to call and touch base Wednesday afternoon. Seeing as how he had mentioned being a runner, it would be reasonable to call. His phone rang straight to voice mail. My message short and sweet –

'It's Melissa, just wanted to say hi and see how you were.

At our weekly *Girl's-Only* lunch yesterday, Amy had to be the one to ask about Brent. She was mightily impressed that I had gotten his number and an actual date considering apparently I am Not his type.

Which by the way is CRAP! Having a 'Type' is like saying you are going to the grocery store to pick out the person you want to spend the rest of your life with. As if there is such a person as being our 'Type' all bundled up in one nice little package. Are you KIDDING me?!?! Such a thing in the real world now a day's can't possibly exist.

*We may be starting to understand why the status is still blinking: **Single**.*

Luckily Dana disagreed with Amy's thought process. Not to pounce on Amy or anything but sometimes I wonder if the hair dye hasn't burnt a few cells.

"You can't assume Melissa isn't Brent's type. He may be rich and handsome, yeah fine, but what makes you think he would only want beauty?" she sassed to Amy innocently, I could see the fire in her eyes however. Dana may be all calm, cool, and collect all the time, but it's the look in her eyes that people tend to miss. She secretly disliked Amy's ability to walk in a room filled with men and leave with her pick of any she desired. Only to later discard them like a candy wrapper.

"No offense to you Melissa," Amy started again, "but Dana, think about it...Brent is from a different social group than us. He is high society. We are talking about upper-east-siders that do galas and charity events twice a week. They spend money like it's meant to magically reappear. And Guess what- For Them, It Does!" her obvious fluster had us all chuckling.

"I keep telling you, the man is a flake," Ivy chimed in. "His track record sucks, and he is basically married to his career. His uncle is all but letting him run that conglomerate. You'd be better off not even bothering. Not that I wouldn't Love to have my bff on the inside of that social calendar and clientele, but I don't want to see you hurt." Ivy's buzzing had me thinking.

Why hadn't he called? Is he really married to his company??

See, this is where women and men are complete opposites. I like a picture painted for me. If you are not interested, flipping Tell me – Flat Out! I can deal with it, but by golly don't leave me wondering. That would drive anyone into a crazy frenzy of attempted communication. Single folk get crap all the time, Especially women, about being crazy and clingy- but when you put a fine tooth comb behind their actions – Men, you are at fault for not being clear from the get go. *If all you want is a booty call- Be Specific...* Otherwise stop all your Wa, Wa, Wa complaining!

After our lunch I stared at the phone on my desk...actually picked it up and almost called. I opened my laptop and eyeballed my email screen as well. It was the blaring sirens inside my mind which halted me every time from making contact.

There must be some logical reason he hadn't made the call, but at the time my insecurities about not being 'good enough' were louder than any Rational thought (Thanks Ivy o_O).

Do MEN go through this same insecurity, or is that strictly a FEMALE thing???

Ultimately, I turned out to be the bigger fool. This morning he called before I woke up, which must be a lovely sound to hear the 'you woke me up' attitude when you are calling a potential interest first thing in the morning…I wouldn't know – I don't make phone calls before 9am!

"You must not be a 'Rise and Shine' type of gal." He chuckled, sounding chipper as ever.

Damn him to Hell, I can't even be angry with him, can I?!

"I am when the occasion calls for it." I couldn't help but smile through the cracking voice and still shut eyes.

"I haven't been ignoring you…." He sighed before adding, "I mean, when Phil showed up Sunday I didn't want you to leave…and then life threw 1 thing on top of another on my plate after that."

"You don't need to explain, Brent." I stopped him.

The tone in his voice had opened my eyes. This was what sincerity from a Man sounded like. It was sad, and so very Real.

"I want to. I need you to understand." He began. "I had asked Phil to come by the coffee shop that morning as my wing man, but you were not supposed to leave. I had planned on calling you Monday but I got a phone call from my sister in MA saying that my brother had been hurt at the race. Even though my relationship is difficult with my family, I had to go make sure everything was going to be fine. By the time I got your message I realized what I had forgotten to do. None of what he said made him sound anything like Ivy was making him out to be – Not a flake at least.

21

So I wondered if it made any difference, can two people from different world co-exist in one happy medium, or were we really so different from each other to begin with that I'm just setting myself up for heartbreak?

"Please tell me you didn't fall back asleep" he mused

"No, I was giving you a dose of meaningful silence." I giggled innocently to lighten the mood. "How is your brother now?" I wondered. For a man who is so dedicated to work – his family still factored in being that the ordeal took him away from the city altogether. This was wonderful news in my book.

"He's fine, at home resting now. The whole situation has everyone frazzled. I doubt he has gotten a good night sleep since, I know I haven't." he admitted, before adding, "Hey listen… would you like to be my plus 1 to a charity event tomorrow night?"

I didn't remotely hesitate. My brain didn't have to think!

Of Course, I would Love to be your date." I've always wondered it if was the over enthusiasm about spending time together which makes us look desperate?

Whatever! I have a date with him tomorrow night. So little Copy-editor Melissa Green is going to a black-tie charity event with 'Mr. NY' himself. Thank goodness it's no longer April Fools week- otherwise I would seriously be waiting for the punch-line to come chiming in.

What do they say about being on cloud nine? *It's the Fall you have to watch out for!*

So we have a date scheduled. Also, Ivy is working the event which means I will get to SEE the girls but stay arm locked with the most gorgeous man in NY all night long. Oh, la la! Maybe ready, willing, and able will apply!

Readers Comments:

Anonymous   April 21, 2013
New Yorkers get a bad rap all the time, but your friends have a point. If you are not from that high society world, you will not fit in. The women are worse than wolves, and very rarely do they give a new outsider the benefit of the doubt that your guy picked you for any other reason than what's between your legs. Hope you had fun at your party last night.

Tuesday, April 23, 2013
Your Match!

Hazard of Single life #101 – The disturbing alarm your body goes through upon waking in a strange bed.

I am a sucker for fruity drinks- this is all I will say on the drinking matter. I am not a lush! Let's be clear about this from the get-go. It is socially acceptable to throw a few back with the girls from time to time, but fact is – I make it less frequently to the 'binge arena' than most blue collar folks do. Let me take You to a party, after 8 hours of correcting the grammar issues of an overzealous writer, and then You tell me what you'll be drinking. Water my Arse! The more colorful the better!!

Anyhew! Saturday was Fan-freaking-tastic! Although I hadn't attended the charity event as Ivy's guest, she made sure I was still in on the Usual pre-Styling fun. She came over that morning before Dana and Amy arrived, which allowed us to catch up and chat. The eye opener was on me.

She laid a bombshell confession out on the table and it was up to me to put on the BFF hat.

"Missy- John at work asked me out." She started her nerves jumbling as she spoke. "He has such a bad reputation for whoring around though. Should I blow him off?" Immediately the coffee I'd just sipped went squirting out all over the kitchen table. Fine! I realized what she meant and how it was innocent enough but OMG, IVY knows how my mind works!

After apologizing, and doing a quick wipe down through a chuckle, I finally asked the one question we find ourselves thinking about when confronted with a 'John'… *Does a reputation ever become old?* Eventually people change, and while this 'John' had a knack for wetting and bedding – does it mean he will ever be anything different? And quite frankly – would that stop you from getting to know someone to begin with?

I guess you don't know until you try. At least when someone has a 'reputation', it's like a Common Knowledge domain. Can't play the fool if you knew he was a dirtball from the beginning, can you.

"Ivy, the bigger question you might want to ask yourself is if you want to try him on, or try him out?" Not every girl wants a relationship with Every man she meets. The guy who labeled women in that manner should be arrested for defamation of the female species. Ivy was just as promiscuous as Amy but she likes to play the 'demur-one' being that she is professional, where as Amy is a carefree spirit and flows from dance to dance.

Meanwhile, Dana called that she was running late. Her excuse was that the doorman assured her a Fed-Ex package would be arriving by a specific time. She'd been waiting for 2 days, and wasn't going to miss it again. Curiosity got the better of me when I asked if this wasn't the same doorman she kissed at midnight on New Years. – A Ha!- her silence whirled a beautiful mental romance between the poor doorman, and little Miss Park Avenue. Knowing Dana, I would be hearing about it soon enough.

Amy came crashing in with a ridiculous story about Tobey, her Friday-Buddy, and how he went through her cell phone in a jealous rage looking for the names of all the other men she was currently seeing. Sadly, he found Thousands of phone numbers that belonged to the penis society. "I kid you not, I have never seen a man so preposterously upset. His hands were waving, his face got all red and sweaty. Oh My God, and I about gagged a few times as spit flew towards me from how he was stumbling over his words." She fanned her chest, swallowing back disgust. "The whole time I kept asking myself, Why I wanted him for Fridays, but when I couldn't come up with a response I told him it was time for him leave. He is crazy, I'm telling you!"

I didn't have the heart to tell her it was her own fault for creating such a monster. Not all men want the same thing, just as not all women want a relationship. Even the single most misleading statement will eventually push a person over the edge. Poor Tobey had reached such an edge and was pushed over it while all Amy could do was gag on his emotions.

"You need to be careful Amy," Ivy warned her, "One day you are not going to be so lucky. And it may be your heart someone is breaking, and not the other way around." Her concern was meant more to remind Amy of the past and how she knew all too well about heartbreak and the effect it has on us.

Heart break ultimately changes us.

The smile that propped up on Amy's face clued us in that a subject change was about to come Blurting out of her rosy red lips.

"Missy, Missy, Missy, you prepared for tonight?? Got your foil packs stuffed in your little black Dolce'?? Or are you going to shove them in your bra straps this time?? Her silliness caused us to laugh. My head shook but it was sad how well she knew me.
 Prime suspect was the Dolce' ;)

It was almost 6 o'clock by the time Dana came rushing in. Flustered and rosy cheeks, my imagination scurried wildly! What had she been doing?!?! Unfortunately for us, it was 'Mum's the word' on the details of her delay. If in fact she was harboring some sort of lovely secret regarding a guy, I would totally understand her. While I sat there and listened to the girls talk about their romantic mayhem, or excitement, I was brewing with my own anticipation. Deep down I wonder, 'Who am I kidding?' – It can't last a life time. Only in fairytales does the girl actually win over the Prince and live happily ever after.

So there I stood, moments before Brent would ring the building, staring at my reflection in the full length mirror and laughed at the idea of all the women at the party being wolves in sheep's clothing. High NY society does get a bad rap, don't they…and I wish more of you readers would state your name as opposed to commenting anonymously.

Needless to say, it was while I sat in the back of his sleek stretch limo that it occurred to me how the only person I needed to concern myself with about being a wolf in sheep's clothing was the gorgeous man sitting beside me. Successful, educated, and supremely equipped with charm, I was climbing a steep hill unarmed. My only shield – a BS-o-meter –currently sits out-of-order due to some kryptonite matter.

"You seem a little flustered." He said as his eyes focused firmly on my mouth.

"Not flustered, merely apprehensive. I don't often frequent galas and charity events." I offered still firmly watching as his eyes roamed from my lips to my neck, and back to my lips again.

"Yes, well, you are not missing much. At least tonight we will keep each other preoccupied." This time it was how his lips broke and his face changed which released a massive flutter of imaginary butterflies' though-out my midsection.

How can one person create such an incredible reaction within us by doing something unbelievably minute?

I bit my lower lip in attempt to control the intense response but remarkably it sent him leaning over and pulling me towards his body. Our mouths firmly pressed against each other, and my mind went blank. There in the back seat of his limo, I proved ready, willing, and able were the only three words he needed to know anything about. And when he realized that no part of me felt like stopping him, he asked the driver to make a few turns around the block and the middle window was quickly rolled up.

Have you ever driven around the Upper East Side in a private limo? Tinted sound proof windows, cushion seats, plush flooring. The word 'Scalding' isn't hot enough for the limit we reached. You know you've found a right fit when Everything he does, every movement he makes creates a blur in your reasoning. Exhilarating and fun, we created a memory I would never forget, especially when he found my red lacy panties shoved in the pocket of his tux.

"I would let you have those as a souvenir but I'm rather fond of them at the moment." I giggled, taking them from his grasp.

His hand went straight up to his heart. "And here I thought you would give me something to remember you by." He baited tactfully. Curious, was that his way of saying he was a limited-time dater?

"You don't need to remember something you have often." The statement came out before I had a chance to contemplate what I meant. *Thinking- a Valuable commodity in single life* -By which time was too late to take it back. "Really?" he mused, "Often sounds inviting." He smiled, reaching out for me again. This time I leaned back in opposition.

"You made a promise to attend this event, Brent. Wouldn't they be disappointed if you didn't show up?" I asked, the mature responsible Melissa rearing her unpopular face.

His head slumped down as he took a deep breath. I realized it was his, 'What I want to do **vs**. What I should do' reaction.

"I'm sorry" I quickly added reaching out to touch his arm. "Don't get me wrong, I would love nothing more than to go around the block a few more times…"

He looked up at me, wanting my words to stop altogether. "You're right." He threw a soft fake smile, picked up the phone and asked the driver to take us to the Plaza. I could hear the lining of disappointment in his words.

"You look beautiful tonight, by the way." he complimented.

Fine, I will be honest and admit that it threw me off guard. It's not because I've never been complimented before, it's because of how he had said it. He used the statement to change the subject while using me as a buffer topic. This is what I do when I want someone to think of something other than what's being discussed, using their vanity to change the subject.

So it seems I have met my Match. After that statement, the night flew by. Other than to disappear in the ladies room for a few minutes of gossip with the girls, I was locked arm and counting down the minutes for him to say it was time to leave.

The following morning, I woke in a very bright penthouse master bedroom. It was Past 9AM, and he had been watching me sleep.

Or in his words, 'Waiting for you to wake your Arse up so we can spend the day together.'

I haven't stopped smiling yet.

So what do you do when you finally meet your match?? Do you -
    *A: Go with it, **B:** Challenge your opponent, or **C:** Change your tact altogether*

Readers Comments:

> **Anonymous**   April 24, 2013
> I say, B: Challenge your opponent. There's nothing like a good challenge to get the "fires and desires" heated up!!! ;)
>
> ~ALF~

Friday, April 26, 2013
What Had I Done?!

Have you ever woken up in the morning with the sun shining
brightly on your face and felt like something Important was going
to happen to you that day? That type of feeling that seems to have
come from a dream you'd completely forgotten, but the notion
lingers at your core that everything was right in the world. – That
has been me these past few days. And even when I worried I'd
made a mistake, somehow buried deep within I had this blind faith
that everything would work itself out.

Who Knew!

Sunday I spent my day parading around the city locked arm to arm
with my Mr. NY. We went to the museum, the park, and ended up
eating Chinese take-out at my place. Sadly, the perfect night ended
with a sleepy-eyed goodbye kiss at my apartment door. "Goodbyes
are the worst." He started, "I always think of things I wanted to tell
you on the way downstairs." I kissed him and let him leave. I
found myself reacting in the typical fashion, back against the door
after it's been closed. Not really wanting to have closed it in the
first place, but knowing that if I hadn't I'd somehow regret it later.

I've been single for such a long time; this guy has made foreign
land an ever present issue. Dana insists that I take things 1 hour, 1
day at a time. To go slow and enjoy the ride, but that statement is
like wearing shackles on my ankles, the heavy iron preventing me
from running, from dancing.

So Challenge him, I would.

Tuesday night, Amy found herself at my doorstep, buzzing to get
up, bustling to get me out into her nightlife. After Tobey flipped
out on her, her whole entourage was in for an upheaval. She started
making comments that she wanted to change everything up and
date just like everyone else. But as much as I want her happy, I
think she's merely rattled. Tobey had been with her the longest out
of the weeknight buddies. Everything she was saying pushed me to

sit back on my sofa and think for a moment, then it struck me…
Drunken girls say the damn-est things!

"Melissa, Who am I going to find to replace my Friday Mess?
There's never been anyone to compete with him, whisssch is why
he was Friiiiday….and now I've lost him." Her pout was pitiful,
but it was her slur which signaled a need for massive coffee intake.

"Sweetie, let's go down to the diner and we can figure all this out."
I offered, getting up and putting on my jacket without waiting for
her to agree. She followed, and I didn't expect anything less. In
this case however, I needed Amy as much as she needed me.

We sat in Tom's diner, sipping on black coffee, and I caught her
up on my Fantastic Sunday with Brent.

When I was done she asked me 2 essential questions.

"Do you think you're ready to be in a relationship?" and "What
makes you think he is the guy?"

When after a few moments and an immediate response didn't
present itself to either one of her show stoppers, I shifted back into
the booth and thought about what she was really asking me.

Goodness Gravy, while I want to say that I'm ready for a
relationship, I really do like hogging the bed, and not having to
wake up before 9. I mean, who likes having to argue with their guy
to flipping put the toilet seat down. Imagine rushing in the middle
of the night to take deuce, but accidentally fall into the porcelain
bowl. Men don't really get the point to that either. Obviously,
they've never fallen into a pit of cold, wet arse water, having their
boys chilled like a martini on the rocks. There's a way to open
your eyes at 2 in the morning.

Her second question indeed had me thinking. Being the rational
analytical type a pros vs. cons list would fix the question on if he
was 'The One'. Let see…He has a Big____ ….and…..he has nice
teeth…and he is charming, but not in a 'politics' sort of way where
you tend to wonder if everything that comes out of his mouth is a

April Gutierrez

form of manipulation or if he really is merely complementing you. Also…he is wealthy… and…he has a Big___ … Oh Wait, I already said that. HA!

Sheesh! Of Course he is the right guy. He would be the right guy for Elizabeth Taylor if she were still alive, he is the IT guy. Like George Clooney was back when he was of 'dating' age. No matter what, When you hit the lotto, you don't forget to claim the prize.

So the answer to both questions was I couldn't possibly know. I would have to take the leap to see for myself.

Wednesday morning Brent called at precisely 9:05am. Somehow, I knew it was him before I answered it. Who else had my number that didn't realize the full extent of my morning routine, even Marcus -(a client of mine) knew that mornings were not my highest in production.

"Good Morning, Beautiful. Were you dreaming of me?" he quizzed mischievously.

"Of course, and if I were a man I'd have a big arse boner to show for it." The immediate early morning baiting produced an eye opener of a chuckle from him.

Yes, indeed he didn't mind the push back.

"So what are your plans for today?" it was how he asked that really had me curious. As if wanting to hear I had No plans at all, As if not wanting to be disappointed.

"What day of the week is it?" and you can't expect a girl to remember these things while half dressed, still hiding under warm covers.

"Today is Wednesday, and there is an art exhibit that opens up at lunch time. I would love it if you'd attend with me." He asked. His voice still lined with doubt.

Shaking my head, I knew I shouldn't ditch another day of work to spend with him, but if I didn't say yes, I knew he would just call someone else and my chances would start to fade out.

"What time are you coming to pick me up?" I asked, knowing exactly what I would tell Marcus when I called him to say his pages would be late.

"I will see you at 12, wear something green, the artist is Irish and loves all things Green."

Opening my eyes, I realized I had to get dressed quick anyway; otherwise I'd be late for brunch with the girls. As I sat up I felt it, the sudden dread that something important will happen. Those are the worst!

You'd never admit to anyone that you have a 6th sense but sure enough it's a female intuition that's never failed in the past. The Spidy-sense of being a Single woman I suppose.

Brunch was interesting. Dana spilled the beans about the doorman romance, but the only response came from Amy who only asked if there had been any elevator sex yet. That was 1 thing I didn't know about our dear Amy, she had a thing for elevator sex. This had me curious and wondering what it would be like on the way up to Brent's penthouse. 53 floors up…I'm sure we'd pull the stop button somewhere around the 10th.

Fires and Desires Indeed!!!

Lucky for Brent the art gallery was a 2 story brownstone on the upper-east side. Unlucky for me, it meant seeing more of the wolves that fashioned their tips for eye dart throwing at the last get together. It is no wonder that some of the men choose not to marry into the society, the women really do seem to suffer from a royalty inbreeding issue. As Eddie Izzard says it, best to spread the genes apart as much as possible. No, high society keeps breeding with high society creating the Dullest prunes on the planet.

The constant interruptions came from the shrill laughter of Brent's female 'friend', Abigail. Fact is, I don't really think she realizes how annoying she comes across. I will say however that the afternoon took a turn down an interesting path when Amy's Tobey sashayed ahead of me. Come to find out, it was Abigail herself that invited him as her date. It hadn't even been a week that he played the 'destroyed character' in front of Amy, and now he's found himself a 'Dime Duchess'-(rich trust-fund socialite). What a jerk!

And it's guys like Tobey that really get under my skin. I marched right up to him, and did what any friend would do.

I slapped him! Right across the chops. I only turned around when the gasp from the crowd was louder than my thundering heart.

"How dare you make Amy feel like crap! It hasn't even been a week and you are already dating someone new?!" I seethed at him.

Sure, Fine, it was a bit much. I mean, quite frankly it's none of my business, but the whole situation had Amy turning in knots. When Tobey didn't answer, I felt sheepishly embarrassed. More so as I turned around to find my Mr. NY, hands shoved into his pockets, with a quizzical furrowed brow directed at me.

Instinctively, it was the typical – *Damn*! I felt my insides shouting at me. The crowd was still staring at me, even though Tobey had stalked off. Now they had begun to associate my hot mess with Brent.

What had I done?!

"What was that all about?" he quizzed apprehensively as I approached him.

"It's a long story, but I was defending one of my best friends honor." I started, pausing only to look behind him to notice that everyone had begun to get back to the art in the gallery.

"Then I suppose she is very lucky to have you for a friend. I've never known someone to go so out on a limb that way." The moment his face softened with a smile, I knew I was in the clear.

"Damn straight she's lucky." I replied, reaching out to hug him. Maybe I just needed to feel his warmth to settle the tension going on in my brain.

So while nothing much really happened these past few days, my big moment was realizing that I could still be the me I've always been and not scare him away.

Tuesday, May 7, 2013
Spring Fever

Spring Fever....two words placed together to create one whopper of a label no one takes the time to really talk about. In the world of 'plus none', this is typically the time of year where you tend to notice a surge in promiscuous activity. Spring not only brings the glorified budding roses and the return of chirping birds, No...it Also unleashes a period of undeniable horniness amongst the single crowd.

Yes, I will lower my head and admit I have fallen victim to this spring fever craze, but in all fairness- it was bound to happen!! In years past, the partaking of hasty romantic interludes has always been about the game involved in the season. Central park during the dusk runner hours, or a bathroom stall located in the back of a certain Irish pub on 7th. It never really mattered where or with whom because none of the guys were 'Keep' material; they fell into the 'Use-em-lose-em' category.

This year however I find the game wasteful- but then again, I may just be looking at it in a different light. When the girls started chatting enthusiastically about their plans for the weekend, I realized I didn't want to go clubbing, bar hopping or any of the other ideas Amy and the rest were drumming up. I found myself dreaming up cozy ideas for Brent and me all the while wondering if he had ever gotten caught up in a Spring fever romance.

Okay ....this is what women who like a specific guy do...we make the mistake of *Wanting* to spend time with the guy we like, forgetting that we are not in a 'Real relationship' with them. Wants are all well and good until we actually put an emphasis behind them. That's when reality comes bargaining in and your guy realizes that there is some sort of expectation. It's like the confusion Amy had been going through with her hell-of-a-mess Tobey. Dating and Relationships...the unwritten rule is that when you are dating you can (If you can keep it straight) date several people at once. While, in a relationship the rules are clearly stated that you will be the only one taking up the free time, thus the realism of Expectations. Amy hadn't made things clear with Tobey, and while she basically lied to herself about what she really felt for him, when it came down to it, He is a guy and the quickest way for guys to get over their women issues is Under the grasps and gasps of a new beautiful woman. Literally!

During Spring Fever- EVERYONE (single) is Dating! Just sayin!

So it left me thinking where Brent and I fall into this Fickle little season. I mean, we have managed to spend oodles of time together in these past 2 weeks, but the moment girls started talking about their secret spring fantasies they were going to try this year, something inside of me snapped.

Call it jealousy, call it not wanting to share, but I can tell you, without a shadow of a doubt that I am Not interested in having sloppy seconds where Brent is concerned. My status is still Clearly blaring single, Blinking light and all, which is perfectly fine with me, but this year I don't want to jump from guy to guy to play into each fantasy… I want it to be Just Brent.

Is that my being Naive?? Maybe, considering we've only known each other for roughly a month.

Anyhow, our -Girls Only- lunch on Thursday ended with everyone deciding what they would try out first this year. Dana, as embarrassed as she was when she admitted it, she decided she would pick-up a retail salesman.

"Oh, You should so go for one of the higher end shoe store clerks…that way you can get us a discount for the new spring lines coming out." She smiled and giggled. Probably wishing she had thought of the idea first.

"I'll make sure to send him your way when I'm done with him, then he can give you some pointers." She teased. Thus creating Amy's blueberry lollipop shaded tongue to burst out of her mouth like a child. Their innocent banter echoing through the coffee shop.

"No, this year I am going for a Real business man type, Wall Street or something like that. I want him as nerdy as I can find-em." She sighed, so very sure of herself. It was a jaw dropper indeed.

"Why in the world would you want to spring fling with someone you can't possible have Anything in common with, Amy?" Ivy spat out. Sadly, it was once the words were said that we realized our own judgment regarding Amy.

Eyebrows furrowed, with a quick roll of the eyes, "Seriously, all I need to know is if his body speaks the same language as mine, Honey." And as Usual it is her thick skin that makes it easy to be friends with Amy, although deep down I'm sure it bothers her that people think her uneducated.

"What about you Ivy?" Amy countered, "Who will you try to tackle?"

"Tackle indeed ladies! I'm thinking a football player this Spring…Who knows, maybe even baseball. They have the tightest arses I've ever seen." She sighed, rosy cheeked. In this one instance, Ivy actually didn't need any commentary- she could pull it off easily.

This was when I got the eyeball from all three girls. It was well known by all of New York City that I am seeing "Mr. NY" himself, so it isn't a matter of whom but Where, and How.

"Seriously, I have No Clue!" I started, I'm not sure he has the nerve to be as adventurous as we are."

"Back seat of his Limo, Missy!? What do you mean he doesn't have nerve?" Amy almost shouted at me before they all chuckled after her.

I shook my head, still not sure what they wanted from me. "We will see, maybe I can just persuade him into a little of this, a little of that."

Which was immediately followed by Dana's, "I'm sure knowing you, it will be a Lot of this, and a Lot of that. Your inch is closer to that mile than you realize, Honey.

Needless to say, riding up the mirrored elevator to meet Brent for lunch at his office, my reflection proved the doubt I was feeling. God Knows I want him all the time, but spontaneity isn't something we plan, it happens all on its own. So talking to Brent about our status as two people was pointless when all I really want to do is tear his clothes off every time I see him. The trade off would have to be, Hope. A glimmer somewhere that all this *Want* isn't being wasted on the wrong guy.

The test...yes, that came during lunch.

The walk from the receptionist desk to his corner office was filled with anticipation galore. Who knew that staring at a man's butt for only a matter of minutes would have that effect on a woman? Well, It did! I realized however that I wasn't the only one who was eager to get back to his corner office. The moment I made it all the way in, he shut the door behind me and flipped the lock.

The clicking of the lock had me turning around to face him. His gaze was filled with a desire I knew all too well. Within two steps I was in his arms and I wasn't worrying about anything other than matching his kiss and returning the passion he was clearly seeking to satisfy. His arms pulled my figure closer to his, crushing it tight against his body. Hands didn't have to wander to know how hard he was, the pulsating heat was clear as it was being pushed up against me. Backward steps led us to his desk which had a spectacular view of the city. Breaking the kiss and with a slight pant, I took a peek out at the city. With eyes still out the window, Brent began unbuttoning my little dress with kisses to the bare skin he revealed. The soft smooth skin erupted in goose pimples, creating a slight chuckle to release from his lips. After the third scorching kiss, I faced him and quickly caught up with unbuttoning his shirt. Although he was clearly at the advantage where buttons were concerned.

Eagerness got the better of us, my legs wrapped around his waist and the rest left us in a daze. We remained on his couch for the better part of the hour not saying much of anything. While I hadn't thought to mention anything about where we stood as two people interested in each other, I couldn't help asking something that he still hasn't answered.

"What are you doing for the rest of Spring?"

 Nine words, obviously forming a question which is clearly filled with *Wants*.

Should I just lay it all out on the line for him? Or would a guy even care?

Reader Comments:

Anonymous   May 07, 2013
No, don't lay it all out on the line for him. Just keep having fun and enjoying him and see where it goes after a little more time goes by. You've only been seeing each other for a very short time and if you do lay it out, you may scare him away and you'll keep your status: SINGLE! ;)
~ALF~

Anonymous   May 08, 2013
No, do not lay it out there. Make him work for it while having fun. All things worth having are worth the work. If you want to be rid of that single status, you both have to work at it while you play.
sh

All things mysterious are a point of interest. We may not be of the Feline family but I dare say the human race has some of their tendencies. For a curious cat knows no satisfaction until they please their wondrous mind. The problem with this mentality is that we often find ourselves seeking a little too much information, and when all knowledge (skeletons) are revealed, what we are left with is not enough to sustain our interest.

In this journey of blog writing, I have come to realize that my odd ways of thinking has been the greatest cause for sustaining such a long single status. My level of honesty is what perplexes them-the male masses- and even you, my readers, I suppose. When it boils right down to it, a part of me can visualize the other shoe dropping where all relationships are concerned.

What it really comes down to is an emotional connection between two people. Fear prevents most relationships from truly taking off. Up until now, all the men I've encountered have never fit. They've played the games, they've made themselves out to be something they are not.

Sadly, and it's not a knock on men or my trying to be harsh, but: They are just Too Damn Picky! Which is even MORE shocking when all you hear is 'Wa Wa Wa, I'm still single!' - Well, get off your high horse and come down from your absurd perception of women.

Okay – So my little rant stems from a conversation Brent and I had while in the company of his best friend, Adam. After a spectacular Spring Fever rendezvous in the park, Brent invited me over to his place. The whole elevator ride up I couldn't help think of Amy's elevator fantasy and what it would be like if Brent pushed the STOP button…..hmmmmmm I might need to give it some more thought, the ride up to the pent house really is Long enough ;)

Anyhow, not but 5 minutes at his place and Adam gives him a buzz to see if it was okay to stop by. First case of Curiosity for the

evening – Brent asked **ME** if this was okay- *Nice*! Second case of curiosity came 20 minutes into their conversation when Adam asked if I had any single girls like Me I could hook him up with…..
Jim Carrey's, Reeeeehhhheeeeaaaalllyyyyy instantly sang in my brain.

What on Earth has Brent been telling his friends?!?!?!

"Well Adam, what type of girl are you expecting?" I asked cautiously. I mean, really….let's face it, I am Nothing like Amy, Ivy or Dana. The only reason we've stayed friends for so long is because our differences allow us to mesh well with each other.

"You know, great body, big boobs, a nice arse and a hell of a sex drive." His reply had me pausing, looking to Brent and furrowing my brow…. So this is what Adam's friends think of me…. *Hmmm*

"See, that is really interesting…." I began. -realizing that my blood had started to boil and a part of me which Brent had never encountered was about to rear her ugly face.

"You have just given a set of qualities that any pole dancer, porn star, or high school drop-out is capable of having." I sassed.

"Well, I'm not ready for any type of relationship. I just want to have a good time, get laid and move on to the next piece of arse." He replied, almost dumbfounded why I was even upset.

I merely shook my head, looked at Brent and waited for him to interject before I said anything more. I huffed only after a few moments of a returned blank stare. Seriously, this guy is his friend?!?!

"This is why women of sound mind reject men like you. Your vanity and lack of maturity limits your attainability. I wouldn't even recommend even a needy whore to walk anywhere near you!" I replied to Adam.

I got up off the sofa and headed towards the elevator, not even thinking twice to look around to see if Brent was even following me. By the time I pushed the down button I realized that Brent was hovering just behind me. The door opened and he walked in after me, standing on the other side as the doors closed us in.

The second we began moving Brent turned to face me. "That was harsh." He said quietly and as calm as I've ever seen him.

I shook my head and wondered how he was keeping calm knowing how upset that had made me. "Shesus, seriously....maybe it's because he seems to have this perception that my friend-Like Me- would meet his criteria, and quite frankly –I am not just another piece of Arse pole dancer that doesn't have a brain. If that is what you want..." I paused, still shaking my head not fully thinking about what I was about to say, "I think we should just stop seeing each other." it was then that I wished I have just Shut the Eff Up!

He closed the distance between us, that made the elevator seem safe, took my shoulders in his grasp and bent down so that his face met mine. "You are not just another girl to me, I am not like my friends, and I do Not want 'us' to stop seeing each other..." he paused, slightly tilting his head to the side, "It's because I don't talk about you, that they have come up with their own assumptions about the type of woman you are, and while that isn't fair to you, I'm happy you have a fire inside you to bite back in my world. Believe me, Adam will get over it quickly. He is probably laughing about it and wishing he hadn't said anything about still being single to begin with.

Foolish little ME!

I didn't even say anything. I reached out and hugged him, wrapping my arms around his back and buried my face in his chest taking in his scent. The elevator finally opened and Brent pushed the P button to go back up.

"You have to admit it though, Melissa, you are a mysterious one." He sighed, his arm still wrapped about my shoulder.

"You know all you have to do is ask..." I started, thinking that maybe it has been my lack of curiosity that brought all this about.

"I just don't like strangers knowing my life's story; it always seems that judgments follow soon after and everyone stars airing your dirty laundry."

"I know what you mean, not everything should be made public knowledge." He replied quickly.

*In comes the **Curious Cat**!*

"What wouldn't you want being public knowledge?"

He huffed and chuckled, throwing me a sideways glance. "Our relationship for starters, after Megan- the press has been keenly interested in my relationship status and lack thereof."

Just as I was about to counter his statement, the elevator *binged* open. Brent, towering over me smiled and kissed my forehead and tried the interaction with Adam all over again.

Lucky for Adam I was a little less fired up but in all honesty my mind was severely distracted.

I couldn't help but wonder what had occurred with Megan that made him want to keep our dating status as private as possible.

Should I care that the phrase will forever state: Curiosity Killed the Cat???

Reader Comments:

> ***Anonymous***   May 11, 2013
> Don't worry about his past relationships. That can only lead to trouble. Leave the curious cat at home.
> ~ALF~

Tuesday, May 14, 2013
Misunderstandings

Misunderstanding...the word alone gives me the heebie-jeebies. I'm Serious too! When you get to a certain age, you would think an adult gene would magically turn on and people in general would learn how to communicate. Sadly, it is the comprehension of what communication truly means where misunderstandings begin to develop. Not Only do they develop (the misunderstandings), they expand into every aspect of your life until KABOOM, you wake up one morning and it's as if life has taken an enormous shit on your plate...HA! (That's gross!) But you get my point... we are then left with 2 choices 1. Eat the shit and move on, **Or** the less ideal 2. BooHoo complain and make everything Worse!

Honestly, I have seen so many people waste so much time and energy by choosing the lesser of the two choices. They complain about things they can't change, or could have but refuse to see the lesson in any ordeal. These individuals play the victim card, drawing more negative attention their way. Negativity breeds negativity. Sometimes, it takes the 'Grin and Bear it' mentality to casually walk through life gracefully, even if the silver lining comes after you are unable to make sense of anything.

 *Where am I going with this.... Well, I am a magnet for misunderstandings, especially when men are involved. On many occasions it has been these communication confusions that have lead to my status changing Back to Single. You would think that after a few break ups, I would get a clue of what not to do, say, or act. Miserably I fail to grasp the concept of 'Think before you Speak'. HA! Or better yet, 'Think before you Speak while Typsy!'

Weekends in the spring have always been filled with parties and Spring Fling Fun, and this past weekend was no exception. Only difference came in the fact that Brent agreed to join my excitement with the girls. At first it was a Grand idea, Yeah, Sure...Until Ivy decided to jinx the whole damn idea and mention her doubts at our Thursday brunch. This should have been my 'I should have known' clue.

"Is he going to be like a babysitter or something? How is that going to work exactly?" she started, "I mean, when Dana brought that lawyer of hers he stayed, what? -**Maybe** 25 minutes before he got fed up of our sex-capade conversations." The memory of the poor 'fella had us giggling over our mimosas.

'Brent isn't like that, and I've already talked about you guys. I'm sure he will be okay with our silliness.' While I tried to say it as confidently as I could, they completely read between my Bullshit.

I get it, Brent has No Flipping clue what we are like as a group of women going out to party. Jesus! Men in general have no idea what women are like at All, otherwise everyone would be happy and getting laid whenever they wanted. Relationships would be easy and simple and Honestly, there would be peace on Earth. (Yes, I just laughed out loud writing that)

So they had their laugh, but at the time I was bound and determined to get the last laugh. And don't get me wrong, while I may be cynical at times, I would never see myself as an overall cynical person. Even now, I'm still looking for the silver lining.

Friday night rolled around, and so did the limo, right on time too. Hand in hand, we all sat together in the back of Brent's sleek black limo and drank a bottle of Dom with not a care in the world. At first I wasn't even concerned with the playful banter the girls had going with him. They joked about my previous entanglements but it was great to see how he nodded his head and found things to ask them that they hadn't been expecting.

'So did she ever tell you if she took her panties Off for that, or just, what exactly?' He asked Amy with a cat like smile spreading across his face. The question came from a story about a previous Spring Fever choice I'd accomplished a few years ago with a doctor.

Amy's spine stiffened, her posture impressing the rest of us as she smiled in my direction. 'You know, Melissa dear, you never did explain that to the rest of us in Full detail." Tossing the imaginary ball back into my court.

With a loose wet tongue, I giggled and proudly stated "A girl **Never** tells what she does with her lace in the heat of the moment." For that I received a, 'Bravo' from Dana and Ivy. Brent nodded in acceptance, while Amy merely chugged down the remainder of her champagne. So the start of my night was Perfect! My guy was fitting perfectly and my girlfriends weren't giving me dirty looks.

It was at dinner that Everything changed. Ivy had made the reservations and it never occurred to me to ask, at any point in the planning process, Where we were dining. Unbeknownst to any of us she had booked us dinner at a restaurant Owned by an EX of mine. The moment our limo pulled up to the Lavish entrance of, The NoMad, my heart sank lower than it's ever been in my entire existence!

Of course Brent noticed too! "Hey are you okay?" he whispered, "Why did you tense up?"

I could only shake my head insinuating that nothing was wrong while staring at Ivy's backside as she left the limo in a flash. At first I figured, "What's the worst that could happen?" but that is the Dumbest thing a girl can contemplate while arm-locked with the most eligible bachelor in all of NYC.

Unfortunately, I was up a creek without a paddle on this one. Ivy was making it clear she wouldn't stand or sit anywhere near me. I'm sure she was dreading the harsh hell I would whisper in her ear had she dared to come close.

The moment came where I was grasping Brent's hand while staring up at the charming yet unfaithful, Jeremy Borbone. He greeted the girls first, praising them for how well they all looked. Ironic how pleasant he was considering how much he had once blamed them for ruining our relationship. It was obvious Ivy had specifically chosen this restaurant based on her interaction with him. The moment finally came when he looked at me and said 'Hello'.

It is incredible how 1 single word can Ruin a whole evening. I would have been happy had he just ignored me altogether, but No…he was never capable of being reasonable.

"How have you been, Melissa?" he started, "You look great."

Because I have No Flipping Filter "I'm great, this is Brent Bishop, my new boyfriend." The moment the words slipped out of my crimson red painted lips I could feel the regret brewing.

I looked at Brent, who had already begun to stretch out his arm to greet Jeremy and waited for the disappointed expression to start weighing on his face. I focused on Brent throughout this brief conversation with my despicable Ex and never once did he look my way. After about a minute, I felt the squeeze in the hand being held by his….he gave me a sideways smile but the disappointment was there, hidden in the lines on his face.

Why? It's always me. And Yes…that IS me complaining….Life took a Huge Effing shit on my Happy Plate and quite frankly I'm upset I handled it the wrong way. Who freaking cares if we come across an Ex. They are there, a part of our past. They helped mold us into the people we are today, and a part of learning to love yourself is also learning to accept the past we have lived and the people who make up that past. And while Jeremy may be a sore spot, I should have known better. I should have handled the situation differently. (See, the adult is in there somewhere)

Anyhow, I got tipsy after that. Brent asked a few times throughout the night if I wanted to go home but Amy kept answering for me, and I didn't argue. The Whopper of the night came when I was the last one in the limo.

"So, how serious were you with what you told Jeremy at the restaurant?"Brent asked, taking my hand in his.

It brought me to attention. This time I found only hope in his eyes. Is this what he wanted? Did he want to take the chance?

"I wasn't thinking when I responded to Jeremy. He just brings out a very bad side in me."

"So it's a bad thing to be in a relationship with me?" he countered quickly.

"No, that's not what I meant.' I stammered, "I just blurted that out, and it's not quite my being honest. I mean, we haven't talked about our relationship status."

He nodded his head, and created an enormous amount of anticipation on my end. Was this the moment I'd been waiting for....was he going to ask me to be his Official girlfriend???

"I think I would have done the same thing had it been my Ex as well." He said.

This is what KILLS me about life. So he goes and says that, kisses me, then the limo stops. Then next thing I know I'm standing outside of the limo, saying goodbye to him and that's the end of that.

Shesus Flipping Cosmos! We may not have had an argument but I swear that was the worst misunderstanding I've been through yet.

And if things couldn't get any more confusing...Jeremy sends me a text the following morning *Lets have Lunch soon*

O_o   Seriously? While I refuse to 'Wa Wa Wa' about the whole thing, I will ask this...What is it about being in a relationship with a great guy that makes your Ex want to revisit YOU?

Reader Comments:

Anonymous   May 15, 2013
I think the ex's look at you like a prize or a piece of property. You belong to them and now that they don't

have you, they don't want anyone else to have you either. They can have as many girls as they want but you can't have another guy.....NOOOO! So they call you when they see you with someone else, especially if that someone else is better looking than they are, and want to revisit your old relationship. This is just their ploy to distract you from your present relationship but they really don't have any intention on making good on any promises so don't fall for anything they have to say. Leave them "kicked to the curb".

~A loyal follower~

Anonymous May 16, 2013
Sounds like your status still says Single, what's so bad about seeing what Jeremy has to say? You seem like the curious type, I have to disagree with the previous commenter. If anything else you can add some closure to the thing with Jeremy.
oriolecal

Anonymous May 16, 2013
You don't know what you have until someone else is plucking her!

Tuesday, May 21, 2013
The Replaceable Ones

The idea of being replaced sounds so…well, it sounds so fascist, like such a chauvinistic thing to say. The concept of taking your fill and moving on should really be described in a more eloquent way. It should be spun in a way expressing the need for change. A chapter closing and a new one shining brightly in another direction. But alas, life is never viewed through rose colored glasses. No, in fact we find our ignorance and naive beliefs to be our foolish method of coping. "Poor me, I was dumped". Or my favorite, "poor me, he left me for another woman". Well Bah humbug, let me beam some rays of sunlight and feed you a giant dose of reality. If he left you for me, it wasn't because you were the best piece of produce on the meat stand.

Oh and IF you happen to be a guy reading this, and I'm sure a penis will cross this blog eventually, you are not the only sirloin steak that's been passed up for a filet mignon. I use meat as terminology in this topic of conversation because human nature has been a revolving door of meal choices. Human nature in the romance department, in my book at least, falls in such a category. Relationships could often be categorized as different levels of dieting choices. You choose to get into a relationship as easily as you choose to be a meat eater or veggie person perhaps ;) It is safe to say that occasionally you will refuse to spicen up the meals, and other times you pound on the sauce, all based on how you feel.

Well, relationships seem to be the same. But the kind that continues to baffle me are those who insist that they must Change their choice of "meat" every single meal!

Now, to be clear, I don't care, I am just a complex observer. I have come across many a men who are hiding, or searching, wanting and occasionally needing to find in me what they long for. Bear with me, let's break it down. They are my version of a buffet, I've sampled and now it's my turn to evaluate.

The married men that I end up having relations with are usually hiding from their responsibilities. The ball and chain is no longer dragging them by the heels, it's severally choking them at the neck and they refuse to grow the balls to be truthful with their wives. These men have usually disappointed me. They expect me to replace their dull existence with a fiery passion they are lacking in their shared bed. These men become tiresome. They initially attract me with their good qualities, but then the hypocrite in me hates that they are cheating on their wives. Their character tarnished in my eyes.

In the beginning of my twisted hobby, I realized that there are plenty of men searching for the "right" girl. Go figure that each and every one of them saw me as that one and only. Minus the fact that I insist regularly to each and every one of them I'm not relationship material, these men had all the qualities I would look for in a man. Responsible, handsome, charming, Great in bed, and occasionally the well endowed. These men always left me questioning myself. The single most let down was their inability to bend in their requirements. The ONLY reason they stay single…are you ready…their picky arse nature. They want the physical, the vanity. Heaven forbid a girl is packing 10 pounds, they are running as fast as their insane arses can take them. The saddest part of their existence is the fact that if they were blind, they would have found their bliss a long time ago. These are the men that have a longer check list on their dream girl than any crazy I've come across who has one for the guys.

The wanting men drive me bonkers. They want you…to be what they want. They want you to call them, text them, they want you to be the romantic lover that they've been waiting for. Well, it isn't gonna happen. You can't make someone be who you want them to be. And if you actually accomplish the impossible be sure to take a picture, because they won't be around long. Most women resent a man changing them, DUH as most men despise women attempting to guide her man into "her man". The man whose want is insatiable often finds himself alone quicker than the man who has learned what patience is. Eventually, people grow out of their phases, and if you have any common knowledge, human nature is an ever changing evolution.

My favorites of oxymoron's are the needy men. These men are similar to the wanting type, only difference is the fact that they are miserable if they don't get you. They need you in their life or they are incomplete.

Honey, this isn't a movie where a man walks into your living room and proclaims that "you complete him". My comment which usually follows is "what do you want?" Yeah I need you too... ;)~smiles~ I need you so I save some batteries. I need you to take the sting away for just a little while longer so my fucked up life doesn't seem so bad.

So what does all this have to do with replacement? Well my unidentified type of man is the replacement man. He jumps from each of the precious four categories until he reaches the needy phase. Which at this point he had wasted most of his life fucking and replacing every chick in the city and has to move. He needs to get into a relationship because he is reaching the over-the -hill mark and sees his hypothetical kid's graduation...he being the one in the wheel chair sitting off to the side. Fine, so that man typically has a hot young wife nearby, but you better be damn certain that her lover is somewhere nearby too. These men bitch and moan most of their bachelor years "poor me, I'm always getting myself into crappy relationships" or "poor me, why do I always get the psycho bitches."

~smile~

These men make me want to scream. Not out of anger but out of annoyance. Jeez Louis, take off the Damn chip on your shoulder that makes you honestly believe that you are perfect. You snore, you hair is starting to thin out, you drink too much and usually the women who have sex with you fake their orgasms. ...trust me, they do! They frustrate me because they are the cause of their own doom. The reason your relationships are crappy is because you never quit talking about yourself...me me me...and when you do happen to listen to a single word a female says, you do it at all the wrong times. It's like the mute button in your brain is pressed 24/7 and SHIT the 5 minutes you hear anything is when we are bitching you weren't paying attention.

I like my steak thick and juicy by the way, the kind of meal that keeps me satisfied every time I get it!

So my Rant for today is brought to you because Brent spent the better part of the week showing me sides of himself that has reminded me of every man I've ever dated since being with Jeremy. The confidence I'd built thus far in having grasped the attentions of Mr. NY himself has utterly faded and I've returned to the fickle idea that it just isn't worth it......A man who marries his career should learn to have an emotional OFF switch in their personality. Sadly I haven't told Brent I want all this to end...I'm almost waiting to see if he turns out to be like none of the men I've categorized. But how long does one wait for it to rain in the desert?

What's so bad about hoping he isn't a douche bag??!?! Am I just being Naive? And as pathetic as I find myself asking this....Is Brent a replaceable one?

Reader Comments:

> *Anonymous* May 23, 2013
> Sounds like a cop out! Brent is probably just busy and here you are thinking he is a bad guy. Seems to me you are looking for a reason to let go of a sure thing. You talk about being such an adult but you haven't been open with him which is the adult thing to do.

> *Anonymous* May 24, 2013
> He is Mr. NY! He can have any woman he wants but he chose you. Give him some time to see what turns out. Maybe he isn't a douche bag but is just having an extra busy time right at the moment. However, with that being said, he always had time for you before. Are things cooling off? Is he getting bored? These are questions only

you can answer. If you are really into him, talk to him. Ask him "what's up" point blank. Is Brent replaceable??? If he's not the one to make your heart skip a beat every time you are together, yes, he's replaceable!
~ALF~

Anonymous   May 27, 2013
Based on everything you've posted it sounds like you are scared you have found someone irreplaceable. Again, Grow some and stop being such a coward!
Replies

   Anonymous   May 27, 2013
   Wow, really! You keep telling her to "grow some" but I notice you still post as Anonymous! Maybe YOU need to grow some! Be nice....
   ~ALF~

April Gutierrez

Tuesday, May 28, 2013
Clear Communication

I will first start by addressing my harsh commenter...~ Echem ~
You know who you are!

Anonymity or not, the silver lining of your response forced me to
take a step back and look at what was really happening. It is your
choice of words I beg to differ on however...Coward just doesn't
define me the way it does you. A coward faces nothing in the light
of day, and chooses to hide behind walls that have been built to
protect their personality. My mother always warned me: Be
cautious of judgments, for it is much like a dodge ball which is
bound to pounce you in the face.

Hmmmm...Now, I really don't think I need to say anything more
about the Anonymous commenter who lashes nasty comments
about my being a Coward...the oxymoron is Obvious.

On the same subject of commentators...ALF!!! I LOVE your
DEVOTION!!!

So, to the topic at hand, am I indeed IN a relationship, or have
decided to let Mr. NY go about his merry way?!?!?!

The girls were not much help when it boiled down to the subject of
Brent. When I tried to get feedback at our weekly brunch, it was
furrowed eyebrows and confusion as to why I would even be
having inner turmoil.

"Sweetie, come on, it's Brent you are talking about. You knew he
was married to his job." Ivy reminded me...again.

"Yeah, and seriously, if Brent wasn't in to you he would have
already had his assistant break it off. Have you even talked to him
about all this?" Dana seemed to agree with Ivy.

Beyond that I had to look over to Amy who always had something
colorful, while brilliant, to add as far as opinions are concerned.

56

"Well, I just think you're nuts. I mean, you know he isn't seeing anyone else. Otherwise the tabloids would be all over him. Gotta look at the bright side buttercup." For as much as Amy avoided relationships like the plague, it sure seemed like she was actively trying to keep me in mine.

"I think you should just talk to him and see what he says. Guys are so absent-minded- he may not even realize he is ignoring you into a file folder of lonely." Dana added positively.

I left our weekly brunch and did the UNTHINKABLE....I met Jeremy for a drink. In my mind it was just 1 Drink. The way I justify it is: there is nothing wrong with catching up with an old boy friend who seems to want a platonic relationship. Ya can't have enough friends. Sadly, you never know what men want until they open their mouth. That was my first mistake.

I found Jeremy sitting at the bar, already having had a few by the sound of his slurring.

"Sheesh, Jere, couldn't wait for me to get here?" I started out sarcastically.

His chuckle and shake of the head put me back 4 years. Nope...some people just don't change.

"Didn't you know that it takes a few to sit in front of an Ex?" Yes, Sir! It was obviously by that point that I was not going to go down this road.

"Well then, I suppose you drank them in vain as you will not be sitting in front of this Ex." My voice sweet and exceedingly clear.

While I wanted to yell at him what an Arse he was, I thought better of it. Why should I give him any amount of emotion...he'd stolen so much of that already on our wasted relationship. Walking out of that smoky bar I came to the conclusion that closing 1 door meant another was being opened. Closure Indeed!

April Gutierrez

I'd spent all this energy worrying about Brent. I hadn't been the adult I'd prided myself being. It was my epiphany....somewhere in NY City there were church bells ringing and a chorus singing...I had to go see Brent!

Now, when I make comments that Brent is married to his company, I'm not really exaggerating. His assistant has her own assistant, neither of which care, quite frankly, if I just had my huge epiphany. Brent was in a closed door meeting, one which was going on its 3rd hour in progress. While Janice (his assistant) assured me I wouldn't be waiting long if I sat in his office, Gloria on the other hand, rolled her eyes and tapped her wrist watch.

'That man has been in marathon meetings all week; I wouldn't get your hopes up." Gloria sassed humorously. Can I say, I adore older secretaries...they are so Flipping honest!

I told Janice I would only sit in his office for a few minutes. I was being spontaneous and all. I will blame his comfy sofa....because it wasn't the bright sunlight coming through the enormous glass windows in his corner office. I sat down, staring at the incredible view and dozed off.

I'm still shaking my head tonight, writing that I was so tired I hadn't even noticed falling asleep on his sofa.

BUT incredible things happen when you are pushing the pendulum. Yes, indeed they do.

Brent had come into his office and found me sleeping comfortably on his sofa. I'm not sure how long he'd let me sleep, Janice wouldn't tell me later. She merely smiled and said, 'Go with it, Honey."

When I woke up, the sun had already set in the NY view. Brent was sitting at his desk, leaning back in his chair and reading a document through his stylish reading glasses.

The moment my eyes met his, the whole demeanor of his facial expression changed. He was soft, and tender, and it made me feel like it was only he and I in the world.

"Well, hello there sleeping beauty." He said, putting the document down and getting up from his desk.

I stretched and took in my surroundings. That was when I saw it. Brent had ordered us dinner and had a table in the corner of his office set up for us to eat.

"Yeah, when you didn't stir I figured you were tired and would probably wake up hungry."

I let him reach the sofa and sit with me for a minute. We kissed and for a moment I wondered if we would even make it to the table to eat, but a lingering issue needed to be resolved before I were to stay in that office.

"Brent, I need to know where you see us going." I started.

"I don't understand." He replied rather quickly.

"You've been ignoring me these past couple weeks."

"I've been giving you time to figure things out. I saw the look on that Ex of yours, and I've also been in relationships that have needed closure. I don't want us to get serious to later have you leave for another guy." He said it, and then he stood up.

Fine! He caught me off guard; he said exactly what I wanted to hear.

"I want you….and I want to know that you will find a way to fit me into This life, that the rumors of your being married to your company won't have you leaving me when it's all said and done."

Honest and clear communication…..

We ate dinner, talked about what I meant about 'rumors' and how I left Jeremy in the past where he belongs.

Wanting everyone in the world to know, Brent asked me to change my status to: **TAKEN**

Reader Comments:

Anonymous   May 28, 2013
Yay! Do you see how communication can clear up doubts? I hope you are going to take him up on changing your status...... :)
~ALF~

Anonymous   May 31, 2013
Lucky girl! Brent sounds dreamy. Do you think that jumping into a relationship with someone you hardly know is the right thing?
Sally N.

Anonymous   June 01, 2013
When it sounds too good to be true, it usually it! No man can be that perfect, and if there is one out there his wife is ruining him.
CalPal

Anonymous   June 06, 2013
WHOO HOOO!!! Always keep the lines of communication open :)
Sarah

Tuesday, June 4, 2013
Lightning Strike

Theoretically, it has been said that lightning doesn't strike twice in the same spot, thus IF I were a betting woman, I wouldn't place a wager on the same guy twice. Now…my 'Gifted' mind did do some research behind this silly little thought process I had going and boy was I in for a big surprise.

After a whirlwind few days with Brent, we decided that it would be in our own best interest to create a schedule for each other. Come on now, don't knock it- you have to realize the ONE thing I had been forgetting all this time….Life is BUSY!

I had been in fact, procrastinating from work, which in my case is a **bad thing** since I am a Freelance copy editor. Meaning = I only get paid for the work I complete, and sadly that hasn't been much recently. A schedule would suit me well, and I'm neither complaining nor feeling left out in the matter.

I also had a feeling that I would need to make room in life for more work. Marcus Roberts, my oldest and dearest client, who writes nothing but romance, has just completed his 49th novel. It will need work, and being that I am the only copy editor he will work with, I know the publishing company will be calling soon after our meeting.

"Sweetheart, when are you going to write your own book? Doesn't it weigh heavy on your heart to read and make my stories perfect for printing?" he wondered insistently. Marcus has been a lot more like a father to me since I moved to NYC. We get together every other month and work out the details for what I will be doing next for him. With all this Brent business, I realized there at the coffee shop on 5th that we hadn't spoken since March.

"I will write something when my muse decides to linger long enough to create anything with depth." I quick wittedly replied.

Marcus tilted his head and paused a moment as if wondering with which color palette he would use to paint a portrait of my face.

"Muse, huh." He began and began nodding. "Okay, I will make a few phone calls, I think I know just who to talk to."

It was the achievement look on his face that worried me more than I wanted to admit. His heart is so grand, but it is his loose attachment to reality that has always come back to bite me in the Arse!

"Marcus, what are you talking about?" I asked as cautiously as I could.

"Darling, you will write your own novel if it breaks every damn rule in your playbook." He stated firmly.

This was the first time he'd mentioned my playbook in the time I'd been working with him. To this I was taken back.

My playbook is a very carefully decided upon life I would live. The must-do and never-wills I'd decided upon long before I ever met Brent. Years and years ago when I sat down and analyzed everything I knew I wanted to accomplish, the only way I thought to record my goals was to create a 'playbook' for them. In my official interview with Marcus all those years ago, he asked me what I wanted to be when I grew up…I pulled out my 'Playbook' note book and read him off my goals. What originally caught him off guard was my assertive reaction to the date stamps next to each one, and that no where listed on my playbook was a goal to write my own story. It has forever been a topic in our conversations, like the black plague that never vanishes from our history.

I shook my head and changed the subject back to his newest romance novel. His hopes were for me to be done by August, which meant I would have my work cut out for me.

"I am going to give you a call this week, please don't argue with what I ask." He said firmly at our goodbyes.

I agreed, only because I could never say no to him. Not only because he is my biggest financial benefactor, but also because he is the sweetest soul I have ever met.

"Give Jennifer my love and wish her a happy birthday for me." I asked.

"You should just pop in on her some day. She lights up after every one of your visits."

The girls found the recap of my lunch with Marcus hilarious. Looking at the encounter from their perspective, I can truly see why others find my interactions with him amusing. It's like playing a verbal game of tennis with a senior citizen. While he doesn't display the usual crotchety personality as others his age beam of, his skills in meddling far surpass any from his age group.

"I want to know the minute he calls." Amy insisted. "The last time he meddled with your 'muse', or lack thereof, I had the most amazing sex for a month with the actor he tried to have work with you. What was his name, Jerry or something?"

"It was Nathanial, and yes, I very much remember. I still have some of the things he gifted me that month." I recalled bashfully.

"Honey, it wasn't your fault he turned out to be Amy's type. Or should I say, Amy being His type." Dana shot at Amy.

We all started laughing as Amy, mouth filled a lemon filled donut, coughed and nodded that she was genuinely sorry.

"So how is everything on the Brent front?" Ivy asked, desperately wanting to change the subject.

"We are still working on a schedule for each other, but all in all, great." And as if the smile had never left my face, I was cheesing as I had before my meeting with Marcus.

"I don't get this schedule shit. You haven't even changed your status to 'In a Relationship'." Amy huffed.

YES, I know! I am a horrible flipping freak. I have this great guy, who is working with both of his assistants to fit me into his schedule as often as possible and I haven't done the one thing that is Killing me to do….. Is this a sign? My inner gut screaming, don't Commit with this one???

Lightning struck me the night I met Brent Bishop. The mere fact I met such an incredible guy who actually LIKES me back is a big deal, as it would be for Any NY woman. And Lightning doesn't strike twice, so I should just jump on his boat and just row with it, Right?

I contemplated that question for a brief 24 hours before becoming infinitely distracted. Brent left NYC for a meeting in LA. He was so rushed we didn't even have a chance to say goodbye. I got the text that he was boarding a plane for the West coast right about the same time Marcus called and asked me to join him and Jennifer for dinner.

A preoccupied mind is far worse than an absent one. It is in the little things we tend to miss the obvious clues which eventually make a crater size impact.

Marcus had mentioned Jennifer, thus innocence spread like a calming balm in my thoughts. I should have known better. The moment I was taken to their table in NY's 21Club, I was confronted with what a mischievous romance novelist perceives as the muse who will make me write my very own novel.

There, next to Jennifer sat- Benjamine On'rie, Europe's #1 romance novelist on the market. My breath was not only taken away by the mere fact I was sitting next to 'Literary Royalty' but also because his tall 6'3'' 240lbs build intimidated my little self. I'm not sure I have stopped blushing since dinner.

Maybe it was his emerald green eyes carefully placed behind delicious long lashes that almost seemed to bat every time he ginned at me. Who knows, it could have been how the bronze glow of his skin made me want to make love to sunlight as I had as a child.

All I know, is I'm in BIG TROUBLE because lightning has surly struck me twice!

Tuesday, June 11, 2013
The Frenchman

Let's play a little game of Fairy Tales, shall we!

Once upon a time there was a girl who spent her whole life in search for this elusive Prince Charming character. She'd heard distant whispers that he didn't exist, but still she was always looking for him, always looking for the silver lining. After many unsuccessful years she realized that the whispers had become louder for a reason and while she so desired him to be true, it seemed as though he was a figment of her imagination. A ghost looming in a future that would never exist.

He was an idea someone had created to fill a void in their sorrow, loneliness, and unfulfilled life. They'd spread his description throughout the land like a plague against man. The balance was forever disturbed in what women would come to expect from the male species.

Go ahead, think I was a cynical little creature wandering about all my life...I was. I won't deny it at this point. Ever since I started this blog I've been fighting the inevitable- throwing myself into a relationship that I didn't believe in. The hope that Brent fit the Prince Charming complex was based on a desire to change my status from Single to Taken, but I ended up fighting that too.

So here I sit, staring out my bedroom window speaking to you as a person who has finally met a bona fide, living breathing Prince charming character. He is no fictional being, no alien from another planet. The problem had always been geography. Had I ever gotten on a plane and flown to good o' Paris, I would have eventually run into him- sooner rather than later. Rather than now for example, when everything is so utterly in a mess of confusion.

Marcus really did me in this time. His intentions, while pure and wonderful, have stirred a sleeping giant in my center. After a night filled with wine and loads of laughter –my own included- he put me in a cab and reminded me of what his intentions were all along.

"One must give himself completely to his art and not hold back. Throw caution to the wind. Embrace the muse. Make love to your art.' We can thank Harley King for that one." He chuckled innocently. His eyes sparked in the evening light. The old man was forever trying to encourage the inner writer in me.

With the cab door closed, I warily reached into my **Tory Burch clutch** and gently caressed the napkin carefully placed inside with On'rie's number scribbled on it. Recalling a similar moment, I realized that my bubbling excitement was twofold, for I was holding a proverbial time bomb in the palm of my own hands. And with that realization, I sat stone cold the whole way home.

I kept the topic of On'rie to myself when I had brunch with the girls on Thursday. They were more interested in the photo moment I had with the paparazzi. 'What happened was' ~Brent asked me to pick him up at the airport when he got back from his trip and Spring in NY is a rather windy time of year. Sadly, I wasn't wearing a fabulous white dress like Marilyn Monroe. Needless to say, I think boy short styled underwear is soon to make it's round two in popularity.

"Sweetie, just be thankful you had a cute pair of lace on, otherwise it would have just been embarrassing." Ivy started, huffing and focusing more on her nails than the conversation. "At least all of NY's upper society is now aware of your smoking hot body and that Brent has taste of course."

At first I didn't know how to take Ivy's comment, being that she seemed annoyed, but then Amy put a few things into perspective. (She must have noticed my confused gaze)

"Ivy, I think all of NY is now aware of Missy being Brent's hot girlfriend, which seemed to be the point of the picture to begin with." Amy snapped.

Ivy stopped fiddling with her nails and squarely looked at us. "The point of the photograph was to embarrass both Melissa and Brent. That is what the paparazzi always intend to do. Don't elude yourself into thinking they are anything positive and good." She shot back unnerved.

"What's your deal Ivy? Why so hostile?" I immediately shot back at her.

She shook her head at us, "They called my office, they wanted an inside source for their story. They wanted to know everything about you. And it bugs me to know what else they want, and who else they are going to call." She admitted, her eyes easing up, filling with concern. It was killing her, the worry.

"Why would the paparazzi care now, it's been almost 2 months since you guys started seeing each other."Dana added, "I mean... you haven't even changed your damn status yet."

"Brent is part of the elite. He is old money, and because of that he represents a status in NY that everyone wants to be a part of. Melissa is now a part of that world, like it or not." Ivy informed.

A slowly sinking feeling began to grow in the pit of my stomach. What if Ivy was right? What if this dark cloud of looming cameras is an omen of some sort, warning me to proceed with caution?

Unfortunately, the concept of caution has also eluded my grasp of comprehension. The inability to clearly 'Think' first has been something of a challenge. Brent called and let me know he was off to a conference in Tokyo. This time for a week.

How does that old saying go, 'While the cat is away, the mouse is sure to play'?

Yeah, that's me, the silly little mouse squeaking about. By Friday morning I was staring at a laid out napkin from 21Club with On'rie's phone number on it, the ebony black ink playing tricks on my brain. The longer I stared at the numbers, the more they seemed to dance around the stark white background.

I had to do something. I couldn't call him. It just could Not happen. While Marcus' intentions were pure and wonderful, I wouldn't play into the devil's game of, 'Let's dance around the fire'.

I got up and left my apartment. Where did I go? I went straight to Dana's- My only Logical friend who never judged my thoughts. I called her down from her office on the 46th floor to have an early lunch with me.

"We need to make this quick, I have a meeting in a little while I can't reschedule." She insisted. "What's going on?"

We walked, and I talked. She listened, and I confessed everything about having met On'rie. And there on the sidewalk of 91st street I openly admitted to Dana what had been driving me crazy these past few days.

"Dana, I want to call him."

She didn't gasp in disgust; she didn't even seem to flinch at my declaration. She kept us walking at the same pace until I reached out and tugged on her arm to stop.

"Did you hear what I said? I want to get to know him." I repeated.

"Then call him, get to know him. Get it out of your system. But realize that when Brent comes back in a week, everything will be different, and you will be the only one to blame for it." She said calmly and then tugged her arm out of my grasp.

"I have to get back to work. I love you." She kissed me on the cheek and left me there to watch her walk back up the street. The moment her figure disappeared into a crowd I knew what she meant.

I decided to take a walk through Central Park as opposed to catching a cab back home. It gave me time to think. I get what she meant by everything being different. I would be the one to ruin things, but haven't things already changed. The mere fact that I Want to get to know someone different, on a more personal level, is an indication that everything was already different. Brent isn't new anymore; he is someone that while I don't know everything about him, I still know the basics. On'rie on the other hand is a brand new penny with no smudge marks on him.

Fact of the matter is if I want to know what a real relationship feels like. Playing the fickle card only ends everything I've built up so far.

Doesn't the princess ask for a sign in cases like this? I whispered to myself.

And as if the fates were right on the money, around a curb came walking the gorgeous Frenchmen himself. It was like being transported into an older Disney film. I saw him through rose colored glasses that I'd sworn I would never wear again for any man. He had a soft flowing light following behind him, and everything around his gracefully moving body faded into a pallet of pink and green hues that blended in an almost De Vinci style painting. The moment I caught his eye, it was a passionate, ~'it's so wonderful to see you again' demeanor that would make any woman melt a mile away. His step picked up and I was moved by the spirit in his walk towards me.

I'm not blind. I'm not deaf. But boy do I feel dumb in having wondered if I should see him again. If not butterflies, a swarm of eager bees were let loose in my very center. While I had never written what most would consider a novel, I could feel the story he was creating...a disastrous all-consuming fervor to love a man like him.

Il n'y a qu'un bonheur dans la vie, c'est d'aimer et d'être aimé

There is only one happiness in life, to love and be loved. (George Sand)

Reader Comments:

Anonymous   June 12, 2013
The grass isn't always greener on the other side!
Susan

Anonymous   June 12, 2013
Better watch out. Karma is a Bitch!

Anonymous   June 12, 2013
I have to go against the other two comments and say that
if you were truly happy, you wouldn't even be thinking of
playing with the Frenchman. So, on that note, play
away!!! :)
~ALF~

Anonymous   June 12, 2013
Not sure you really know what you're getting yourself
into. If you really care for Brent, then don't play, but if
you are unsure then talk to Brent about it before taking
any leap with your Frenchman.
Advice from an old romantic, Tiffany H.

Anonymous   June 12, 2013
I'm a follow the heart kind of person, but if she's only
having these thoughts about the Frenchman because she's
unsure of her status with Brent then that isn't a good
reason to go after the Frenchman. I say she should check
with Brent, if they are only dating each other and her
heart doesn't flutter at the thought that he only wants to be
with her, then she should set him free or agree to date
others as well as each other. But she shouldn't throw
everything with Brent just because of one good convo or
because her heart does a little flutter when he smiles.
Sarah

Tuesday, June 18, 2013
The Other Door Opened,
Season 1 Finale

How many times do you find yourself saying, 'If I knew then, what I know now...' or hear the saying 'when one door closes another opens.' I suppose I will be repeating both of those statements to myself while this rather immense sting takes its time to grow wary of my heart. Meanwhile, all I can do is shake my head and ponder what I could have done differently, if anything at all.

Last Tuesday I didn't listen to the few loud sirens coming from reader responses, and now I wonder why...maybe because I wanted a 'heartbreak-free' happily ever after, with whoever managed to provide it. For that to happen however, I would need a free base to stand on. I had been, feet firmly placed, in Brent Bishop's world of idealistic relationships. The loudest unspoken truth: I don't want what I've been living. Schedules and text messaged goodbyes are not my idea of the 'Romance of a Lifetime'. No, I have not been happy with Brent, and while I realize this now, after the fact, the past week has been an enormous eye opener of what we 'Should and shouldn't' do in situations that we are thrown into. Hindsight is 20/20.

The moment I watched Benjamine walk around that corner in Central Park last week, I knew that I was meant to wonder about my Frenchman. And don't give me crap about fate and destiny being an excuse for the romantic folk to hide behind choices. We all make choices in our lives. Some turn out to be horrible mistakes...the kind we grow awfully old regretting. While other choices change our lives, charming us with the greatest of riches...Love.   In my case, our chance encounter unleashed a can of circumstances. One foot in front of the other, leading down a path that I should have known only had one certain outcome.

As it turned out, On'rie was leaving a meeting with his literary agent, a gathering where I was the topic of discussion. In fact, I too materialized in the park from thoughts that afternoon- his thoughts that is. Romantics could have a field day with that wormhole but instead they snapped meaningless photographs. Yes, what would later be construed as a steaming affair, for the afternoon, we set ourselves up quite profoundly for what circumstances confuse for fact.

Even now, as numb as I feel, my lip gently curls at its corny thinking about that afternoon I spent with my literary genius…………..

"I was just thinking of you, my dear." On'rie mused, planting gentle kisses on either side of my smiling cheeks.

Playing to his affections, I took his arm, twisting my body to face the direction he was headed and snuggled up to his delicious body.

"And what would these thoughts consist of exactly, dear sir?" my inquiry sounding of childish curiosity, but his playful nature made comfort a way of being.

The hearty chuckle erupted from his throat, and his free hand patted my hand holding his arm. "Marcus warned me of your mocking demeanor. Do you do that often; make light of others thinking of you, and of things that are supremely important?"

While I could sense he meant well, it was obvious I had wounded his pride. "I do it often enough for an old man to find a fault in it apparently. Excuse me, I'm sorry, continue." I apologized.

I didn't try to make a distance between us, only because he would clearly have known how much it affected me to be called out on a fault of mine, but I did become apprehensive as to where this conversation would lead. Knowing Marcus was involved in our having met, all intentions where On'rie is concerned are curious to me.

"If you please," he began looking down at me, "I brought your name up to my agent, apparently he has heard of you from a colleague of his. I mentioned that you were working on a book of your own and he is interested in reading it when you are willing to share it."

We hadn't known each other long enough to share a deep understanding of each other's reactions, which is mainly why I kept my initial reaction concealed. However, the bomb he had just set off in my mind created a cataclysmic sized crater. The only thing I could muster was a meager, 'Wow'. Three letters put together that stopped him from walking a step farther and letting go of me completely. The sudden movement left me feeling naked, alone.

"Was I wrong to say such things?" he asked confused, staring deeply into my eyes.

I couldn't help but break the connection and sigh softly.

"No, it's just that I am not a writer On'rie, I haven't thought much of Marcus' ranting all these years. I just don't have it in me." And though the words were coming out of my mouth, the look on his face was wreaking havoc on the conviction behind my words.

"Should you not give it a try before you disregard an opportunity such as this?" his question thick with accent. "You are talented and beautiful and see so much of what others disregard. Only a writer does this. Believe me when I say, I know when I meet a writer, and from our first conversation, I felt the story that you have within you. "

Indeed he was right, any logical person in the literary world would agree with him. But you see- I am not a Logical person. The idea of writing something of my own for everyone to criticize and pick apart is terrifying. And before you go on and enlighten me that this blog is such a thing, well, it's not. Reality does not beget fiction. What he and Marcus are asking of me is so much more intimidating than anyone understands.

 What does one say to a handsome Frenchman when he is trying to hand you a key to his fabulous world? ~shakes head~ I wouldn't know…I changed the subject, and let it go…for a while at least.

"How long are you planning on staying in the city? You must visit Grand Central Station. It's like being transported to a different time. The writer in **You** will appreciate it." I mused, focusing on the way he leaned on his left side.

"I will only go if you come to appreciate it with me." He responded, almost in a challenge like tone.

While Ben is and has been anything But innocent, the idea merited innocence. I'd already spent 15 minutes walking arm locked with him. What would be so bad about an afternoon adventure?

"Sure, my schedule has been freed up this week anyway." I huffed, not thinking how much it sounded like a complaint.

"What is this?" he began, "Left lonely by a lover?" his accent again catching me off guard. He took my arm again and we began walking out of the park to catch a cab.

"I'm not sure exactly what he is, On'rie, but yes I suppose lonely covers it." What was weird was the fact that at the time, I didn't feel dirty by admitting to him that I was a little lonely. It didn't bother me either that after that moment, he upped the ante with his 'French Flirting'.

"So if I was to say, Mon Chéri let me be your companion in loneliness so that our hearts can wander as one. What would you respond?"

Closing my eyes, I giggled a little, looked into his gorgeous green eyes and shook my head at him. "You are a terrible flirt, has anyone ever told you that?"

"Indeed they have, but only by women who have had intentions of sleeping with me." He tossed me a sideways glance, "Are your intentions on this level?" he asked plainly.

"They are not. Does this change your affections towards me?" I quick wittedly replied.

"I could no sooner tear you from my heart my dear, you are a new simple pleasure I wish to hold on tight to."

That was the first time I felt he was being openly honest with me, and not just a French flirt. I mean, he was clearly flirting, but I believed that he too believed he was being sincere and open. Our cab ride those 20 blocks was hilarious. He imitated several American copy editors of his own, making them sound as prudish as I'd ever heard. Makes me wonder if I respond to my clients the same way. Needless to say, by the time we realized it, the cabby was pulling over at 45th street.

"Why did we get out here? He asked me curiously.

I'd always laughed at the idea that some people just didn't get it. The whole point of being in the city was to feel the ambiance. New Yorkers walk. It is part of the life style. NY Landmarks are not meant to be driven to, they are meant to be walked to…unless we are talking about Liberty or Ellis.

"How else are you going to understand what I mean by, being transported, if you don't just go with it?"

I'm not sure if it was On'rie's presence, or if maybe I was having a taste of my own medicine, but walking into that building woke something pretty incredible in my imagination.

I watched as On'rie walked ahead of me. His awe of the whole place could have been what inspired me. I felt as if I was being washed by a tidal wave of a story hidden deep in my subconscious. Characters, back story, history, struggle, and intrigue. I suppose I too was transported to a time of romance and desire. Forbidden desire.

That was when a malicious snap startled me. A few feet away, a man with a bulky black metallic camera stalked the walkway where we were headed.

On'rie reacted first, and without thinking of consequences either. "Would you leave us be, there is nothing to photograph here."

The man ignoring On'rie snapped another picture. He pulled the camera away from his face and mocked, "She is not your girlfriend. In fact, I have it on good authority the two of you are with other people. I will Snap as I please."

Just as the words left the man's mouth, On'rie was charging at the paparazzi scum. The guy ran off, camera in hand. In that moment, I knew everything had changed. On'rie came back and asked if I was okay. My head nodded yes, but deep down in the pit of my stomach I worried. No, in fact I was not okay. Far from it indeed. The smart thing to do, is not always our first thought. No, usually our first instinct is to ignore that anything happened at all. We left Central Station, startled by the events. I invited him upstairs to my place only because I was still trembling when we got out of the cab. The only thing I could think of as I poured us a stiff drink was what I would say to clearly explain the events that lead to that moment.

Did I need to explain it?

Oh, I needed to explain…of that I was sure. Otherwise I wouldn't feel guilty all of a sudden.

The longer On'rie sat on my sofa, the more I became aware of the guilt I was dancing with. The kind that changes everything. I knew who I was dealing with. I'd crossed the line and no matter how I saw this going I'd lose Brent in the end. Tonight, tomorrow, in a matter of time it wouldn't just be a matter of circumstances, I would find myself so lonely that I would really be that horrible person that made a wrong decision.

"Can I make a call without you saying anything?" I proposed to On'rie. There was a worry in his eye as he nodded his head.

That was when I called Brent. The right thing to do was to call him and tell him the circumstances…prepare him for the storm brewing.

"Hello?" he answered, the gruff sound meaning I'd just woke him up. I'd forgotten about the time difference from NY to Tokyo.

"Sorry for waking you but this couldn't wait" I paused, collecting my thoughts.

"Baby, it's really early here, can it wait?" he pleaded softly. Wanting to give in to him, I almost agreed, but then On'rie smiled weakly, proposing strength for me.

"No, it can't wait. Tonight the paparazzi took pictures of me with a friend of mine, Benjamine On'rie. I ran into him at the park and we spent some time together.

I wanted to go on, say that it has been plainly innocent, but I couldn't give in to a happiness that will eventually be destroyed by his lifestyle. I am not the type of woman that will make him happy. Look at how 1 lonely week puts me in front of another incredible man. No, Brent needed to believe that I'd done something wrong.

"And what shall the caption say on page six tomorrow, Melissa?" he asked, his tone clearer.

"I'm not sure... you know how they muddle the truth all up." I offered sheepishly.

That was when I heard the sigh....disappointment. The one thing I'd wanted to avoid and yet caused all on my lonesome.

"You would know, you're a writer."

I will admit, I deserved worse... but damn did hearing the words come out of his mouth surely sting.

"I suppose you're right." I agreed. "I'm sorry I woke you up."

"Before you hang up, let me get something off my chest." He halted quickly.

"Go ahead."

"All this time you've been waiting for some grand epiphany to hit you that would have you change your status to, ~being in a relationship. You never once stopped to think, that the moment you came to my office to be with Me, that our relationship had changed. We have been in a relationship. Maybe you are more like your Elizabeth Bennett that you want to admit, except you are more a foolish girl than I thought…I didn't think I had to say three words to make you believe how much I care for you."

I didn't reply to his declaration, frankly I couldn't. I hung up the phone and lowered my head.

If On'rie hadn't been sitting right in front of me, I would have cried myself to sleep that night. Instead, On'rie followed me to bed. I curled up in his embrace and fell asleep in his warmth. That next morning Amy woke us up with the 20 question phone call about the story and pictures on 'Page-6' blasting me for cheating on Brent.

On'rie smiled at me through the whole conversation. He seemed dazed and confused. At times it seemed as if he was contemplating many things all at once. Finally, Amy agreed on a cease fire and I was able to hang up.

That was when, 'The Other Door Opened'.

"Come to Paris with me. Stay with me, not as lovers…unless you want to, but stay with me and write your book. Let me help you forget him, and this romance that left you lonely. We can spend the summer basking in the light, the romance of the city. Every writer must come to Paris, come with me. Let's not be lonely together."

It is an offer I can't refuse.

Happy Summer Readers,
~Melissa Green

Readers comment:

Anonymous   June 19, 2013
Oh Melissa...go to Paris with your sexy Frenchman and "not be lonely together!"
~♥~Au revoir et profiter de votre vie ... Statut: Taken~♥~
~ALF~

SEASON 2

Tuesday, August 13, 2013
Home
Season 2 Episode 1

A blank screen and this little familiar cursor blinking anxiously at me to create something magnificent- This has been the daily routine going on 9 weeks now.

I have…So much…to say about this summer, but I'm sitting here tonight not even knowing where to begin.

Life finally happened to me. I grasped at an opportunity without thinking every aspect through and took a leap of faith. That one single action changed my life and for that I have On'rie to thank.

My wonderfully handsome Frenchman, who's proven in his own little way, what an incredible writer he is, altered my path. The world has known it for years, but on a more personal level, he is the Shakespeare of our era.

When he initially asked me to jump on a plane and go to Paris with him for the summer, I never imagined how things would turn out. I can tell you this, if nothing else about my summer, we left New York City in June with 1 agenda. To find myself, not just my literary self, but to acknowledge the type of woman I genuinely am and boy did I ever. I left firmly believing I wouldn't find the writing bug and have returned with a completed manuscript... Inspiration intact.

Early, upon said return, I surprised the girls at the usual spot for our '*Girl's only*' lunch - The three of them let out a shrill cry upon seeing my beaming face. The encounter making me realize how great it felt to be home.

"You have to tell us <u>Everything</u>!" Amy pleaded the moment she hugged me. I was sure she meant details about my relationship with On'rie, but anyone can guess what happened there. (Come On! Please... did you seriously think I wouldn't succumb to the seduction of the Most Romantic man on the planet??? HA – I actually think he got that label in a magazine somewhere!)

~Shakes Head~

Anyhow – As we sat down, Dana covered my hand and asked quite demurely, "Did you get any writing in?"

Nervous by the question, I looked to each of them like a silly deer caught in the headlights. It was the first time I'd spoken of my accomplishment to anyone other than On'rie.

Vulnerably, I nodded before the words could escape my mouth. "Yes, and I finished it. It is a full length novel." It hadn't felt real till this moment.

"Wow, Melissa this is wonderful news." Ivy commended before asking, "What will you do with it now?"

Fine....I will admit, I'd thought the same damn thing when I wrote, 'The End' when I was done, but hearing my best friend ask me what I would do felt like she lacked the enthusiasm for it to be shared.

"I have to wait for On'Rie, he hasn't flown in yet but he's made some feeler calls out. Knowing the immense pull he has in the literary world I'm hoping it will find a publishing home."

Amy patted my back, the typical 'Good Job' motion she tended to do when she was getting ready to change the subject. It was nice to be back amongst people I could read well.

"Well, my summer was great, you didn't miss too much on this side of the ocean. I mean, some of it you might need to brace yourself for…" she hesitated, looking at the other two "but other than that New York City has been quiet with most of the residence out in the Hamptons."

I found my head slightly tilting to the left at her almost News-like report. More confused by where she was going with it. Clearly I had missed something and they were fixing to break it to me nice and easy. I looked to each of them and realized that it was Ivy who drew the shorted straw in the draw.

I actually held my breath, knowing deep down it wouldn't be good.

"Sweetie, we didn't want to tell you over the phone or in an email much less. I actually would have thought you'd seen it by now, but seeing as you haven't brought it up…."

"For Pete's sake, what is it." I halted her, releasing the cushion I had built up.

It was she who took a deep breath before saying the one thing I honestly wasn't prepared to hear.

"Brent is engaged."

Would it be a dangerously female thing to do to admit, out loud (in the fine black print of a blog) for thousands to see that my body went cold. Everything just kind of stopped.

It stung, but maybe if I'm honest with myself, I'd admit that it felt like being trapped in a tiny room with a thousand bees on a suicides mission, with me as their target.

Oh, but how the snap in women occurs... The faces we have learned to use to mask the emotions that run rather deep in our being. I learned a long time ago that no matter how much it hurts, there is a time to let each emotion run its course, and a restaurant is neither the place, nor lunch with your girlfriends the time to mourn a man who's place in your heart is still unknown.

"Hmm, that is interesting news." I started. "I'm glad for him. Somehow it makes me feel less guilty for having left with On'rie."

"Page-6 has decided to make their reunion a big thing." Ivy admitted, reaching down into her bag to withdrawal a newspaper article."

"Seriously Ivy, Why would you hand that to her?" Amy sassed, unsuccessfully trying to snatch the paper from her hand.

"You know she is going to go back on her own and find all the information on these two.." Ivy countered, reaching out farther so that I could take hold of the paper.

Indeed it was what I had suspected.

'Brent Bishop reunited with Ex-Fiancé, Megan Moore after a steamy summer courtship'

"I'm glad I wasn't in town to see it happen, I suppose." I quietly admitted.

"Tell us about On'rie, Melissa. What's he like?" Dana asked, her sweet voice bringing my attention away from the black and white callousness.

Her question instantly brought the smile to creep across my face. Yes, the mere mention of his name does that to me. He's like a summer breeze, making everything cool and calm again.

"Oh Dana, he really is the white knight in shining armor our mothers told us of, but at the same time he is so real. He understands me and all my little quirks, he never questions the silly ways I do things." I sighed, "One night, we were sitting on the veranda eating dinner when we started talking about my novel. Our conversation went from fiction to reality and back to fiction, like a language others are not meant to know of and only writers can comprehend. And he knew exactly what I meant when I said things."

"He sounds like a dream, are you sure you're not just fluffing him up?" Ivy asked, apprehensively.

Admitting it to myself, most of the things I do say about On'rie seem too good to be true, but then you're around him for 5 minutes and you realize that it's not this dream you've wandered in to.

"He is very real ladies."

"Well....tell us....did he inspire any romantic scenes in this novel of yours?" Amy giggled as she asked.

The four of us erupted in silly laughter. It is only a matter of time before I admit one thing or another about my Beyond words sex entanglements with the Frenchman.

"Let's just say, I had to force myself to make it clean on paper or it would just be an erotic novel for the masses."

"So tell us, are you guys an item?" Ivy inquired innocently, still giggling from before.

With a sweet tantalizing smile I replied, "We are Off the Market ladies, if that means anything."

In the short few days that I have been back I realized that Home is not where your heart is. Home is where you feel whole, NYC is my whole. This entire time away I came to grips with who I was as a person but deep down I was homesick. I know I wouldn't have been able to write a complete novel this summer had I not left.

My blog ends with today's interesting eyebrow raiser.

This morning consisted of a particularly important pre-scheduled meeting. As soon as I had made arrangements to leave Paris, Marcus insisted that I stop by his office and drop off a copy of the manuscript. It was his conversation with On'rie that had him enthralled.

What do they say about forgetting to put your guard up???
 -Something is going to be thrown your way unexpectedly.

Indeed, I was not expecting to find a 6 foot, blond, blue eyed bombshell standing next to Marcus as I walked in to his office unannounced. Her presence was intimidating and I didn't even know who she was. Looking back, I could smack myself for even asking, for that matter, even being nice to her.

The moment Marcus glimpsed at me walking into the room he halted the conversation and greeted me as the old friends we were.

"My dear, it has been a long 9 weeks." He whispered, kissing both my checks like the French do.

"While Paris is remarkable, New York City is my diamond heart."

He nodded, "Yes, well, from what I'm hearing, you should make a trip again soon. Ben says you've created something magnificent."

"I would say that his admiration for the creator might be having a field day with his word choice."

Marcus jumped quickly, "Oh, forgive me, Melissa this is Megan Moore vice president for Costner's Publishing."

The name didn't immediately strike me. It was right about the time she started talking, telling me how she heard of me that the light bulb flashed on. (Brightly, I might add)

"You are Brent Bishop's fiancée? " I asked, but when the words were out I realized that it came out more like a statement…and with a bit of humor attached to it. (Only I could laugh in a situation like this)

Damn Fates are against me, I'm Sure of it!!!

The curve of her mouth indicated how precisely she knew who I was. That was when I nodded. (mmhmm)

"I can assure you that my relationship with your ex has nothing to do with our interest in your work."

The rest of what she said fell on deaf ears. Even now I couldn't tell any of you what gibberish flabberghastic shit that might have been coming out of her mouth. I stood there and looked into the eyes of the woman who was 'Engaged' to my Mr. New York.

I left 9 weeks ago, running away from a decision I knew I wasn't sure of, chasing an idea- that if I had time I could 'find myself' - but in reality I ran away with a broken heart because I don't have faith in Love. I may have accomplished what I set out to do…and lucked out with the company I've kept but is <u>That</u> going to be enough?

Is giving up on love worth achieving a dream?

Readers comment:

Anonymous <u>August 13, 2013</u>
If you give up on love, you can kiss your dreams worthless.
You should never have left Brent!
Christa M. In Winnipeg

Anonymous <u>August 13, 2013</u>
Only true love lasts the test of time. Follow your dreams and if love finds you, let it in or welcome it back!
~ALF~

Anonymous <u>August 17, 2013</u>
Welcome it back? Why would she go back to Brent...I can't see why she would do that, she made it clear before she left to Paris that Brent wasn't meeting her 'boyfriend' expectations.

Anonymous <u>August 14, 2013</u>
I dont get why it bothers you that he ended up with his ex, You Left Him. You made your bed, no you have to sleep in it.

Anonymous <u>August 15, 2013</u>
Maybe when she went to Paris to find herself, she found her true feelings for Brent and realized she'd made a mistake. Also, Brent must have still had feelings for Megan because she went from his Ex to his Fiancée in 9 weeks. Hmmmm, makes you wonder!

Tuesday, August 20, 2013
5 Million People
Season 2 Episode 2

Every once in a while, (maybe more often than I'd like to admit) I
find myself frozen in a situation where I'd later wish I had said or
done something differently. ~Shakes Head~ Believe you me, I
kick myself after those moments. Mostly because all I really
should do is keep my mouth shut, let people dig their own graves,
and watch as they fall in their perfect little hole.

This week has been a series of rather abundant highs, and one
significant low.

On'rie's flight (home) landed right about the same time Marcus
was blowing up my phone Wednesday morning. Initially, I didn't
answer because I was afraid I would be distracted from seeing
On'rie walking out the gate at the airport terminal, but after the 4th
repeated call, I knew I couldn't put him off any longer and
answered.

"Good Morning, Marcus."

"Don't ignore my calls honey, you know I will just keep calling
you until you pick up." He started, his voice filled with annoyance.

"And in this case, you really want to hear what I have to say."
With my eyes still firmly affixed towards the gate, I felt my
eyebrows rise in instant interest.

"Hmmm, let me guess...You finished the manuscript?" The
question came out and the fear in the pit of my stomach created a
nervous ache. *Is this how I'm going to get every time I hear
someone has finished reading this book?*

"Sweetie, this book has everything women want to read now days:
Romance and a thrill of not knowing what is going to happen at the
end of the next page. Bravo!" he beamed.

What was I to say to that?? Thank you doesn't seem sufficient enough, but it was how I reasoned. A simple thank you and I was incredibly humbled.

"I'm going to pass it along to an editor I know to get some buzz going. We should talk soon, sometime this week or next. Send me a text when you get some free time."

"I will, I see On'rie coming out of the gate so I will talk to you soon." I replied the moment my eyes captured that handsome French face.

Putting the phone back in my pocket, I found myself walking towards On'rie with a jump and a hop in step. I hadn't even noticed the paparazzi waiting in the wings for a photo-op of the European writer. Needless to say, they ended up with a front page winner. Not that it matters, but I hadn't realized how interested they were in our relationship until we were asked a dozen questions on the way back to the car.

No one understands how difficult it is to keep your private life private until being faced with a pushy gossip columnist that insists on following you a thousand steps. On'rie had warned me in Paris what it would be like, so I can't even say I didn't know. I did, I do….but I suppose it will take some time to get use to it.

Best question/response in those thousand steps was found bright and early the next day, printed in black and white - clear for the whole world to see on Page-6 of the New York Post. It was the very first thing shoved in my face that Thursday morning when I met up with the girls for our brunch.

Amy's perfectly manicured fingernails held the paper squarely in front of me as I sat in front of her.

"Is this not the most romantic thing anyone has ever said?" she mused.

"It was pretty sweet when it came out of his mouth." I replied greeting Dana who was sitting next to me with a kiss on the cheek.

"Has it sunk in yet, I mean that you are dating such a public man?" Dana inquired, the creases on her forehead signaling more than just her concern. *Doubt maybe?*

As I took the paper from Amy, Ivy interrupted before I could answer. "My dear, you shouldn't care if they are parked outside of your apartment. By the time they get use to On'rie being in a relationship you will be glad there are gone."

Her disdain for the PapZ is a love-hate relationship. In one aspect Ivy makes a living off of what they publicize on her clients. On the other hand, unless you have deep pockets they are pretty much Uncontrollable.

Deciding to keep the article as 'keepsake material', I took one last look at the blurb before folding it up and placing it in my bag.

"She is the best thing that's ever happened to me" Announced world renowned writer, Benjamine On'rie when asked about his relationship with Brent Bishop's ex-girlfriend, Melissa Green. While their relationship has yet to be cleared, it is safe to say that the two are a couple to watch. This news comes only weeks after the official announcement of Brent Bishop and Megan Moore's engagement.

When I looked up, I found Amy giving me a curious glare. "What is it?" I asked.

She shook her head, and I could only guess what was about to come out of her mouth. "Are you sure you are okay with this whole ordeal?"

Sigh~ Speaking before thinking 101: When annoyed take a 3 sec pause before saying anything. Usually you will catch yourself before you say something you will later regret~ o_O

"If I were to pass him in the street I wouldn't flinch." I lied. The moment I said it, I knew none of them believed an ounce of my insistence, but as my friends they went with it.

"Okay, I'll say nothing more in the matter." Amy agreed hesitantly, taking a sip from her coffee cup.

"Changing the subject however, Marcus called yesterday to let me know that he is sending my manuscript to some of his colleagues.

He wants to get a buzz going before it even hits a publisher's hands."

"That's great. Are we going to get to read it, or do we need to wait along with the rest of the world?" Dana asked.

Fear again. "I will get some copies made and sent to you guys, if you all want a copy," was all I could respond and it triggered a change in subject with nodding of heads.

"Well, I will be on the look-out. I hate to cut out so soon but I have a meeting that can't be avoided." Dana said, grabbing her purse and saying her goodbyes.

The three of us watched her walk out of the restaurant. As soon as she was gone we turned to each other, as if reading each other's minds.

"What are we doing for her birthday?" almost simultaneously asking.

Ivy won the conversation lead. "I want to throw her a surprise party. It shouldn't be too difficult. I will fill you in on the details and you show up."

I am always down with someone else planning a party. I can't even imagine what all it takes, detail wise, to make the events we go to turn out successful, but I'm grateful Ivy loves to do this sort of thing.

A few days later On'rie and I walked into River Café under the Brooklyn Bridge utterly excited to see Dana's face when she and Ivy walked in later. Amy waved us over to the table set up for our dinner party.

The ambiance of the little place was perfect. Just what Dana would love for her birthday dinner.

"What time did Ivy say she would get here?" I asked Amy, interrupting her conversation with On'rie about Paris models vs. Milan models.

She flipped her wrist and smiled, "Any minute now."

"I'll be right back, ladies room." I whispered in On'rie's ear, kissing his lips as I pulled away while the smile and twinkle warmed my heart.

Can a girl get any luckier? HA! Because the moment I think such things, you'd imagine seeing me duck in response to any disaster Fate would find to knock me out.

~Yeah, no such luck!~ And let me tell you that I never *Expect* shit to happen to me. I forget, Each and every time that I live in a city of over **5 million people**.

Some faces are harder to forget, however. One in particular was staring at me the moment I got up from the table, I felt his glare before I realized it was him.

Brent Bishop stood with another gentleman by the bar that had been set up outside. When he nodded at me, I couldn't help but purse my lips together in a pained smile and nod back. I disappeared into the ladies room and dreaded the retreat from the safe enclosed room. The door literally felt like a safety lock. I stared at my reflection in the gilded mirror. The woman I found was not who I imagined seeing and the comments from last week's post honestly came to mind.

Why did it matter that Brent is engaged, I chose On'rie.

Somehow, I'd been lying to myself. I jumped from one ship to another and forgot to wear my lifejacket. It was nothing but my running away from the fear of not being good enough. And yes, that makes me a coward, something I adamantly argued to Not being, in April.

So what now? I found myself asking the reflection.
Nothing else but to face the bear head on and pray I won't get mauled.

Leaving the bathroom I appreciated Brent's consistency. He was waiting for me right outside the ladies room door. The undersized darkened hallway seemingly smaller with the two of us taking up much of the available space.

"I hope it's okay that I come over to say hi." He started before I had a chance to say anything.

"It's fine. How are you?" I asked, regretting the question. I didn't want to hear that he is doing Fabulous! I am a WOMAN! When that damn torch is still being carried, a woman only wants to hear how much she is missed. Anything else is Bla, Bla Bla!

"I'm okay, I guess. Busy with work, as usual." He replied, shifting his weight –noticeably uncomfortable.

"Some things never change, I suppose." Squinting my eyes, I felt like saying: The first time shame on me but the second time shame on you for egging it on.

"Look, we should probably talk." He started, "I said some things, and we never had a chance to talk. You left so suddenly…"

"I can't imagine what your fiancée would say if she knew we were meeting for a… talk." I interrupted him.

"M, you don't understand. I want us to talk." His sincerity cut deep. The way he stared at me, as if looking through me, not at me, knowing exactly how to control my emotions.

"I don't think it's a good idea Brent…" I started and lucked out because Amy rounded the corner and found us standing there, alone.

"What's going on guys?" she asked, looking at me for a reasonable explanation.

"Nothing, everything's fine. I'm sorry, have I ruined the surprise?" I asked, and starting walking away, not thinking to wait for a reply.

Sure enough, I walked outside for the air my lungs needed. Maybe I had been holding my breath that whole time, I wouldn't know. But I felt like I was being suffocated. I walked out to the edge of the balcony and stared out at the river and watched the way the waves danced under the Brooklyn Bridge.

On'rie joined me a few minutes later. While the fact remains that having seen Brent threw me off, the admission I made in that moment should probably have been kept to myself.

"I feel I've made a horrible mistake and now I don't know how to fix it."

He turned to face me, while I still stared out at the water. The breeze kicked up and I felt the chill. Was it the fear of admitting a flaw, or just timing?

"What do you want me to do?" he asked softly, knowing that I was talking in circles.

The only problem was that I knew exactly what I wanted. "I need some time to think."

He nodded, turned my body towards his and just held me. "I have to go back to Paris for a couple weeks. Enough time for you to realize how good we are together." He whispered into my ear.

I pulled back far enough for him to see my face, "I adore you, you know that don't you?" I asked.

All I'm left wondering now is, *'Can one Fix Love?'*

Readers comment:

Anonymous August 20, 2013
Sometimes in life, we tend to make hasty decisions because of a misunderstanding or not talking out a situation. These decisions often come back to bite us in the arse. Take some time to reflect on your relationships and be honest with yourself and your heart. Love can be fixed but it can also be destroyed!
~ALF~

Anonymous August 21, 2013
Are you kidding me. You can't fix love, and what's worse is I don't think you know what love is! You didn't make a mistake when you left the city, you knew you didn't love Brent back then.
Nancy

Anonymous August 22, 2013
You must not be married or in a relationship. Being in a relationship is a series of 'Falling in, being in, and fluffing out of-Love' Melissa, just Go with it!

Anonymous August 22, 2013
I agree with you Anonymous...Many relationships are on again/off again in the beginning but if there is real love, it CAN and WILL be fixed! Go after him Melissa!!! :)

Tuesday, August 27, 2013
Fate had Another Idea
Season 2 Episode 3

"Denial is not just a river in Egypt." Have you ever heard that expression? Yeah, well, my granny would tell me that as a teenager, and I never quite understood why it mattered....Funny how I do now. For all the paths we take in our lives, the longest to overcome are the one in which we are blinded by denial.

To go days, weeks, and even months ignoring the white elephant in our mind – This is the set back from moving on. You know what my white elephant is....Mr. NY, and quite frankly I was a little taken back by the comments on last week's episode.

Just because I am confused doesn't mean I can't fathom what love is...but I'm also not saying I am **IN** love with anyone. And while I never thought of it before, I totally agree with love having a lifespan of series. You either Love someone, or you don't....there is No shade of gray in that. But once you love, everything changes.

Hearing about Brent and Megan pushed me to the level: 'You don't know what you have until you lose it', and while I didn't technically lose Brent, I still don't have him. Honestly, the fear of ruining something with 'perfection potential' is what did me in from the onset.

So here I sit, getting ready to tell you how the nail got one more whack from the hammer this week.

The night On'rie left was the first time since spring that I'd been bitten by the lonely bug. Luckily, I have friends like Marcus to come banging on my apartment door at the crack of dawn to spread good news of success.

Yes indeed, Marcus knocked no less than 50 times that morning before I made it to the door to greet him, disastrous hair and all.

"The sun hasn't come up yet, Marcus." I complained as he made his way to my plumpy purple sofa.

"Our futures don't wait for the sun to rise and fall, my dear," he began, "and besides when do I ever wait for everyone else's day to begin?"

Rolling my eyes, the only thing I could think of at that moment was the shiny new coffee maker in my sad empty kitchen. If I was going to be forced to stay up when the world was snoozing, I would certainly have a cup of Joe in me.

"So tell me why I'm the privileged one this morning, Marcus." I asked, pulling the coffee bag out of the cabinet.

"Your book, my dear, has been picked up by none other than Random House Publishing. They asked Megan for an interview with you as soon as possible." The expression he held was of stone cold excitement, and yet he was holding his breath, almost waiting for me to drop the other shoe for him.

I stood still, eyes slowly lowering and squinting together as the confusion peeked.

"Why is Megan Moore involved with my book getting picked up by a publishing company?" I asked him as gently as I could muster.

"Tosh, Tosh, Melissa. You need to stop being so nervous about that woman. She really does seem harmless."

"Yes, like a cobra waiting to attack in daylight." I snapped at him quickly. The coffee bag almost flying out of my hand towards him. Turning around I went back to the distraction at hand, coffee.

"My dear, regardless of who pulled the strings, the fact is, your book is something rather special. It needs to be out there. If On'rie were here he would agree with me, and you damn well know it.

Most authors spend years trying to strike it big. Here you are, ahead of all the rest and ready to start your complaining."

With the coffee brewing, I finally turned back to my dear friend and beheld the expression that spoke volumes. He cares, so much so, that he doesn't give a darn bit how things are happening, as long as they are happening.

"So what's this interview going to consist of, hmmm?" I asked plainly, hands of submission both perched on my hips.

"They will of course ask what you are willing to do to get the word out. Which shouldn't be a problem seeing as you are in a relationship with Benjamine On'rie. Your association will peek interest from his followers."

"On'rie is in Paris, Marcus, and I'm not sure what our relationship is at the moment." I admitted, the sadness in my voice apparent.

"As far as the world knows, you are still together, he is just away on business." Marcus stated, moving on with the outline. "They will also ask you for a preview of what you are working on now, and it's important for you to accept this request as they could potentially be your publishing home for the foreseeable future."

This was where my stomach began to ache.

Nerves maybe?

Nope!

Something **FAR** worse.

"I, uh…um. Marcus, I don't *have* anything new." I admitted fearfully.

With a 'Marcus Double Take', he all but lost it, "What do you *meeaaannnn* you don't have anything?"

So, there is a perfectly good explanation for this madness…Maybe not appropriate but it was the first thing I thought of at 5 in the flipping morning.

"I can't help that writer's block is my equivalent to Love's cock-block, Marcus!" I snapped at him.

The silence in my kitchen was stunning. I couldn't take it back, but I wish I could. He stared at me, speechless, but more because of my meaning. The crazy part of the whole situation is that Marcus wasn't confused by what I meant. He could see how everything in my life was preventing me to accomplish what I had this summer. NYC is home, and it's also where my reality is muddled. Paris was carefree and where I found my fictional world.

"Melissa, I say this with the utmost amount of love for you... Learn the language your heart speaks. Love isn't confusing, it's just *complicated*." With that he turned around and left me standing alone in my kitchen. Left to wonder how I would actually accomplish this feat.

Sadly, there is no Rosetta Stone for the most complex emotion known to man.

After that, I spent the whole day staring at a blank screen on my laptop. I had so many things I wanted to put on that blank page, but I was trying to listen to my heart. Marcus was right in the sense that I don't know the language it's functioning in. Most of the time I just, Act....and can never explain the reasons behind those actions.

Not fancying another wasted day, I made plans to have lunch with Dana Friday at South Gate near the park.

She was sitting at a table, sipping from a wine glass looking at the menu when I walked in. She was a sight for sore eyes, and I think she noticed how I felt when I sat in front of her.

"Hi, honey. I hope you don't mind, I ordered us each a glass of, Patrimonio." her voice innocent and sweet.

"It's lovely, thank you." I said raising the glass to my lips to sip the yumminess.

"Are you okay?" she inquired plainly. The tilt of her head signaling she was aware of my change.

The sigh came out before I could think. "I'm fine, just sorting things out." I admitted.

"Anything you want to share that I may be able to help you with?"

"It's not much more than not being able to write anything at the moment. There is too much going on in my head. I'm just frustrated because Marcus said I'm going to need to present what I'm working on now to the publishing company when I have my interview with them." I explained, taking another sip of the fabulous wine.

Dana sat for a moment, waiting to see if I would add to my complaint.

When I didn't she asked, "What's going on in your head?"

I looked up, and faced the facts. "I want to bump into Brent again." I started. "Ever since last week, I haven't been able to get him out of my mind. It's like being blinded. I can't see anything other than his face every time I try to think."

Even I had to take a moment with such the admission. Putting it in any other way wouldn't have done it justice.

"You need to make sure you know what you are doing when it comes to that man. He is engaged, and you are with On'rie. I wouldn't recommend seeing him again, but that's just me."

As per my usual motif, I changed the topic of conversation and we finished our lunch saying nothing more of my absurd desire to see my Mr. NY again.

I will admit that life has a funny way of showing us the right path to take, or even how to get ourselves out of a rut. I left South Gate thinking that the fresh air would push me to wake up from the darkness of writers block....**FATE HAD ANOTHER IDEA**!

I beheld his exquisite figure before he even noticed me....and the mere fact that I knew his walk still stung a little. Last week I'd finally accepted that at some point or another I would run into him. It is New York City, after all. But never while I was thinking about him.

Not wanting to seem insensitive I sat at a bench and waited for him to reach it, figuring he would join me. I looked out over the lake and focused on a group of ducks floating in circles.
I didn't look at him as he sat next to me, merely nodded at his presence.

"Isn't this dandy." He whispered.

"Indeed it is." I replied, the smile unavoidable. The humor in how life tries to throw curve balls is Always amusing.

"How are you doing?" he asked for the second time in the span of a week.

This was when I turned to face him. "I'm just dandy, Brent. How are you?"

He shook his head, "So you've resorted to sarcasm then."

Taken back, "Do you find it unreasonable that I would ask my ex how he's doing?" Curious if he'd mistaken my reply as sarcasm...Then again, It would be something I would resort to. ;)

HA!

"I'm good, M....Just Fine."

"What now then?" I asked.

...And before you start thinking that I muddle things up here, just realize this one little Fact....Every second I sat at that bench with Brent, only inches away from me, my heart was breaking in the worst way possible.

"When you called me that morning in June, I wasn't thinking, and I'm sorry for what I said to you." He offered.

"No, you hit it right on the money...I was waiting for this grand epiphany which would wipe away all my fears about our relationship, something that would ease the worry I was going through." I admitted.

He sat back, "What worry?" he asked suddenly.

I huffed, "While words are not necessary to solidify an emotion, your presence is. Every time you left on business, I was here wondering if what we had was strong enough to withstand our limited schedule."

"I run a company, M – You knew that. It was always part of the package."

"You don't get it. You hardly ever made time for me to at least come say goodbye before you left on those trips." I said, pausing to notice how he realized my point, "Once, you even sent me a text message from the plane. You seriously mean to tell me that was part of the package?"

Crickets! He turned to face the pond and I could see the muscles in his jaw flex.

When the silence reached its peak I stood up and took a few steps away from the bench. Away from him.

"I'm sorry." Brent said behind me. He had gotten up and made his way to my side. He reached out and grabbed the inside of my arm turning me towards him.

"I'm sorry for giving up, Brent." I offered in return, looking up into his dazzling hazel eyes.

I'm not going to lie, it was nice feeling the warmth vibrating from his body. The energy his touch created still has the power to hypnotize me, but this time I just went with the moment.

He leaned in closer, heading in for the kiss we were both magnetized for. I closed my eyes, and prepared myself for what my heart was racing for.

That was when his cell phone rang. Our eyes instantly flew open and he scrambled to answer the call.

While he acted like nothing was taking place on his end, I took several steps distancing myself. The safe space a sure bet that I wouldn't feel regretful later.

Eavesdropping, I realized that it was Megan calling him. With pierced lips I welcomed the reality check.

The moment he ended the call, he looked at me with guilt spread throughout his face. That was all I needed to see to know what was coming next.

"M, I plan on marrying her before the end of the year."

I simply nodded my head. Connection or not, you need more than just love to have a relationship.

"Congrats, Brent." The hallow meaningless words left my lips and simultaneously the tear that had formed on its own at the corner of my eye unfortunately fell as well.

I turned around and walked away.

......**I walked away**...... and it felt, in that precise moment that my heart would shatter into a million pieces.

Readers comment:

Anonymous August 27, 2013
If he leaned in for a kiss, all is not lost. He must still have feelings for you. Don't give up again. Turn around and go

after what you want.
~ALF~

Anonymous August 27, 2013
Plans can change! Collect those heart pieces honey.
Deb

Anonymous August 28, 2013
While I'd love to agree with ~ALF~ that all is not lost.
Remember that he is with a woman and was about to kiss
you... cheater? This being the same woman before you, so
I'm thinking with guarded heart and think that if he would
kiss you while with her what would stop him from
jumping back to her while with you. He too seems lost on
the road of love.
Sarah

Anonymous August 28, 2013
Sarah, I understand what you're saying and I thought
about that too. But, Megan was his ex before he got
together with Melissa. I really think he loves Melissa but
was heartbroken by her so he was going to settle for
Megan, who just won't leave him alone. I really don't
think he's a "cheater" per say but more confused. Like you
said, he seems lost on the road of love.
~ALF~

Anonymous August 28, 2013
What I keep on wondering is how you can continue to
feel as though you're not good enough for this Brent guy?
I don't trust Megan, sorry. A woman who puts that much
interest in her man's Ex has a hidden agenda.

Tuesday, September 3, 2013
Words Cut Deep
Season 2 Episode 4

Champagne and designer dresses really should be considered the 'chicken soup' cocktail remedy for a broken heart. If nothing else, the distraction is well worth the effort to make any undesirables fade away. In my case, it has been the temporary band-aid to the heart strings issue.

On'rie came home from his trip to Paris bright eyed and bushy tailed, and with news of an invitation to a ceremony being held in his honor at the Plaza. Of course he forgot to mention it to me sooner, which is never a stellar idea when the information involves a woman who needs a red-carpet gown for said event.

Lucky for me, I have the top PR chick on the upper east-side in my corner. Ivy knew just who to contact when I filled her in on my dilemma. She was also especially excited when I mentioned that On'rie had scored her and the girls tickets to share our table.

"Limo Party!" she squealed into the phone.

In which my response was, "Just let me know when you have the dress situation handled and we will make a date of it."

By the following morning, between Dana and Ivy, my cell phone was ringing off the hook.

"Are they always so eager to get your attention so early in the morning?" On'rie asked, sipping casually from his coffee mug as if the world had not a care.

Not being able to help it, I leaned back in my chair to take a peek at the digital clock on the fireplace mantle. It only read 9:45am.

My face scrunched into a saucy confused expression. "It's not that early. Your timing must still be set to Paris my dear."

Flipping the page of the newspaper, he decided not to add to my comment. Instead he paid closer attention to the articled he had just uncovered. Huffing a few times before grasping my full attention.

"What is it?" I hesitated, knowing that his noise making was more opinionated than anything else. That was when the corner of the paper folded down revealing his now amused face.

"We have apparently made 'Page-6' again, but this time they have taken it to a whole new level of Joyous misinformation."

I stood slowly and made my way to his side, leaning over his shoulder ever so gently to read the piece myself.

'While the Cats away the Mice will play. New literary Pre-Madonna, Melissa Green was seen in Central Park last week chatting it up with her ex beau, Brent Bishop. While their relationship has been off since June of this year, a source tells us that there may still be some cobwebs in their break, blaming Benjamine On'rie for the split. Our source also reports that On'rie is not publicly claiming their relationship is an official thing, only that their time together has been the best for him. He should probably make his trips out of town shorter if he wants to have a relationship with her stick.'

Quite Frankly, some things are just better left unsaid . I shook my head and went back to my seat on the other side of the kitchen table. Picking up my coffee mug, I waited for a question I probably wouldn't hear leave his mouth. The best part of On'rie has always been that he doesn't care for an explanation, especially if it is half concocted because one can't comprehend a situation themselves.

Brent was never a talking topic for us. We never talked about him because I couldn't...can't explain my feelings simply.

"I hope you know that I do value our relationship, Melissa." He said softly, folding and putting the newspaper back on the table.

I smiled at his comment. "I have never doubted that one bit." I replied, in equal softness.

The morning light gleaming through my kitchen window caught the corner of his eye and it's hue changed from hazel to light blue. The simplicity of the moment reminded me of something that had happened while in Paris.

The first week we were together, I recall spending little time in a vertical position. The seduction very much intoxicated us into a drunken-like state and we would stay in bed for what seemed like days at a time, only really leaving to eat and get cleaned up.

One of those mornings, I had woken up before him and caught him slowly waking up. The light was shining on our bed and while I know the color of his eyes are hazel, he woke up with an almost clear blue hue that morning.

Startled, I gasped, "Your eyes are so blue." It really was the most beautiful thing I'd ever seen.

"They are only that color when I'm happy." He replied, following it up by a kiss that makes me forget what the rest of the day was like. I will never forget that morning, but only because it was the closest thing to hearing how happy he was being with me.

"What is it?" On'rie asked, pulling me out of the memory. Instantly a smile grew on my face. "Your eyes are blue this morning."

It's incredible how 6 words can make clear the depths of a connection two people share really. Words are nice to hear….some words will always weigh heavier on the heart than others, but an action-while involuntarily as it may seem, is worth so much more.

Ivy sent the girls and I a text message directing us to Madison Avenue's InterMix with hopes that we would all find something to wear to On'rie's event.

Dana was the first to join me outside the white pillared building, waiting for the others to arrive.

"So I see you've made Page-6 again." She began. "At least this time it didn't seem to scathing."

"Makes me wonder who's her source." I quickly shot back. It had been bugging me ever since.

"Indeed, that is curious. I know none of us would say anything to anyone about your private affairs."

The moment she said it, I snapped in her direction. The word affairs circling my head like concussion stars.

"I didn't mean that like it sounded."

"Don't worry, I wouldn't blame you if you did. I admit to thinking about it once or twice, but then On'rie shows up and I realize how wonderful things are with him. I could smack myself for ever wondering if I'd made the right decision leaving Brent."

Dana pursed her lips together and nodded in agreement. She seems to be a Team On'rie.

Ivy showed up with Amy at just the unfortunate moment to hear my statement. "You wonder because of your lack of closure. Next time make a clear break and just maybe the guy will get a clue."

"She's right you know. The only reason it felt weird seeing him again is because you just kinda up and left. Most people have a post break up that gets them through to the next level. Closure really is a process." Amy tried to explain.

 My question is: How does Amy have ANY opinion about relationships???

"I'm not sure this place is going to work Ivy." I changed the subject. "I'm just warning you, I've been here before."

"Little faith, my dear. I spoke to my connection here and she has pulled some spectacular dresses for us. She even has a *Marchesa* for you, M that she promises you are going to die for!"

A stunning two hours later I was back in my apartment, beautiful sage-green semi beaded *Marchesa* hanging from the door frame of my closet. While it was hard to admit that Ivy was right, I would give her the credit that staring at my dress did make me go a little starry-eyed.

The night of the event, On'rie and I were the last to get picked up by the limo. He failed to inform me that he would be receiving a special award that evening. It was Ivy who had done some PR research and gave the little tidbit up on the ride there.

"I wanted it to be a surprise, my dear. You've had a lot on your mind." He said innocently.

We made it to the Plaza right about the same time as every other attendee was arriving. It was fun to see the cameras flashing as people left their limos and started to make the walk down the red carpet, and into the building.

"Do you want me to go in with the girls?" I asked him, not wanting to intrude on his moment.

"Absolutely Not!" he scolded, "I want you by my side, why would you ask me that? You are my Mon-cheri!"

With that being said, the world-wind of a red-carpet walk with Benjamine On'rie was breath taking. Reporters asking dozens of questions and camera's flashing like rapid fire. Every now and again he would squeeze my hand and whisper in my ear how beautiful I looked. The giggle it created was probably the desired effect, they ate up every moment of it.

Once we made it inside the building, Ivy had a glass of champagne waiting for me in hand.

"I thought you could use a little pick me up after that delicious mayhem."

"That was all sorts of invigorating." I admitted sheepishly.

On'rie greeted a few people, introduced me to a dozen more and we were off to sit at our table. Every person I was introduced to knew of my book and how I had just been picked up by a publishing company.

The congratulations seemed to be followed by daggers but still, they kept coming and the smiling faces were everywhere.

On'rie had mentioned that he had wanted the award to be a surprise, but more-so because of the speech he was planning on giving. The shock moment came when his most recent work was presented and eventually he was summoned to the podium. Before he left the table, the crowd in the frenzy of applaud, On'rie leaned over to me and planted one square on my mouth. PDA for all of the literary world and NYC's elite to witness.

Once at the podium, the spotlight was finally all on him, but boy was that short lived.

He removed a perfectly folded white paper from his breast pocket. Stared at it, then addressed the crowd.

"I had written a nice little speech thanking the committee for this honor, but if you would allow me, I would like to wing this." His attention reverted back to me before he continued.

"When I started writing, many years ago, I realized that we must have a passion for the craft, otherwise it becomes a function. Like brushing your teeth. You have to do it or something inside of you turns dark and rots. I have been blessed to accomplish so much in this industry, worked hard to win awards like this one tonight but something had been missing. My work was becoming a function, and no longer held the vital passion we all thrive on." He paused, and inwardly laughed. "Then my good friend Marcus introduced me to an exquisite American girl....Melissa, my love, it doesn't matter what the world is saying as long as you are speaking our language. Thank you for being my girl and reminding me of this passion we share, both in our relationship and in our craft."

He raised the crystal trophy and thanked the crowd, walking back stage with one of the ceremony presenters.

I turned back to the ladies at my table who were each blotching their eyes at the corners with their napkins. Being that I was about to implode from embarrassment, I excused myself quickly from the table, walking as nonchalantly as I could to the door heading out into the lobby.

Rounding the darker corner and halting my steps, I noticed a familiar figure in the distance pacing between the pillars. It was Brent, talking to Joseph, an old friend of his.

"Man, you really just need to let this go." He offered Brent, "It shouldn't matter anyway, you are engaged, dude."

"I can't help the fact that shit like that is going to bother me." He retorted sharply. "He all but admitted to falling in love with her from the moment he laid eyes on her. Words like that cut deep, no matter what your current situation is."

"Can you blame him? Melissa was the one man." Joseph asked. His statement and Joseph's response caught me off guard. I turned too sharply and the heel of my shoe clanked hard on the marble floor. The noise bounced off the walls, pulling both of their attention in my direction. Seeing Brent look squarely at me felt like an anvil plunging inwardly towards the pit of my stomach.

Turning quickly I came face to face with Dana and Ivy who both walked me back to our table. They saw who was in the lobby area. They knew perfectly well why I was trembling. But thankfully neither one said a word for the entire evening.

The distraction came, On'rie's speech created a curiosity from those in the literary world that hadn't heard of me. Little by little I had managed to woo the remaining leading literary figures before the night was out.

All in all, I'd say that on a professional level, the night was a success.

On a personal level….Well, Ivy said it best before we dropped her off.

"I think it's about time that I picked you up as a full time client. Tonight's performances have made me realize that in one way, shape, or form, you my love, are going to need the help of my services. If not to promote this incredible book you have, or tidy up an inevitable mess."

"Well it's about time someone wants to clean up my messes." I joked.

"Baby girl, you need to stay away from your Mr. NY. He is a heart grenade waiting to explode on your newly built love nest. The mess he could bring to your table is not what you want associated with your book release." She warned.

So basically it boils down to: **Stay away from Brent at all cost**…… Why does it then feel like he is a magnet North, and I a polar South?

Readers comment:

Anonymous   September 06, 2013
Seems to be you feel that he is your magnet North because you tend to do things you know you shouldn't. Benjamin sounds dreamy- keep him around!
Nancy

Anonymous   September 06, 2013
I know your heart is confused but take time to analyze things clearly. You don't want to lose On'rie over something you really don't want.
~ALF~

Just so you know, I have spent the better part of the week writing my new manuscript. Go Me! It's incredible what eavesdropping on an ex-flame does for the inspirational pallet. The fact remains that the key words in my initial statement are, 'better part of', seeing as I've had a visitor drop in on me this week.

Visitors are always fun, especially when they come rapping on the door at a bright and early, 8am Thursday morning. *I don't think I have to say anymore* and seeing as you, my faithful readers probably can easily understand what the problem with that situation is, begs reason to be thrown at those in my life and why they simple don't get it.

Before I go into how my dear old friend Andy Henderson is staying at my place whilst on his vacation, I must address my faithful readers.

Dear Ms. Nancy - You know who you are...You're right, I do tend to do things that I shouldn't do. In fact, I have become aware that I more often go against the grain and do things I am Specifically told not to do. My mother always seemed to have a problem with that little fault about me.

As an adult, when someone said, 'Oh, you can't do that." It practically seemed like an open invitation. My response after the fact would surprisingly be, 'Really, why not?"

Unfortunately, I will admit there are times I should just simply listen to the wiser folk pleading the good advice, but where Love is concerned, I haven't done much listening. But then again, good advice from reliable sources are hard to come by.

Well...Anyhew...Andy Henderson is a childhood friend. Do not, my any mistake, assume that he is or has ever been a love interest because he isn't. While I will openly admit that Andy is supremely attractive, he is not my type on an emotional level. There is just something about a guy that plays video games as a hobby that turns my oven off. ;) And while there is nothing wrong with having such an intellectual hobby, I just can't play the damn games myself, and feel a twinge of anger every time I see one on. *call it jealousy ALL you want!*

Seeing Andy in my doorway that morning immediately had my head turning to see if the banging had woken On'rie. *See, there is a good girlfriend move shining bright*

"Hey" I whispered, quickly ushering him inside.

"I'm sorry I didn't call. Why are we whispering?"

"My boyfriend is sleeping." I admitted, looking back towards my room once again.

So very much like Andy, he didn't miss a beat. "Your Boyfriend?!?!?!" his voice no longer in a whisper.

"Ssshhhhh, you're gonna wake em up!" I hushed him.

"When did you get a boyfriend, Missy?" he asked. Sadly, I realized there was disappointment lined in that sexy voice of his.

My head slightly tilted to the right, "Honey, we have been together for a while now. I thought you knew."

"How would I know, I've been in Australia for the past 5 months." He stated matter of factly.

Sighing, I turned around and had him follow me to the kitchen. 20 minutes later and a delicious cup of coffee in hand, I had Andy all caught up on what he had missed.

Quite frankly, I should have just sat him in front of my laptop and read this blog, but then again he might catch on to a little too much information.

"So he is here then?"

"Of course he's here. His home is in Paris, and most of his business is there as well, but he's been staying in the city for me.

So, it kinda has just worked out so far."

"So far?" he asked harshly.

"Yes, Andy, So Far." I snapped. "I don't have all the answers, and you know….this whole real relationship shit is new to me."

"Of course it is, you never agree to commit to Anything that means longevity."

Refusing to argue I reached out to his arm. "Ivy is so going to want you to come to our lunch. That's okay, right?" and while I essentially was 'asking', it's because he knows it's always 'Just the Girls', I ask because he isn't my 'Gay boyfriend' he is just my wonderful understanding 'Guy friend'.   **Hopefully you followed that**

"That's fine, I'm actually working my way up this time to asking our Amy out. Maybe she has gotten past the oyster debacle from last year."

I kinda hoped she had too, I mean, she spent a solid 3 months complaining about Andy and how she could still smell fish on occasion.

Before I could say anything about that, On'rie walked into the kitchen hesitantly. Seeing his expression made me jump to his side.

"Ben, this is Andy. He will be sleeping on the couch for a few days." I offered.

The handshake that ensued made me realize that a boyfriend usually needs more than that.

"Andy is a childhood friend, we grew up together. He usually just stops by and stays with me when he has work in the city."

"It's nice to meet you Andy. I'm sorry we don't have anything more for breakfast, Melissa did not tell me you were coming. I would have made sure we had food sent over."

"Oh no, don't worry about me. I am pretty simple. I hadn't thought to call. Missy hadn't informed me that she was in a relationship."

~shakes head~ Oh boy…I knew it was coming…On'rie is BIG on proper etiquette. He had been brought up by royals and in such an upbringing silly little things bothered him about modern society.

"It doesn't take much more than lifting a phone and dialing a number now a days." Was all that came out of his mouth. I guess I counted my blessings on that one. He turned around and went back to my room leaving me with my eyes wide open and my arm held out to Andy as to not reply to the comment.

"Well, let me go get myself presentable and we shall be on our way to brunch." I told my dear old friend.

My room had a funny uncomfortable vibe in it when I walked in.

Seriously though…I get jealousy, but not for EVERY single man that walks into your eyesight.

Maybe it's a French thing. I mean, On'rie isn't overbearing, he just seems leery of men lingering too long around me. The whole idea is fascinating considering the one man he should feel threatened by, he doesn't seem to be. But like, someone of Andy's personality comes strolling in my orbit and KABOOM, his demeanor turns on the Green power.

"What makes you think that having another man in your apartment is 'all well and good'?"

My head fell back at the absurdity. "Are you Flipping kidding me, this is Andy we are talking about. He is like my b*r*o*t*h*e*r, Jesus!"

"I don't care what he is, Mademoiselle, he is a man with a God Damn Penis, he doesn't think with his brain, he is controlled by his lower region!"

I huffed at his argument, however accurate, and quickly dressed, leaving only after planting a short lip lock on his puckered lips. He wasn't pleased-Obviously, but I wasn't about to go explaining something that wasn't worth the time.

Andy is a friend. Has been in friend zone since our senior year in high school and has stayed there. This isn't a Ron Weasly-happily-ever-after story, this is reality.

So there we were, sitting at a now 5 seated table, waiting for the bombshell question.

"So what did On'rie say about your just showing up like you usually do?" Amy asked inquisitively.

10 minutes even. That was all it took. Seriously, my friends know me Too well!

"I would say his feathers were rather ruffled by the whole situation." Andy teased.

"It's not funny!" I snapped.

The immediate silence was awkward. But their stares were rather amusing.

"Missy, you really need to just introduce him to your chill pills." Andy joked, but the inside joke wasn't understood by the rest of the girls.

Their ears peeked and their heads tilted. I could only imagine where their minds were traveling with that statement.

"I'm not on drugs dear, and it's 2013, we don't joke about that shit anymore." I scolded Andy.

"I really think we should all get together to make Andy's visit worth wile. Something to keep him thinking about when he goes back to boring ol' Iowa." Ivy insisted.

They settled on location and plans while I played with my crisp white napkin. Drugs, old boyfriends, and never ending parties.

These were memories Andy had hidden away with me in them. A word…Shame. I could easily become ashamed by the memories he could recall. The nights where he had held my hair back while I slept on the porcelain bowl.

You would think I wouldn't look at this as a YOLO challenge. Shake your head now, that is exactly how I thought of it Saturday night after about 6 Long Island Ice teas at 'The Tippler' .

Some nights, wining and dining just isn't enough. On'rie was at a late night business meeting and I was free as a bird. As free as my clipped wings would take me. When the clock struck 3 Ivy and Dana had said they were ready for bed. Amy and Andy on the other hand looked at me as if I knew the secret to Fun.

My kind of fun begins and ends in an imagery world were rules are something of an unknown element.

We assured them we would catch a cab back to my place within the hour. Funny thing how that hour never came. We left the bar and walked right into the park, drunk off our arses.

Bright Idea #1: Andy suggested we play nude-man-hunt in our bare feet.
        NEXT DAY RESPONSE: Seriously?

Bright Idea #2: Amy suggested we go swimming in the fountain.

        NEXT DAY RESPONSE: Seriously?

Bright Idea #3: When all was said and done, I drunk dialed Brent to come pick us up.

NEXT DAY RESPONSE: Are you Flipping kidding me?!?!?!

So yeah, needless to say, we ended up in jail after a few complaint calls. YOLO is officially out of my phrase choice and I'm waiting patiently for the Page-6 story about what a train wreck On'rie has gotten himself entangled with.

Worse moment, after all the madness came when Marcus bailed us out of jail.

"My dear, no matter how much of a mess you've made, always know the hole can go deeper yet."

"Marcus, it was bad judgment. It won't happen again." I tried to tell him but his hand went up.

"Spiraling out of control, for whatever reason, will not win you Brent's affection back."

"That's not what I'm doing." I countered.

"No?" he asked, "Then why did you call him?"

.....Why did I call him?.....

Readers comment:

> ***Anonymous***   September 12, 2013
> First of all, I can't believe the way On'rie acted toward your friend Andy. I can't stand jealousy! Time to grow up On'rie!!! AND as for why you called Brent...simple...because you still LOVE him and really want to be with him and not On'rie. Time to go after what you want and stop settling. On'rie might be a nice guy, except for that jealousy, but he is not the one who holds your heart. ♥
> ~ALF~

119

April Gutierrez

DancingQueen September 17, 2013
Nude man hunt? That is AWESOME! Drunk dialing your
ex? That is freaking hysterical.

Tuesday, September 17, 2013
Faux Princess
Season 2 Episode 6

Remember when you were a little kid and the most randomness of people would give you a nickname? Often times, kids with nicknames were those whose parents were clueless on the date of delivery. They didn't think of the longevity and how names indeed effects a person ability to fit in.

As an adult, however, we tend to pick up nicknames for specific reasons.

In my experience, it has always been arse jacks attempting at humor. I've never found those people to be very funny, in any which way or form.

Now. If you are a woman, and another woman strikes up a label when referring to you....this isn't a spectacular notion. Most of the women who I've nicknamed are real bitches. The nickname serves only one purpose and that is to put a smile on my face whilst I am being required to mention them for some ungodly reason.

The key, to this WHOLE concept, however, is to never let them in on the joke.

Seriously. It's just not a good reaction when you hear that people are referring to you in a different manner.
Say for example, 'Faux Princess'.

Okay... I will admit it, I've been laughing ever since I heard it. Yes, indeed, I recently overheard a conversation in which I was referred to as a 'Faux Princess'.

My week has been unreal to say the least. After Marcus bailed me out of jail we waited patiently for the Page-6 story to appear.

On'rie had a field day as to my behavior, which of course has him still frowning in Andy's direction.

Mistakes are made so that we may reflect on our bad judgment, to then wisen up and say that we have matured into knowing better.

While the article itself was precise, it failed to mention my darkest of bad judgment calls. Literally, the one call itself, I made that night which I knew I shouldn't have made.

~Sigh~ ALF, I agree with you to some extent....Brent is obviously not out of my system, but in regards to On'rie's jealousy...I've given him plenty to worry about.

The 'wisen up' became apparent as my week progressed. Marcus, still upset with me, didn't return a single call. That is to say, not at first. My apology voicemails became stale and I turned to the classics.

When dealing with a writer, the safest bet of reaction falls on the pen. Yes, paper, pen, little white envelope, and a cute Forever stamp. We writers are all fools for the classic snail mail. The thrill alone of receiving a letter in the post is enough to accept any sort of misdeed. So I played dirty, sue me.

By week's end, Marcus had called me to thank me for the just apology. He also relayed a meeting message that somehow ended up with him.

"Ms. Moore has scheduled a meeting with you to sign some papers. She said she tried you several times and you had not returned her calls." Not that he sounded annoyed, but I sensed a twinge of concern in his voice.

"I have not received one single phone call from that woman, my dear." I promptly replied, immediately wondering what she was playing at by complaining to Marcus.

"I just don't know then, Melissa. My darling, you must take this publishing contract seriously. Otherwise, you will lose it before you even sign the damn papers." He scolded.

"Marcus, I'm telling you, she has not called me once." I reiterated.

"Fine, Fine. I will email you the details. Just make sure that you show up."

"Thank you sir," I teased, "Send my love to Jennifer, please." My goodbye was sweet, but more so because he had proven to be a true friend recently. His inability to soften reality was a sure way of knowing how gravity keeps him in my life.

Megan's statement to Marcus rubbed me the wrong way.

Why would she say that she had unsuccessfully tried to get a hold of me, when in fact, I hadn't heard from her in quite a while?

It bothered me to the point of getting a few other opinions on the subject.

"You see what she just did there, don't you? She just promoted a negative response to come from one of your closest colleagues." Amy began.

"I mean, if she can easily get Marcus to think ill of your work habits, it won't be difficult to have others believing something that isn't."

"Why would Megan Moore want to shoot down the one client she 'Wants' to sign in to her company?" Ivy asked Amy, then looked at me. "It's madness, you are just making a mountain out of a molehill, Melissa."

I couldn't help but shake my head and disagree. "I'm sorry but she is playing at something here. She gains nothing by having Marcus thinking I'm not reliable."

"You need to be careful with her, sweetie," Dana interrupted, "If she is playing a game, the only victim is going to be your book." She added.

Ivy took my hand in her own, "If we need to work overtime to get this straight, I am all yours."

"Would this be the first client request then?" I asked her teasing.

"I am at your service, my Lady." She replied in her fake British accent.

The four of us giggled and waited for the servers to leave us to our freshly laid out brunch. I spoke directly to Dana, being that she is in the business world.

"What do you think I should do?"

"Honestly... publish with a different house. There is no way around it. If you think she is up to no good, then the only way to be sure of making the right decisions is to find someone that is interested in your work alone. Based on your professional credibility, it shouldn't be too difficult, considering." She advised.

It was good advice. The only problem I faced was worrying about the obvious. Was I burning a bridge before I even crossed it. Were my concerns about Megan –The woman- so great, that I could think her capable of petty indifference professionally?

What else could I do but seek out the only person which could answer my questions at face value. I left brunch with the girls and found myself in the lobby of Brent Bishop's office building.

The receptionist remembered me and buzzed me in without even asking questions. Sadly, the elevator was empty on the 30-floor ride up. How often do you get to stare at yourself in the reflection the elevators doors offer.

It's there, that doubt begins to from. Too many elevator chimes later, I steps off and was welcomed back by Brent's secretary, Janice.

"Melissa, what a pleasure to see you." she greeted me as I neared the front desk.

"It's lovely to see you as well." I began, "Is Brent in by chance?" I asked.

She leaned back in her chair and then sat up staring out into the distance of the office before facing me again.

"He is in, but is going to be having lunch with the soon-to-be Mrs. soon."

"Is he in his office?" I asked plainly, fully planning on doing the unthinkable.

"Yes, he's in there." She replied.

I turned on my heel and walked the well known path to his corner office with the spectacular view of the city we both love.

Not bothering to knock, I pushed the large wooden door open to find him almost waiting for me, seated at the edge of his desk.

The look he held was of humor mixed with a dark inner desire to defeat. It was a look I knew all too well.

I'd seen it before. In this very office in fact.

"And to what do I owe this pleasure?" his silky voice asked as I neared him.

Thrown by his choice of words, my step weakened, my courage faltered.

"I, uh…" and the words and conviction left me. *(Damn Conviction All to Hell!)*

"You never cease to amaze me. You do everything wrong, and yet, here you are, in my office and I'm still waiting to hear what will come out next."

God help me! My heart bleeds for him.

He sighed, lifted himself up from where he sat and met me in the center of his office.

With his body in front of mine, I felt the heat from his mouth on my forehead. His hand touched my chin and he lifted my face so that my eyes could peer into his.

"What do you want from me, M?" He asked. His words thick with the same struggle I'd been fighting all these weeks.

But what use would it be to give in, to go back, to acknowledge something that will end up causing us more pain in the end. As soon as the thought formed, the conviction returned to my core.

"I need to know that your fiancée isn't in the market to ruin my literary career." The words were sharper than a knife I hadn't intended on using.

His features changed, and the softness disappeared. He let go of my chin and took a swift step back, the immediate distance creating an emptiness I was sure we both felt.

"You're being absurd." He started, his body then taking several more steps back. His mind obviously toying with the idea that Megan was playing games. "She isn't that type of business woman, Melissa. She wouldn't offer you a deal, if she didn't think your work held merit."

At this my head tilted a little higher. I know a thing or two about women and what they are capable of when it comes to the love they are trying to protect.

"Brent, she isn't who you think she is. She lied to Marcus, she is playing at something."

"Sometimes, you need to realize that people in general are not who we think them to be. Sometimes, we believe so much what we want, that we are blinded by the truth."

"And what's that Brent?" I countered sarcastically, not thinking of the reaction it would cause.

He closed the distance between us with 3 sharp steps, grabbed both of my elbows and brought my body to come crashing into his.

"That this right here, you in my arms….this is what's real. That everything else is just a filler to a story that has no ending."

I couldn't help but be pulled in by his desire, his lust. His mouth crushed over mine and his tongue began to dance in a rhythm I knew all too well.

MADNESS! I didn't reason with myself, I just kissed him back with equal passion and let myself become dazed in that moment.

As the moment slowed, and reality came crashing in, the room filled with the light our bubble had eluded. Our eyes opened and what we saw was disaster.

Janice had walked in and was standing there at the entrance of his office. Perhaps waiting for the right moment to stop us in our tracks.

My body jumped away from Brent's but I was still speechless.

"Mr. Bishop, Ms. Moore is waiting in the conference room." She informed him, while looking at me.

"Thank you, Janice. Please tell her I will be right there."

Mortified, I wanted to run from the room. Run from the building. She closed the door and he walked back to his desk, leaving me wondering what else there was to say.

We had just kissed. And not just any ol' kiss, no, the type of kiss that sends an obvious message.

"I suggest you find yourself another publisher, M. It may not be best that you work with Megan after all." He said, staring out into the view.

Without another word, I turned and left his office. I couldn't help however but walk a little slower as I passed the conference room. It was Megan's voice that had me gravitating towards the semi opened door.

"Don't worry, John. This Faux Princess will not be getting any type of contract deal from our house. I merely want to ruin her chances of getting picked up by any other publishing house while Benjamine On'rie is in New York City."

It was all the ammunition I needed.

My mother use to say, Trust a woman's intuition. I went straight to On'rie and told him what had happened. All minus the kiss of course. What point is there in going into something that I wouldn't be able to explain anyhow.

Within the hour, we were standing in front of Johnson & Stein Publishing House getting ready to sign a deal on my book. The whole situation was unheard of, but that's what I get for being in a relationship with On'rie.

Then, as if saving me wasn't enough, he insisted that we interrupt Megan's afternoon meeting so that I could publicly decline her offer.

I didn't have to say anything but you should know I said enough.

"Excuse us for barging in like this but it couldn't wait." I said as we walked into her board room.

"Pardon me, but this is extremely inappropriate." she complained.

"Yes, and I do apologize. You see, I will be unable to sign with your house after all. The term 'Faux Princess' has just been patented under the company I have just moments ago signed with." I countered, looking around the room. "Again, excuse me for the interruption."

On'rie held me the whole way home, and by then my shaking had calmed.

It was there, in my apartment, while On'rie was out picking up dinner, that everything became muddled.

My phone rang, bringing me out of the haze. The screen blinked, Mr. NY.

At first glance, I hesitated. I could only image why he was calling, he must have heard what happened with Megan.

"Yes?" I answered.

"Thank you." He replied. His voice soft and smooth.

"For what?" I asked, curiously.

"I missed you, and seeing you this afternoon made this ache in my chest disappear."

Stunned by the sideswipe I responded without thought, "Nothing has changed though, Brent. You are still with Megan. I am still with On'rie."

"Weren't you the one that told me, things can change as quickly as the wind does?"

Funny how my words always get thrown back at me.

Readers comment:

Anonymous   September 17, 2013
You need to be honest with On'rie. If he finds out about it from someone else it will not be good. Always trust your instincts. You knew Megan was up to no good. It's obvious you still have feelings for Brent. You need to be

true to yourself. Take the time to figure out who has your heart.

Anonymous <u>September 17, 2013</u>
OMG!!! First, I'm glad you signed with another house and not with that BITCH! AND the way you barged in on her meeting to publicly tell her was priceless! Kudos, to you!!!
As far as Brent goes....YIKES! How can you resist that kiss and "invitation". You know he would leave Megan and go back to you in a heartbeat, if you just said so. Decisions, decisions!!!
I'm still hoping for a reunion! ;)
~ALF~

Anonymous <u>September 19, 2013</u>
You should be ashamed of yourself.
Nancy

Anonymous <u>September 21, 2013</u>
....Shame is a funny business.... Always remember that when you wag your pointer at someone, it's a reflection of your own character!

Anonymous <u>September 23, 2013</u>
Why should SHE be ashamed of herself?
~ALF~

Tuesday, September 25, 2013
That Three Letter Word
Season 2 Episode 7

Before a word is said about my week, I will address the comment shocker from last week's episode.

First off, "OMG! …. Seriously! …. You should be ashamed of **yourself** for suggesting that any other person should feel anything. Whatever!"

If I were to feel shame about something, that is for ME, MYSELF, and I to work out, not anyone else to force the feeling on me. I have openly admitted that I am **not** Proud of my actions, and have rightfully accepted some of the mistakes that I have made. Suggesting that I feel Shame for any of my dealings would leave room to believe that I regret any of it, and I will tell you one thing…I Do Not Regret as a general rule!

What happened between Brent and I, alongside with the comments that started to filter in, I took into consideration that I was being an introvert with On'rie. I hadn't disclosed the events that took place in my Ex's office because, up until my actions were being thrown in my face, I didn't think there was anything to divulge.

The morning following the big Megan beat-down, all I could think of, as I watched On'rie make us breakfast, was Brent's phone call the night before. I weighed the pros and cons of my situation and ended up with a basic life response.

Be Open with the man in front of you.

"I have something we need to talk about." I began, noticing how he turned and slowly raised his right eyebrow in his typical comedic way.

"I'm being serious, Ben." I scolded softly, which caused him to remove the pan from the stove and walk over to where I sat at the kitchen table.

131

"What is it, my love?" He said, as he crouched down in front of me.

That was it, the 'do or die' moment. Full disclosure and let the pieces fall where they may.

"Yesterday, when I went to see Brent about Megan, right before I overheard her making that outrageous comment, something happened with Brent."

My chest was beating a thousand miles a minute, and it wasn't fear. It was the failing courage to be honest with myself about what had happened. Luckily, On'rie's lack of demeanor didn't deter me from getting it out.

"Brent kissed me….and I kissed him back." After the words had released from my mouth, I inhaled and waited for the reaction.

He stared at me. Looked from one eye to the other. His features were stone cold, neither upset nor angered.

"Do you want to be with him?" he finally asked.

And in response my head reacted before the words came out. I shook the no and I grasped for both of this hands.

"I don't know why it happened, but it changed nothing, and that has to mean something. Doesn't it?"

He stood up, breaking our connection. My body followed his, not wanting to give him too much space.

"I would want to believe it means you choose me, but I'm a simple romantic, what do I know." He offered.

My body quickly lunged to his, molding in his warm embrace. "I do choose you." I whispered before I kissed him.

****And for those of you that want to knock on my Sins. *Eat That!*****

Things got a little bumpy after that morning, however. *Page-6* had a field day with the report of how I acted towards poor ol' CEO Megan Moore. The Buzz, in fact, took over our brunch Friday morning.

"While I am uber happy for you taking the reins of your career, Please, Please, Please let me know beforehand next time you go barging in to someone's conference to withdraw a contract petition." Ivy scolded almost the moment she sat down across from Dana and me.

"Everything happened so quickly, I hardly had time to think, much less make phone calls."

"Well, who arranged everything?" Dana quickly darted the question at me, her hand coming up to my forearm.

"On'rie did most of the coordinating…I'm the one to blame for the blah, blah, blah in the board room, I'm afraid."

"I have to give it to the source of the story. They gave some pretty juicy details." Ivy added, her face buried in the menu.

I shook my head at her. It wasn't like I had created the mess to begin with. Had I not acted harshly, Megan would have ruined my chances, more so than she already had.

"I'm just glad you cut the witch's broom to pieces!" Amy encouraged.

"Something else happened, that may have obliterated her broom all together." I said softly, my eyes directly focused on my carte du jour. I could hear the other three menus slapping down on the glass table.

It's amusing how we can feel people staring at us before the verification can be made that it's happening. They were waiting when I finally lifted my head to them. Their eyes all insistent, waiting on a confession.

"Brent and I kissed in his office."

The moment I said, 'kissed', Amy and Ivy squealed. I'm still not sure if it was delight or frustration because they all insisted I was insane.

"Yes, I know it's madness. I couldn't help it. I turn to putty near him, I'm a mess." Admitting it is always the first step I suppose.

"But when I told On'rie I realized the one big fact keeping Brent and I apart after all this time," I began, "Nothing has changed. We are still the same people with the same issues. More so really, because he is engaged to be Married to the, 'Wicked Witch of the West'." The sigh came and I gave up. "I chose On'rie back in June, and I still choose him."

"Well I think you need to get to know the man you chose baby-cakes because he isn't who you think he is." Amy spat out.

I could tell she was holding back, not being as blunt as she normally is. A rarity as far as my relationship with Amy is concerned, at least.

"I don't understand?" It was her quick reply that took over the brunch, and more so the rest of my week.

"Sweetie, there is a heavy rumor going around in the modeling world that Ben has been seeing someone in Paris."

Kaboom! And there went all the warm and fuzzy feelings I'd started feeling about my relationship.

There were no words that I could formulate at that point. Really, after Amy had dropped the bomb on us, Ivy did most of the questioning and Dana merely rubbed my shoulder while we listened through the information spewing from our long legged friend.

I excused myself before the food was brought out. I couldn't bear to be around them, much less eat something that would most definitely make my stomach hurt.

I did what I usually do. I walked Central Park and prayed I wouldn't run into anyone I knew.

Sadly, I was unlucky in that department. Half way through the park I ran into On'rie himself.

Just as he had all those many months ago, when I ran into him before we left for Paris, he formulated from thought.

I stopped walking and let him reach me. I'm sure he could see the change in my demeanor as he got closer.

His face tilted as it did when he was confused, "what is it?" he asked plainly.

Then I asked the words I'd hoped never to ask, especially after how honest I had been with him about Brent.

"Are you seeing someone behind my back?"

He huffed, also taking a step back. It caught him off guard, like an unexpected punch.

"You are asking me if I'm seeing someone else, after you admitted that you kissed your ex boyfriend?"

Damn Him To Hell! He didn't answer the flipping question. My head turned to the bridge ahead, my thoughts going down a road I promised I would never travel. Jealousy…

Shaking my head in response, "Ben, I'm going back home. If you show up later, I'm going to assume the reply to my question is that there is no validity to it. Otherwise, just don't come back. I will ship your things back to Paris."

Leaving him there, I took the high road and went back to my place. I waited, my heart racing the entire time I spent staring at the door. I even found myself praying to a God, I hardly ever talk to anymore, about how much I want him in my life.

When he didn't show up by 9 that night, I took it as a sign he wouldn't be coming back.

With my head held high, I got dressed for Ivy's party and left.

The funny thing was, there was no hallow feeling in the pit of stomach. No ache in the center of my chest. For a moment I believe it was shock, but then again, I'd never experienced that before.

I caught Ivy's eye first as I came into the crowded room. She hustled her way over to me, greeting a few guest along the way, generously picking up a glass of champagne and handed it to me as she reached me.

"I hadn't thought you'd come after this morning's debacle." She offered.

I forced a smile, "I just needed some time to think, a little fresh air to settle things out."

"Yes well, steer clear of our Oz guests, I think she's brought her flying monkeys." Pointing towards the stairs, I noticed Brent and Megan chatting with some other fashionably dressed individuals.

"No worries, I will mind my P's & Q's tonight, Ivy." I said innocently, staring at them as I took another sip from my champagne flute.

Why does he always have to look fabulous in a tux?

Now…nights like these have always proven to shake up someone's pot. A new face, one of the girls, an old flame… It's as if Fate hadn't ever really decided whom I would toy with next, only that, in these moments I found some shred of enlightening I hadn't had before.

The longer I stayed in my corner, watching Brent and Megan interacting with other guest, the more I realized how much I truly wanted to ruin her pretty little world. Maybe it was the alcohol making me think a little dark, but then again, the juice only brings out what's directly underneath the surface.

Now....bare with me on this....because it's still rather hazy.

Just as I had made the decision to walk the length of the room, my intention was to ruin their moment, a voice came over the P.A. system. At first I didn't hear the voice speaking , nor the words he was saying. I could only hear the beating of my heart.

Funny how our heart beats to a fantastically rhythmic beat, almost like a war song.

It was the moment I heard my name that I halted and began to back track. The questions I asked myself, now, seem particularly amusing, were at the moment, essential.

1.   Who was on that P.A. system?
2.   Why was I the topic of conversation?
and
3.   Where had I been headed? (A.D.D. at its finest!)

The answers turned out to be fate's joke on me.

It was On'rie talking into the microphone. He was telling the crowd about our whirlwind romance. He even brought up the rumor from that morning.

At that point it didn't matter where I had originally been headed.

My body turned towards him and as if I was being magically pulled in his direction, I ended up directly in front of his handsome self.

He gave the microphone to Ivy and got down on one knee.

Yes, my heart figuratively stopped beating.

"Melissa, my love, will you marry me?"

GOD HELP ME! I responded with a three letter word I'm not completely sure I should have uttered with an entire room filled with New York City's élite citizens witnessing.

YES

Readers comment:

> **_DancingQueen_** September 25, 2013
> Whoop! Whoop! Eat that Megan!

> **_Anonymous_** September 30, 2013
> I'm so happy you came clean with On'rie and aren't hiding any more secrets. I can't believe he proposed! OMG!!! I can't imagine what Brent is thinking right about now. And, I can't believe you said Yes
> ~ALF~

> **_Anonymous_** September 30, 2013
> Aren't you ever worried your man will read your blog?? Seriously, if this On'rie guy ever read any of this he wouldn't be asking you anythhing!

It's funny how getting engaged makes us 'feel' a little different about our relationship….and I don't mean, HA HA funny either. Before last week, I would look at On'rie and think to myself, "Hmmmm, How did I get so lucky?" Fact of the matter is, after he got down on that knee and asked me the most surprising question any man has EVER asked me, I started to look at him in a way I'd never expected.

The morning after the big night, I woke up and watched him sleeping. Okay, so you know I've done that before, but mostly because it's an incredible moment to seize. Your man, vulnerable in his slumber state. I lay there and felt content. The sense of wholeness was something I'd never experienced. I'd seen my parents walk through their entire life happy with one another, and in that instant, I began to believe I was the lucky one in our little duo.

Silly little me, during that first morning ray of light, I let myself Believe.

Nothing else but my ideas about our relationship had been altered. On'rie even sat me down last Thursday so that we could discuss what, 'us' getting engaged meant to him.

Men are Hilarious creatures. That is, when their heads are not stuck up their Arses!

"I don't want you to feel pressured into having any sort of big event…" he began, "but you do know we are going to have to invite a lot of people neither one of us know."

My mind did a double take and I can only imagine what my facial expression appeared to him. Dazed and confused was more like it.

"You know I don't care either way, right?" I asked, wondering if he had paid attention to anything I had expressed about myself in the past 5 months.

Shaking his head, "si,si,si" he huffed. "We just need to be on the same page with this."

Wide eyed and annoyed, I straightened my back and tilted my head. "Ben, you plan and I will just worry about my dress. How is that?" I asked.

A wicked smile stretched across his face and I knew his imagination was pushing him to the max.

Say what you may about writers, but our breed is Always filled with mesmerizing ideas. I'm sure our wedding would top them all. Satisfied, he gathered his things and left me alone to write.

You see, I've been spending most of my days writing this new novel. It's a sad one. By far my biggest setback has been all the tears shed during the process. I've even gotten to the point of a headache because I couldn't stop crying. Makes me wonder if my readers will be crying right along with me....

Anyhow, On'rie loathes the crybaby types, so he has opted not to hang around while I'm working. It's actually probably a good thing too, because all he ends up doing is distracting me with kisses across the top of my bare shoulders. His hands then begin to roam, and writing ends up on hold.

That Thursday morning I sat at my laptop, drinking my coffee, and staring at the screen. The cursor blinking and the words just underneath the surface, ready and able.

This was when an even bigger distraction came knocking on my door, unexpectedly.

What are building buzzers for if the other tenants in my building will buzz anyone up?

Peeking through my door peephole only managed to push my nerves up a steep hill.

It was Brent, unshaven and disheveled. It looked like he hadn't slept a wink.

Only for a single second did I question whether I should allow him to come in.

He didn't look up at me when I slowly opened the door. He took the few steps that he needed to walk into my apartment, my head following in awe.

"Hmmm….little presumptuous aren't you?" I asked, the tone filled with my usual morning sass.

As I closed and locked the door, he replied, "With you, it doesn't matter anyway, you are just like me. You're going to do what you want to do no matter how people feel."

My hand went straight up in pause. "Hold on, let's get something straight. You are not my boyfriend, you haven't been for quite some time. What I do, or don't do….well…Brent, it shouldn't matter to you."

"You see then, that is the problem." He shot back quickly. He sighed and shook his head, almost as if he was arguing with his thoughts.

His head shot back up at me, "Everything you do matters to me. It always has, since the moment you almost tripped in front of me."

The admission stung like an open wound being doused in vinegar. I didn't immediately know how to reply to that. What does anyone say to a man, standing before them, openly admitting their devotion?

"M…you can't marry this guy." He said frankly. "Don't marry him…please." He pleaded softly.

I went from not knowing what to say, to having a dozen things to shoot at him, they were all drowned by the tears I had started to choke back. My body trembled.

"Don't marry him?" I asked between tear filled sobs.

The reaction bringing his body near mine but it was all I could do to keep him at arms distance.

"No, don't do that. You stay over there. Don't try to intimidate me with being near me." I argued, my hands shooing him to the other side of my living room.

"I can't, I can't believe you would ask me Now, to not marry On'rie when you are flipping engaged to Megan!" I shouted, wiping the tears from my cheek.

"That is different, M, and you damn well know it."

"It's not, Brent. It's not different. By no means is it Any different. She is YOUR fiancée, and I have not tried to change that fact." I countered.

"This is madness, you can't marry him while you are still in love with ME!" he opposed, his voice raised an octave higher, halting all of my arguments all together.

Fine, I will now openly admit that I am still in love with him. But still…

"You need to leave. I'm not going to argue with you." I said softly. While the tears had stopped from streaming down my face, I could still see how they welled up in my eyes. The room distorted by the excess water in them.

He moved towards me, and I looked away thinking he would pass me heading towards the door. He did not pass me. He stopped a hair shy of where I stood, clearly taking over my space.

"I love you." He whispered. This was what brought me to look up into his handsome face.

I couldn't help it, he is my weakness. I didn't fight him when his mouth covered mine. I merely wrapped my arms around his neck as if saying, 'Please, don't stop'

And No, I'm NOT ashamed of kissing him back. Not in the least!

His body molded to mine and the morning nip in the air became a vacant thought. A mental alarm, however, did begin to go off in the deepest crevice of my mind.

Almost like a siren that you don't notice until a cold hand is up your pajamas touching a part of your body only your Fiancée should be in charge of.

With as much force as I could, my hand pushed on his chest, tearing us apart.

"We can't do this, you need to leave." I said as best I could.
He shook his head, seemingly agreeing with me and left.

When the door slammed shut hard behind him, I almost felt worse.

Worse because the instant he was gone, the need to be with him enhanced. I missed him and that was maddening.

How can I want someone so much that I spend so much energy pushing away?

By Friday, I was in need of motivation and friendly counsel. I sought Marcus out before my brunch with the girls.

"My dear, tell me you are working hard on that new book of yours?" he begged.

The bright eyed and bushy tail expression lit up my face because it was all good news on that end. "Yes, indeed, I am roughly a third done. I just have to buy stock in Kleenex."

His eyebrow immediately raised, "Elaborate dear."

"It's about a love that dies," I started, "and with every entry I add, I end up crying my eyes out."

"Why on earth would you write about a love like that?" his interest more peaked than anything.

"Love isn't always like you and Jennifer. You know that. Love isn't always fair. Nothing is daisies and fairytales."

"No, but women readers like happy endings, Melissa." He snipped, in his professor tone.

"Yes, but it will have a round about ending. I promise, it will be worth it."

In admitting my belief to Marcus about an ending I had yet to formulate thoroughly...it was almost like setting it in stone. Now my mentor would expect to have a sense of completeness once he turned the last page.

~Shakes Head~ What have I done to myself???

The rush came to leave and make brunch with the girls.

WARNINGKarma....Fate....Destiny....Whatever universal forces you want to pin point on this – Go Right Ahead!

The three dearest friends in my life sat at our table as I walked in late for our brunch. Once I had finally adjusted my stuff and looked to each of their somber faces, I knew something terrible was coming my way.

Dana, who was sitting next to me, placed her hand on my forearm. "Sweetie, we have to tell you something." She started and while my face was directed at her, my eyes darted to the other girls in a curious form.

"Page-6 broke a confirmed story this morning that has to do with Ben. Have you seen him this morning?"

The beating of my heart raced a little faster. It took everything in me to remember the itinerary he had mumbled in his half English, half French language.

"He is out of town, what's wrong?" I asked cautiously.

Ivy was the one to reply to the obvious concern in my voice.

"Hon, he isn't dead, just a deadbeat."

Amy turned to Ivy, "Seriously?" she questioned.

"What does the story say?" I raise my voice.

"It says that Ben got a model in Paris pregnant, and he confirmed it to the press." Dana gentle admitted.

Definitely makes me the bigger fool!

Readers comment:

Anonymous October 01, 2013
It's time to ditch the deadbeat, once and for all. Your heart doesn't truly belong to him anyway. It belongs to the man who kissed you earlier and professed his love for you. You need to tell him you are not going to marry On'rie and that you love him. Megan needs to take a hike too. Maybe Megan and On'rie should get together. They are both a-holes!
~ALF~

DancingQueen October 01, 2013
He confirmed to press before telling M? Oh boy!

Anonymous <u>October 02, 2013</u>
I'm calling Karma! Fits the bill!
Nancy

Anonymous <u>October 03, 2013</u>
What Karma, Nancy? She didn't SLEEP with anyone since she's
been with On'rie. She might have kissed someone but I'm sure
there was some kissing on On'rie's part if he got that model
pregnant. What is your problem??? >:o(
~ALF~

Break ups are never what we expect them to be. Anguish or relief, no one ever truly understands what emotions will linger once someone has started an end. What once was beautiful and all inspiring is easily darkened by an overpowering shadow of emptiness.

Let me be frank, I am not great with my emotions in general. Often times I've hidden the truth of how I feel from even my own conscience, only to face it many years later when its importance is no longer all-impacting.

Call it what you may, denial, deference, or downright genius – I sit here speaking to you tonight still not having faced my most recent of bombarding emotions.

Last week my relationship with the Frenchman ended abruptly.

What few things he had brought over to my apartment were forwarded to his residence in Paris with little more than a note attached. There was no nasty phone call, no midnight arguments, nothing at all.

He did leave me a voicemail…one that I have avoided listening to all week. I'm not interested, if it was important he knows where to find me.

The morning after the official Page-6 article made its debut, Marcus showed up bright and early at my apartment. I'm sure he was looking to wake me up but was greeted by my version of coffee-zombie. No sleep, coffee supplemented, and seriously workin the dark circles under the eyes. I'm sure I was absolutely comparable to the Vogue model On'rie traded me up for. –NOT!

"I'm glad I didn't wake you." Marcus lied, passing me as he headed for the sofa.

I didn't even ask if he wanted a coffee. An empty hand meant a desire for it to be filled as soon as possible in his book. I was happily distracted and worried by his early existence in my day.

"I spent the night writing." I explained. While it wasn't a complete lie, I did only manage to add 3 sentences to the new manuscript.

"Well then, I'm glad On'rie didn't ruin you in that department." He snapped, his voice more annoyed than pleased.

"He didn't ruin me in any department, Marcus. He merely lied and made me a fool." I offered casually.

"And cheated, and ruined something incredible." He countered, the creases on his forehead thick.

The worry on his face deemed a response that would ease his concern, a truth he hadn't heard from me yet.

"If it was so incredible why was I always ready to turn to Brent?" my question brought Marcus to his feet.

"Nonsense!"

I had to stop acting like the coffee I was mixing for Marcus was interesting.

"It's not nonsense, Marcus. It is what it is." I snapped. "As upset as I am with Ben for making me out to be the fool, I'm more upset for not seeing things the way they have been. We were business, and the girl in Paris was romance."

There was nothing he could say to that. We both know the weight of that single truth that tied Ben and I together.

Marcus spent the following 2 hours trying to distract me, to no avail. He went over my new manuscript and made suggestions. By the time we had nothing else to talk about, Dana was buzzing to come up.

She took me out for brunch and a walk through the park. It didn't take long to get photographed by the paparazzi and we were back at my apartment. I tried to write but all I could do was stare at the last three sentences that I had written that previous night.

Ivy came over to review the events she'd scheduled for October, and to solidify the book launch event. Her firm is pushing a November 10th release party. A Sunday afternoon, a day that my career will be changed forever.

Amy came to spend the night with me, and I didn't even bother to argue with her. I knew what they had all managed to accomplish. They didn't want to leave me alone. The problem, I think, has been that it hasn't hit me yet was why they felt it necessary to stay with me.

Do I really seem that monumentally fragile in regards to something so trivial???

The distractions carried on until Friday when I was alone from the early morning light til our girl's lunch at <u>Mexico Lindo</u>. Mind you, I'd spent time with every single one of them, every day, for the previous 2 days, and yet they were a barrel of information as if I hadn't spoken to any of them.

It was Dana that had me intrigued for her simple timid demeanor to discuss her new beau."His name is Kyle, he works at the coffee shop across the street from my building."

"How long have you been talking to him?" I asked, absentmindedly fiddling with my straw.

"Oh, I don't know, a few months maybe. He asked me out last week but I'm not sure…" her voice trailed off as she eyeballed Amy giving her goo-goo eyes.

"You need to get laid, Dana. Just say yes and then you can worry about relationship crap later."

Amy's free spirit worries me sometimes, it almost seems like she is so afraid to get into a relationship that she'd be okay with random sexual partners until she hits her 40s.

"I think it's sweet." Ivy nudged her wrist. "Don't listen to Amy, she is just high on her new boy toy."

Instantly Amy's face went red, "He is not mine, nor is he new. You guys have met him. We hung out a couple years ago. He is just a lot more marketable these days."

"Then you should bring him to tonight's fiesta. The margaritas are going to be Spectacular!" Ivy mused.

My foot in mouth chose that precise moment to find its niche. "As long as I don't see any douche bag I know, I am game."

The three just about choked on their sweet tea but it was followed by giggles that I started. It felt good to leak a little of the built up frustration but sadly there was more leakage ready to let loose.

Ivy followed me home and explained that tonight was part of my PR list. She had invited literary reviewers that I would need to woo over.

Joy! Me, in all my rosy sunshine mood was going to be forced to Grin, and Bear it.

This is all well and good when people care. After a few good strong margaritas, I was dancing to the music playing in my head, and Boy was the melody pumping.

Being that I had made an early entrance, I was the first one waiting for the girls to go on my Margarita Fiesta. Amy sat next to me, giving me the oddest of expressions. "Honey, are you okay?' she asked.

"Yep, I am spectacular." I had to pause a moment to recall if my words had slurred in such a small sentence.

"How many of those suckers have you had?" This time, her question was followed by a steady hand on my shoulder and a silly laugh.

Not remembering exactly, I shook my head and focused on the incredible man-candy behind her.

"Is he my gift for tonight?" I asked, all intention were to make her laugh, but she turned to give him an authorative glare.

"No...he isn't *Your* gift but you can borrow him if you'd like." She sassed back.

"Yes indeed." His name is Jason Rice, an old modeling friend of Amy's from Milan.

While I couldn't help but feel the irony in the situation, it made the night easier. I was drinking, laughing, and even flirting with a gorgeous model, and I wasn't committing any sort of Moral Sin.

As the night progressed, and Ivy was done shoving people in my face to charm, Jason made a stunning proposition. "Want to get out of this place?"

Hmmmmmm...... Let me think.........

Y. E. S.

Leaving the restaurant, I caught Dana asking Jason where we were heading. From what I gathered he told her my place.

Funny thing about margaritas....They have an unusual way for making nights go dark and thoughts vanish.

Jason joined me in the cab....................and folks, that is ALL I remember. The stank back seat of the typical yellow cab driving down a wet New York City street.

Yes, indeed. I woke up the following morning in my bed, fully undressed lying next to Jason who was half dressed. Sitting up, the room spun in a grossly fashion and I could hear the tick, tock of my alarm clock. Even the soft snore of the beautiful man next to me seemed to hurt my delicate brain.

Still to this moment I have No Clue what happened, and honestly I'm too embarrassed to ask Jason if I was any good, LOL!

Readers comment:

Anonymous   October 08, 2013
You aren't tied to anyone any longer so you are free to do whatever you please. I'm just sorry you don't know if you had fun or not. LOL
~ALF~

Tuesday, October 15, 2013
Suitable Benefactor
Season 2 Episode 10

Often times I've thought about human behavior and how the choices made by people in our lives impact our path, our life journey. Let's face it…we can only imagine how the choices I have made recently will impact my little bubble of friends.

Do I feel guilty about most of it? Well, yes…yes I do. Does that mean I am going to sulk in a corner and refuse to live my life? – You're funny if you think sulking for guilt is a choice.

No, I am not sulking. Nor am I even walking around with my tail between my legs. Somehow or another everything will work itself out. And that isn't having a 'fairy-tale wannabe ending' either. No, that is wanting to always look at the glass half full. Too many times can we find a negative shadow lingering nearby. I am choosing to turn on a light and have a little faith.

Waking up, half naked in my own bed with one of Amy's friends was indeed a 'Wake-Up Call'. I hadn't mentioned it before, but Dana was there that night. She had slept on my sofa. Sadly, she had no clue as to whether Jason and I had slept together that night.

It took a couple days, but by Thursday's brunch I was staring at an unsent text to the man in question to see if he was capable of filling in the blanks. Having gotten to the restaurant first, I was able to contemplate sending the retched form of communication or just leave it be. Dana changed my mind.

She startled me with a kiss on the cheek from behind. The phone fumbling out of my hands landed firmly on the hard tile flooring.

"Wow, I didn't mean to scare you." She giggled as she took the seat next to me.

"You didn't…I mean, I wasn't paying attention to the door." I mumbled, realizing my lack of enthusiasm would get called to the carpet.

153

"Hold up. What's wrong?" she asked frankly.

All I could do was shake my head and show her the cell phone screen. As she read through what I had typed out I noticed the methodical way her features changed.

"Amy isn't going to care, Melissa. I'm sure she assumes something happened considering you took him home."

"That's not the point. He isn't my friend. He is hers and I just don't want it to be weird or anything." I said, before adding, "I also don't intend for that to ever happen again, if it did happen to begin with."

She shrugged her shoulders and we both looked up as the door opened. Alex and Ivy walked in, both smiling from brim to brim.

"You will *Never* believe what just happened to Us!" Ivy started, her face was even a tad flushed.

Amy didn't let us reply, "We just got invited to Todd Jones' Charity event Sunday night!" she shrieked in excitement.

Clueless, I couldn't help but ask the dumb question. "Who is Todd Jones?"

Incredible how four words are capable of stunning 3 vivacious women silent.

"Melissa, Todd Jones is the 2nd richest man in New York City…*and* he has recently gotten a divorce from his 2nd wife." Ivy informed poor little naïve me.

What else could I do but roll my eyes and wave my fingers in an *OoooooooOOooooo* fashion. "Fun!" I responded.

"It should be lots of fun, actually." Dana added innocently. "His charity events are usually very enjoyable."

"So, I will set up for us to get decked out and picked up by 4 that afternoon. Just email me a color you'd like selected for you." Ivy informed us.

"You are always so accommodating, Ivy. What would we do without you?" Amy teased.

"You would walk into events looking like a dime-maiden, is what would happen."

Our brunch was filled with tidbits of this Todd Jones. Not that I was particularly interested in the man himself, I was curious who would be attending this event.

Time would surly tell!

I made it a point to pull Amy aside as we left the restaurant. Everything inside me was screaming urgency on this matter with Jason.

"Honey, I wanted to go into something with you."

"Sure, just walk with me to the plaza, I'm meeting up with a few people." She offered.

We locked arms, and walked together.

"The other night, Jason stayed over at my place."

"Yeah I know. He told me that next day." She shot back, her innocent demeanor signaling that it didn't bother her.

"I don't want to be in a relationship with him or anything though. I just felt like I needed to tell you that."

We walked a good 20 feet before she said anything. I could feel her mind at work and when I glanced at her face, she seemed pensive.

"I'm glad you say that." She started. "I really like this one. When he came over the day after, we talked and he told me how much he realized that he wanted to be with me that night before. Not anything against you…" her voice trailed off.

"I'm glad for you, Amy."

She smiled and it felt like the conversation was over. I didn't want to go into it any further. She was my friend and he is the guy she is in to, and apparently it's a mutual feeling.

I stopped walking and pulled on her arm. "Thank you for not being upset." I said and then hugged her.

With her face in my hair, she whispered, "I love you. You are my best friend. I could never be upset with you."

When we pulled away, I noticed her eyes had misted. We smiled at each other, giggled and said our goodbye.

Later that night I sat to write and couldn't shake the exchange with Amy. She had tugged on my heart and while I was glad to have settled things with her, I wasn't sure what exactly I had settled to begin with.

Opening up my cell phone and my text box, I scrolled to the draft to Jason.

This is going to sound odd but, Did we have sex the other night?

No better time than the present. I sent the text and almost instantly he replied back.

IDK

Well, DagNabit!!

The following afternoon I realized there had been one more causality to my innate human behavior – Marcus too had been drug through my turmoil.

'Poor dear Marcus!' Seems like I'm forever sighing that phrase when in the confines of my apartment. He has done so very much for me and it literally feels like the choices I have made recently have taken a toll on him. While I understand that he feels responsible for pushing On'rie on me in the first place, it's not his fault things managed to happen the way they did.

He came over late Friday afternoon to accompany me to a meeting with Mr. Bob Johnson, my publisher extraordinaire. Marcus was insistent about attending the meeting with me based on Mr. Johnson's reputation.

Funny how he says it's the reputation he has a problem with and not the fact that he is as handsome as they come. Good thing the man is married with kids, otherwise I'm sure Page-6 would find something to make up.

Our meeting began all smiles and greetings, but then the Mr. Johnson's cut-throat personality surfaced.

"Melissa….Can I call you, Melissa?" he asked, waiting for my nod before continuing, "Your lack of relationship with Ben On'rie has put a strain on your marketing campaign. What are you planning on doing to market your novel before we release?"

I turned to Marcus, thinking what an absurd question to be asking me. Isn't that something we should ask my publicist? I mean, Ivy would have her game plan face on and ready to fire back with awesome force.

"I have my people on it, I can assure you that there will be no set back in that department." I offered with as much conviction I could muster on a spur of the moment response.

"Your people need to have deep pockets, are they aware of this?" he shot back.

And as if my lips and brain were working without my knowledge, I heard myself say to the man, "I have been scheduled to attend Todd Jones' charity event this weekend. I'm sure the pockets will find a suitable benefactor."

Marcus' hand slammed on my forearm and I could only imagine his eyes bulging out at me.

Luckily, Mr. Johnson wasn't offended by my bite back. On the contrary, he was pleasantly surprised.

"Well thank goodness on that end. Keep me posted on that. Make sure you stop by editing to pick up your proof. The ladies in that department have been dying to get a hold of your next manuscript. Any news you can give me on that end?"

Marcus interjected, "I have been reading her pages as she gets through them. Good stuff, good stuff indeed. The women are going to go crazy over it."

We wrapped up the meeting by setting a deadline for my 2nd book manuscript. They want it done before the book release event.

Bright eyed and bushy tailed, I woke up Sunday afternoon ready for the fun and festivities. Ivy and the girls came over and got ready at my apartment. Getting into the limo, I realized I was the only one without a date.

"Don't sweetheart, I will make sure you get home safely." Dana offered.

While most girls would feel like the third wheel, I had a moment of exhilarated relief!

Inside the Plaza, the crowd was thick with glam and glitz. Beautiful gowns and handsome smiles filled the ballroom. Somehow or another I got tangled in the crowd of guests as I walked ominously through the room. Here and there I would see someone I knew but the mingling was always cut short by stranger interruptions.

Funny how things happen to me. One minute I am sipping champagne and saying hello to old acquaintances, the next I'm being swept off by a complete stranger to an open bar.

"Excuse me, these shoes are not conducive for a half run!" I complained to the well built Armani wearer.

From the instant his face turned in my direction, upper arm still in his grab, I was awestruck.

"We're not running. I was just making sure you didn't get away." He answered plainly, his voice smooth and deep.

Carefully I pulled my arm free from his hold, trying to ease it out as opposed to yanking it out of his fingers.

"What's your pleasure?" he asked, the sharp line of his jaw moving ever so gently.

God Help Me! *I giggled.* In typical fashion, my dirty arse mind worked faster than thought. Luckily he found it amusing.

"Champagne, please." I replied, hoping the save was well worth the effort.

His face lightened with a mischievous grin just before he turned.

I'd been close to money before…in a man it smelt like sexual power.

This one specifically could probably get any woman he wanted merely by smiling and kissing the upper part of her hand.

He ordered our drink and I made the mistake of turning to look out into the crowd. Here I stood next to New York City's 2nd richest man and the first person I notice across the room is Brent Bishop.

Our eyes locked on each other and I felt hopeless. I wanted to walk across that ballroom and jump into his arms.

What stopped me, you ask?

Hmmm…two things really. First, Megan stood at Brent's side. A competition I refused to delve into. The idea that they were still together *IRKS* me!

And secondly, from the moment Todd Jones turned around with the flute of bubbly, he positively stole all of my attention from the world. Even now, days later, I'm thinking of what a charming man he'd been. Don't worry, he didn't get into my dress - Not yet at least. ;) The more I got to know the man, the more I realized that he would be a suitable benefactor...at lease I know Ivy would approve!

It would have been a perfect night..... Brent texted me later on the limo ride home and made everything muddled.

I need to see you. I miss you.

What now?

Readers comment:

> **Anonymous** October 16, 2013
> I know you still love Brent but you need to make it clear to him that you can't go see him anymore unless he leaves the BITCH. Don't let him play you like that!!!
> ~ALF~

> **Anonymous** October 16, 2013
> You leave me wanting to know more every week.
> Good Job!
> Meredith

Tuesday, October 22, 2013
Fine Line
Season 2 Episode 11

Wandering minds are often the most volatile for the soul. Where once you thought an idea was safe and sound, apply the concept of releasing deliberation and there is no telling what the end result will be.

Promiscuous little Ol' me has always driven head first into every entanglement. Some would find that behavior appalling, but I've always taken the stanza of, "You only live once".

I've decided to make that my mantra…. for the time being at least.

What has pining over a taken man gotten me, thus far? Well, let's do the math. A broken heart, for starters. Add a splash of jealousy directed at a woman who attempted to ruin my literary career before it even took off, and what you are left with is a scowl on my face every time I remotely think of Mr. NY.

Brent is still with the 'Wicked Witch of the West', but I'm starting to feel like I get to have the last laugh.

Oh don't worry… I won't get all cocky on you. Believe me, do I know how easy it is to fall once you've begun a steady climb.

The funny part that keeps playing over and over in my head is how much of a bulls-eye I became when On'rie's mistake made headlines. I mean, really…you would think that people would pay just a little more attention to our government being shut down, as opposed to my getting made an enormous fool.

Nope. No such luck. The masses are always entertained by someone else's dark moments, but…like I said- I've been given a redeeming star and have taken to running with it.

Todd Jones, New York City's 2nd richest man….echem, Bachelor, has taken sweet interest in all things Melissa Green. What woman

in her right mind would deny an appealing invitation from an alluring provocative specimen of man…Not I!
Before I get into the good news, I should probably admit the bad.

The wrench thrown into the mix of my week pertains to the lifelong lesson of learning how to let things go, to let people go. Those specifically who tend to drain the happiness right out of our hearts. If indeed I am capable of accomplishing this lesson, is yet to be seen. What began as a text message, evolved into Brent showing up at my apartment out of the blue.

This is twice, in the matter of a month, that seems like desperation, exhumes from his pores. It's not the fact that I wasn't expecting him which bothers me. It's the fact that he doesn't understand why I'm so upset with him to begin with. He pushes, and pushes, affects me in a way I never thought any man could, and then just up and leaves. Leaves, to go back to his Fiancée, No Less!

There is a cunning method to his ability to get into my building without buzzing in too. While I'm not in the swanky part of the upper-east side, I do live in a great neighborhood, that is- if you consider overly helpful fellow citizens part of your thing.

So-knock knock knock, he shows up unannounced. What had me pausing for a moment was the mere fact he looked as though someone had died. I could even Feel the inner turmoil he was carrying about.

"Why are you here, Brent?" my asking was more of a way to express annoyance than actual concern but I doubt he could see it that way.

"We need to talk." His response came slowly as he showed himself in to my apartment.

I often wish I was just a little taller, a little more intimidating, anything to make it to where people wouldn't just assume that my place was open to them at their every whim.

"Hmmmm…" I began, "Let me ask the most vital question here, Brent." But before I could get anymore out, he turned around and gave me one of his, 'please don't' looks.

But since when do I hold back? Oh yeah, that's right…since the day I almost tripped right in front of him and things between us began.

"What do you want Brent?" submission clear in my voice.

"We need to talk."

"We don't need to talk. There is nothing to say to each other."

He took a step closer, and reached out for my hand. Sadly, there is no innocence in letting him take my hand. Since the day he proposed to Megan, there has been nothing innocent about being this close to each other, knowing full well neither of us had resolved anything.

"I miss you so much. When I saw you the other night, it took everything in me to not come over to you."

"Is that because you miss me? Or does it have something to do with my being in Todd Jones' company?" I asked, my sass reaching its limit when I added, "Oh, Wait, or is it because being with Megan terrifies you?"

I had done it. Something I had said, struck the single most aggravating chord in his system and he closed the gap which separated us.

Peering into my eyes, we neither touched nor spoke. His mouth hovered over mine, taunting, teasing. My heart raced and pumped with a blood that gushed of pure passion. God help me but my eyes closed and my body reacted to his presence.

Sometimes the actions we take in life are made without our full conscience. Our reasoning bedazzled by a greater power. In those moments, while later we believe them to be disastrous, in truth, it is our heart's only opportunity to express the emotions we are at war with.

He didn't have to say anything, and I really didn't feel like arguing back. I let him kiss me. Shit, I didn't even realize what was happening until he began to tug on my camisole. By then all the resolve I had to stop him, vanished. Say what you will, but if you were in my shoes, I'd like to see you try to stop yourself from 'Wanting' a man like him...Needing him.

We made love that afternoon and as I lay tangled up in his embrace, the white sheets on my bed half covering our bodies, I couldn't help but wonder if loving someone had limits.

I waited for him to break the silence because nothing I was going to say was going to be easy.

"I don't know what to do, M." he admitted finally. His hand began caressing my upper arm but the moment had already been ruined.

We had just made love and here he was still confused. He still didn't know what to do, what he truly wanted. When in fact he is suppose to want me, love me.

I sat up taking the sheet up with me to cover my chest while I turned my body to face him.

"What do you mean, you don't know what to do?" I could feel the huff coming on involuntarily.

His eyes looked straight up to the ceiling and he softly shook his head. "It's not as simple as you think, M. This isn't my first dog & pony show with Megan."

I smacked a hand off his belly. "What does that have to do with you and me, with this?"

His eyes met mine and the question was answered before he even said a word. It has nothing to do with us, but it was what was preventing us being together.

"So that's it then? You are going to stay with her, even though it's not what you want."

I wanted to vomit. The idea that nothing had changed, even though it was clear how we feel about each other, it made me physically sick.

I got out of bed, taking the crumpled sheets with me and walked out on my back patio. Unfortunately, the fresh air did nothing to clear the muddled thoughts running through my brain. This was it, the end of the road and I felt myself slowly crossing that fine line between love and hate.

By the time I came back inside, he was fully dressed getting ready to leave.

"Please stop contacting me. It's clear that this isn't about me. It's about you, and the sad part is that you don't even get that. This isn't about you wanting us, or you wanting Megan. This is about you being so terrified to commit to something that you are doing your best to ruin it so you have a reason to not marry her."

"That's not…" he tried to interrupt.

"No, hear me out." I shouted. "You can't love me. Not whole heartily at least, because you don't even love yourself enough to get an honest chance with someone. You've hidden behind your company and a half- hearted romance with me, when it's clear that you're just not ready…."

With the little conviction I had left, I walked to the door and opened it. "Forget I ever existed, Brent. I can't hurt like this anymore."

His body walked towards the door but before he walked out, he lowered his face level to mine. "I don't make promises I can't keep, M." his lips gently kissed my forehead and he left.

His last sentence stayed with me all week. I skipped brunch with the girls and canceled my dinner with Marcus. I couldn't face anyone with what I had done, at least not anyone who knows me well enough to catch on that something is truly weighing on me. It was the call from Todd that got me off my laptop and out of the house. I did ask that he come down to my standards and make our dinner something light and simple. While most women are easily wooed by the wining and dining, if Todd really wanted to get to know me, he would have to accept the fact that I am not a part of his world of socialites anymore. I made it a point to stay out of that lime light of glam and glitz all my adult life. A childhood is long enough to endure the pressures of the social elite....

After a dinner's worth of conversation, I was struck by one honest statement. An incredible truth that is still making me blush.

No, Don't go there......Yes, he is extremely attractive, and I can so see myself going there with him, I will admit I wasn't in the mood.

No. it was even more flattering than being told a man wants to jump your bones....

"The moment I heard you had a vivid imagination, I asked your publisher for a preview of your book. When I was done, left in awe, I was instantly curious what intrigue you could create for us....and if you'd be interested?"

I played coy at first, and then I said, Hell! Life is too short.

"Why Not!"

Readers comment:

    Anonymous   October 23, 2013
    This comment has been removed by a blog administrator.

Anonymous <u>October 26, 2013</u>
Okay, Brent really needs to make up his mind. You are not his "go to girl" every time he gets cold feet about making his commitment with Megan. He knows that all he has to do is get close to you and you melt. He is using you! Give him an ultimatum. Either leave Megan for good or don't bother to call you again. Now, Let's see what kind of fun you can have with Todd.....Intrigue, indeed! :p
~ALF~

Tuesday, October 29, 2013
Masks
Season 2 Episode 12

Ever since I was a child, I've been fighting the social class I was born in to. I never agreed with afternoon tea dressed to the brim.

Never felt like being part of the debutant socialites, and yet, somehow or another I have managed to wander back into the arena I fought so hard to flee from all my life. It's actually quite incredible that Page-6 took so long to connect the dots…

What intrigue is this, You ask??

You see, I am Melissa Anabeth Green Bergman. As in, Bergman Industries. The light bulb will gradually light up but you will slowly come to realize why I cut the Bergman out of my name. I'm not so much, ashamed of my heritage, as I have always been annoyed by how people perceive me as an individual knowing that I come from one of the wealthiest families in America.

The girls have always known, but we don't talk about my family at all, that is, we didn't until Todd came into the picture. He knew immediately who I was. Our fathers had done business together many years back. I'm sure, at some point, there was talk of marrying the two companies through us, but Daddy had to have known better. I'm sure he always expected I would run away from home someday.

…And Run Away is exactly what I did.

Come Wednesday morning my cell phone was buzzing off the hook. Ivy was having a baby cow with the newest Page-6 article. The moment they snapped photos of Todd and me eating lunch, someone decided to do some digging.

"They made you sound like a power piranha, Melissa." Ivy complained. I could hear the stress vibrating through the phone. I had, at that point, decided to pull up the article online, just to see what all the fuss was about.

"I'm sure they did, sweetie. But it will blow over like it always does. Weren't you the one that said there is no such thing as bad press?" While I said the words, the article finally popped up on the screen.

The Big Bold Flipping Heading read:

Jones snagged by a Bergman incognito

My heart skipped a few beats and I realized why Ivy was a mess. The article went on to reveal my background and how that changes things in my social standings.

"What in the world?" I breathed helplessly. "Who cares what my popularity is among the social New Yorkers?"

"We do, Melissa. Your book's longevity depends on how well you are liked and talked about in the city." Ivy scolded.

"I understand, so all you have to do is set the record straight. Why don't you just talk to Todd's people, see if they are confirming the dating status between he and I, and we will convey the same message. I will call my mother and forewarn her so she doesn't sue the newspaper for screwing up, why I chose to use her maiden name as opposed to daddies."

Ivy managed to settle everything out with the newspaper. The following day, they issued an apology being that the information, while juicy and almost accurate, was not given through a valid source. The debacle however, got us invited to a masquerade gala hosted by the newspaper's Halloween festivities.

Ivy accepted but it was my job to get Todd to be my date. While it sounded great at first, it was the calling my mother part that set me back a day. I hadn't spoken to mother since Christmas and here we are with this year's holidays upon us.

It's not that I don't want to talk to my parents, or even see how they have been. It's that I've never been one for a guilt trip, and boy do they both like to lay those on thick. It's always, 'I sent you to the finest boarding schools', or 'I paid for your fine education, the least you can do is visit once in a while.'

Usually I nod and agree with them. We do in fact all live in the same city.

I dialed the house number and fully expected Reginald to answer. Astonishingly it was Martin, my brother who picked up. "Not surprised you are calling, little sis." He said in his usual smug tone. "Yes well, I see that you are at mother's side to coddle the situation to your benefit there older brother." My sarcasm was always a last laugh. "I need to speak to mother." I regarded my purpose for calling.

"Let me ask if she will take your call." He began, but I could hear her in the background scolding him for being such a shit.

"Damn boy is never going to learn that it's not polite to speak to family in that manner."

"Good morning momma." I offered.

"Child, what mess have you gotten yourself into now?" she asked, but it wasn't really a question.

"They retracted the story this morning."

"I'm sure they did. Your father called them and ripped that editor a new one." She bit back.

Hearing of the old tycoon ruffled the nerves, "Speaking of Daddy, was he okay with the whole Todd Jones bit?" I closed my eyes and waited…the tick tock of my kitchen clock echoing as I waited endlessly.

Finally she sighed, "He was fine with it. Not what he expected, but he didn't say much in opposition."

"Well, I just wanted to call and make sure I didn't jumble anything up with the article having outted me." I offered, wanting the call to be over already.

"Oh, No you don't little Missy." She began. "Your father has been itching to speak with you. You should have known better."

My eyelids seemed to close involuntarily, the tightness in my gut got just a little tighter.

"I bet he has." Was all I could reply. Believe me when I say, it has never been his voice that makes me tremble. It is the swift manner in which he responds to any and all situations that has never given me any comfort.

I could hear mother hand him the phone, and the slight pause he took as he placed the receiver to his ear.

Finally, "Dear"

"Hi Daddy, how have you been?"

"I've been better, I suppose. No need to ask how you are doing, I get a weekly update as to your shenanigans."

And there it was…all of 2 sentences and I felt 16 years old again.

All I could do was let out the laugh I'd been holding in of ridiculousness.

"Alright Daddy. Thank you for calling the paper and trying to fix the situation. I appreciate your concern but…"

"I called them to avoid the Bergman name from getting smeared in the mud. You have made it clear that you want nothing to do with it, but I will damn well make sure you don't ruin it." He handed the phone back to my mother before I could get in another word.

"Sweetheart, give him time."

And time is what I promised. While I doubt they would come, I invited the lot to my book release event and ended the conversation.

Somehow, and I still can't figure out how, I managed to convince Todd to be my date for the Masquerade ball. It was the first time in as long as I could recall that I didn't attend an event accompanied by my girlfriends, but with the man of the hour.

My imagination couldn't quite put into words the stunning elegance a man could beam while dressed in a tux and a simple black mask, but it was an inspiring moment as I walked out into the street to see him holding the town car door open for me.

"You will certainly be the Belle of the ball, my dear." He said, referring to the gold ball gown Ivy had sent over for me.

"Why thank you, fine sir. I'm glad you approve." I mused.

"Yes, indeed, but where is your mask?"

Without hesitating, I removed the simple sparkling gold mask from my bag and put it over my face.

"As if that will do anything to hide your identity." With that he leaned forward to my masked face and placed a gentle kiss on my lips.

The calm and ease of the gesture put my nerves at ease. Money may make him seem intimidating to others, but with me, he seems so real. *Or is it, surreal?*

Whatever it was, the night began like a fairy tale. The glam and glitz of his lifestyle wasn't a bother, nor was it even a bore. We mingled and he introduced me to most of New York City's social elite, something Brent never did.

When the dancing began, Todd left to find a colleague and I was put to the test. Mingle on my own, and find the girls in the crowd. All I can say….I thought it would be a piece of cake. Not so much!

Out of the blue, a hand extended in front of me. Black tux, Black mask.

I'm a fool. What can I say….I thought it was Todd.

A Strauss waltz began and I was whisked on to the dance floor by the masked gentleman.

I couldn't help but let myself fall a little further into the fairy tale. The room gently spun with us, the mini-lights strung all over the ballroom creating an endless twinkling all around.

But somewhere in the 7th minute, when the trumpets began to sound in repetition, he slowed his pace in the center of the dance floor and pulled me oh so close to him, the palm of his hand on the base of my back. His face leaned close to mine and his mouth covered mine. The kiss. While sweet and sensual reminded me of something.

 That was when it hit me, like an anvil in the center of my chest. I wasn't dancing with Todd.

The confirmation came the moment he raised his mouth to my ear and whispered, "I love you."

Like a flame being doused by ice-water, I jerked away from him. I tore off my mask and stared at him.

Several dancing couples stopped dancing, but as I noticed their attention I thought better of what I was preparing to say.

"The mask suits you."

I turned on my heels and stormed off the dance floor directly in front of the one woman I never wanted to set eyes upon.

Megan, with her smug expression, blocked my way into the ladies room. "Think you are too good for a mask, Melissa?"

I huffed, "I don't need a mask, Megan." I started, half expecting her to say something to protest, "But you should probably check your fiancée's mask, he seems to be wearing his permanently these days."

I gave up on the idea of hiding out in the ladies room and went in search of my prince charming. I told Todd what happened and we left.

In the car, on the ride home, Todd showed a side of himself I hadn't expected.

"I'm sorry I left you alone tonight. Had I known he would do what he did I wouldn't have left to handle some pointless business."

"Don't worry about it. No one could expect something like that to happen." I offered.

"I do worry about it. I like you, more than I should admit, and tonight was supposed to be special, at least, I wanted it to be."

I've never been one to compare but I was kissed by two men that night. Once by a man who meant everything to me, and twice by a man who wanted to mean something to me.

The comparison was simple....Go with the man who wants you to be his First choice.

I kissed Todd on the way home, and haven't stopped kissing him.

Readers comment:

Anonymous   October 30, 2013
Yes Melissa, go with the man who wants you to be his First Choice. Not the one who keeps hiding behind a mask and his fiancé and putting you Second. I'm glad you walked away from Brent and told Todd what happened.

Todd seems to be very much the gentleman and seems to genuinely like you. Try to forget about Brent and concentrate on Todd. ♥ ♥ ♥
~ALF~

Anonymous <u>October 30, 2013</u>
I almost feel bad for Todd.
Nancy

Tuesday, November 5, 2013
Fakest of Smiles
Season 2 Episode 13

Often times the fakest of smiles can be deemed the brightest of realities….for when you do something long enough, somewhere along the line you begin to believe the lie you've created.

Everything is finally happening and I can't help but feel like I'm pretending every waking moment. From Marcus, to the girls, and now this new liaison with Todd….I'm feeling drained. The sad part about it is that I can't even say I don't resent certain aspects of my life at the moment. I'm not complaining…merely verbalizing this absurd confusion going on in my little being.

Let's compartmentalize, shall we.

On spotlight is the Debbie downer of my past week. We'll put it on the plate first and get it over with.

The girls decided on a late lunch this week, seeing as how everyone had something new to share.

Shockers come in all size packages, and Amy decided to make her the whopper of them all. "I'm getting married!" she squealed from across our table once we had finished greeting each other. The talking throughout the yellow wallpapered dining area ceased abruptly.

Amy learned forward, her slender hand hung directly in front of us, direct eye shot of a glamorous diamond rock on her ring finger.

"My dear Word! Would you look at the size of that" Dana gasped, here eyeballs almost bulging out of their sockets.

I took her passing palm and inspected the beautiful perpetual ring.

Don't worry…not even a smidgen of envy surged throughout my system. I have no desire to advance my relationship to a ball and chain status…nor should you worry about my bitterness and eager need to show disdain for the vows of matrimony.

"Jason asked me last night. It was the most romantic thing ever. He had the jumbo-tron at the hockey game pop the question on the screen. When I saw it I thought I would die."

…Hearing the name of my 'might be' one-night-tryst caused more than just knots in my stomach, it caused me to question Amy's intentions even more, but the more the thought festered, the quicker I realized it was fear that was feeding the emotion.

That was the first smile. She bought it, or seemed to as she passed her bling hand to Ivy. Eventually I realized that Dana caught my reaction and empty response.

Under her breathe, "Still not sure?" she asked.

With a shake of the head, I confirmed that I still don't recall what happened with Amy's Jason a few weeks ago. Luckily Ivy and Amy were so wrapped up in the sparkle to notice the almost wordless conversation between Dana and me.

"Maybe some things are better left under the covers."

"Literally" Dana teased.

Marcus saved me from seafood that afternoon. He called and broke up our lunch date, pulling me in for an emergency meeting at his house.

While I was happy to avoid any more conversation with the girls, I felt bad to bolt altogether from hearing everyone's news. Alas, it is what it is.

Across New York City, while waiting in front of Marcus' brownstone for him to buzz me up, I noticed a lone figure at the end of the street.

Against the better judgment I know I've learned to have, I stared in his direction trying to put the pieces together to figure out where I knew him from. This is where, wearing my glasses or contacts would be beneficial towards lowering my embarrassment level. Too far away and you become a blog of nothingness to me.

The door buzzed and I half jumped inside the building. An unexplainable fear took over my being. I couldn't stand out in that cold city weather one more moment knowing someone was staring back.

"Come in, Come in." he ushered me in. "We will all be here in just a few moments, and please have an open mind and listen to everything before you make any un-weighted opinionated statements."

There was my warning bell.

"What's this all about, Marcus?" asking more out of pure curiosity than what it really boils down to how I feel. He is up to something but I can't put my finger on it.

"In a moment." He sighed and walked into the dining room. That was when everything happened.

The doorbell rang, and so did my cell phone. At the time, I didn't even think of who could be at the door, but I had gotten a text message from Jason.

We need to talk.   *What now?*

 I look up from the bright LED screen to find Marcus and Benjamine On'rie standing in front of me.

"For the Love of Pete!" it came out of my mouth without a thought to stop it.

"Nice to see you too, *Mon Cheri*" Ben responded, his voice as smooth as ever.

Is it not unnerving to hear someone speak so calmly, while you yourself are shaken to the core from the very sight of them?

"You need to get over it, Melissa." Marcus scolded.

"He's right. You're relationship with Ben was pretty much an expectation for a successful launch of your novel. We need to talk strategy." Ivy said as she came into the room and rounded the coffee table to sit on the sofa.

All I could do was stare at her and wonder how long she had been planning this mini intervention.

Unfortunately, the longer the thought fermented the more disgusted and exhausted I became.

"I don't have the energy for this people." I started, "I want to be civil, but every time I look at you I am reminded of how I chose you." I directed at On'rie.

"And while I stand here, practically days before my official release date, wanting everything to be okay...it's clear things are Not okay." I said to Marcus.

"Honey, you're book is buzzing interest because of many reasons, but in the literary world- the ONE place it matters the most- it has always been Ben's expertise they trusted in, that they wanted attached to you."

"I can't imagine how anyone would put any trust in a man who builds relationships of lies." I whispered solemnly.

My body trembled standing in that room with the three of them. Everything in me wanted to jump into On'rie's arms and wish everything was as it had been in July. Carefree and warm. But at the same time, I felt like running. Running like I did in June.

This is where the Second smile comes in.

Patterns. Have you ever had an epiphany in the middle of a complicated situation? I can only imagine what it's like to watch a person in said moment.

When life gets just a little confusing, complicated, or downright catastrophic, I find a reason to run. I'm sure if I looked back throughout my life I would find the pattern to be almost exact.

"What?" On'rie asked plainly. His simple question had my eyes shooting up in his direction.

"You win" I gave in. Fighting a giant takes cunning planning, of which I have had none. The public wants me to play nice with a villain....sure....okay, why not.

Does this mean the outcome will be the same? And the answer to that will never be known. I really don't much want to gamble where my book is concerned.

Marcus made a face at me. I'm sure he wondered where I would go with this but playing the mature adult, I sat down and waited for the plan to formulate from Ivy's mouth. On cue, she removed a folder and started her break down of the Sunday festivities.

After about 45 minutes of 'must dos' and 'careful shmoe', Ben finally opened his mouth.

"Are you planning on bringing that Todd character to your event?"

Yes, indeed the Third smile spread across my face. This of course warmed my heart. Could it be, dear God, is he ....Jealous?

Wait for it....

"Hmmm....let me see.....Oh, yeah, that falls in the 'none of your business' category!" I snapped.

Amusing as it was, Marcus shook his head and Ivy found it prudent to mention, "He really should be your date. The two of you have been mentioned together an awful lot these past few weeks."

By the time I managed to leave Marcus' house that evening, my hand was red from how tight I had held my cell phone throughout that mess.

The first step onto the street prompted my text message screen to beam on and by the end of the street I had replied to Jason's message.

As quickly as I sent it, he replied:

>Things can't be weird with us.

Of course, my response was to make light of my thoughts:

>Weird? Why would things be weird? Either we have or have not had sex. One way or another, things are just complicated.

Classic female response: Nothing will be weird

You mark my words, Karma knows Just when to Hit me with a baseball bat! I walked for maybe 2 more blocks feeling as though I was being followed. Making the best choice possible I went into a Starbucks and found an empty seat.

Jason didn't text back so I did what any girl would do….I wasted time. It didn't take long for my 'would-be-stalker' to reveal himself.

Todd planted his sexy self across from me.

"Is it serendipity?"

Shockingly, he shook his head that it wasn't.

"I knew you were going to see Marcus today. I got curious."

At his response my body leaned back in my chair and I stared at him. The muscle across his jaw line flexed and I could tell he was nervous by how he played with his coffee cup.

"Please tell me you were not checking up on me."

"I'm not checking up on you, but I don't trust you 100% either, and I need to stay honest with you if this is going to end up as anything."

The last smile of the day, while mixed with emotions now feels the fakest of them all.

"Honesty is a two way street, and believe me, you have to be faster than a flash for it not to break your heart."

"Yes, well…I have lived my whole life in front of those flashes. I know how to make them all stop." His tone was as clear as day.

"Be my date for Sunday?" I asked demurely.

"Be my date for life? He replied.

How does a girl reply to that?

Readers comment:

> *Anonymous* November 07, 2013
> He doesn't trust you but he wants to marry you? Is it a money thing? Not sure about this Todd guy. He seems fishy to me.
> Janet

> *Anonymous* November 07, 2013
> *How does a girl reply to that?*
> Very Carefully!!!
> ~ALF~

There are very few moments in our lives that we can honestly say we've had our breath taken away. That in one single flash, everything that was, somehow becomes something else, either something more, or considerably less. Today, I write to you as a friend, as a woman....maybe even as a sister. I've taken the rose colored glasses off and realized that life isn't about chance...it is about actions and reactions. While we choose to play at both ends of that pendulum, regardless of what the outcome may be, we are making a conscience decision. Our eyes have been wide open, and there are no excuses.

For the past 7 months, I've been aware of emotions that I haven't been able to control. What is it they say, 'The heart wants what it wants'.... A stubborn little girl who grew up, that's what I resemble.

Don't worry...this isn't self loathing. I've only just begun to shine light on what is finally real, of everything I thought I knew, but didn't imagine could be as twisted as it truly is.

Since last Tuesday, I've probably managed to feel every possible sentiment in the book.

Let's see...I had **'Patience'** with my dear On'rie. While there isn't much to discuss on it, it really does weigh heavy in retrospect.

Ivy made a compelling argument in regards to **'forgiveness'**. While we are all capable of making mistakes, it's being able to forgive that changes the course of our own path. I gave him that. You can shake your head at me all you want, but it's not going to change the fact that the journey I took with On'rie lead me to where I stand today. While I will never forget being made a fool of, the ordeal left me with a valuable lesson to learn...Never believe in a man who offers you everything....the catch is what costs the most.

In there somewhere, **'faith'** was filtered in a few times. The first was when Amy came over to have a heart to heart.

With coffee mugs in hand, she sat next to me on the sofa. This was our first serious conversation about love and understanding.

"I don't want this to be weird, but before life happens to us…I need to get this out." Her eyes were fixed on her coffee mug.

In an attempt to ease her nerves, "You know you can tell me anything, Amy. You are one of my best friends."

She lifted her timeless face, "I know that neither you or Jason know what happened that night, and I'm okay with it….really," she began, "God knows I've had my fair share of lost moments."

In response my head started to shake in argument, "Honey, I don't feel anything for him. Even if something did happen, which I doubt, it means nothing to me. My heart is mute right now."

With a tilt of her face, Amy all but asked what I meant.

"I'm numb. I've been fighting to forget so much for so long that I can't think straight. Sometimes I wake up from a dream where I see a face I miss terribly but then I realize it wasn't real."

"Have faith in love, look at me. I didn't think I would want to settle down with anyone, and when I least expected it, it happened." Amy's face made me want to believe in what she was saying. To give in and let things be, but in truth it was faith in love itself I was troubled with.

"Love is such a fickle little thing, isn't it?" I asked her plainly. "I thought I had made the right choice in running away with On'rie to Paris, but *Look* what that got me." I put my coffee mug on the glass table in front of us and walked to my living room window.

"It got you a published novel, Melissa." Amy replied, following in my step.

As I stared out that window, I recalled another view…the view of the city from Brent's office.

"It cost me so much more though." I whispered, not thinking she'd hear me.

"Not all that's lost wanders, M."

Her memorable words forced me to turn and face her. My friend had faith in me…so in turn, I should have faith in love.

"I won't wander then…I will walk fiercely into every moment." I promised her.

"…And I will be with you every step of the way." She pledged in response.

Being that my week was chaotic, I completely forgot to attend the girl's weekly brunch. It wasn't until Dana caught up with me at Bergdorf's that I realized my **thoughtlessness**.

"Caught red handed, my dear." She scolded innocently as I beamed over a stunning black Gucci cocktail dress.

"I need something simple to wear Sunday." My innocent reaction came from knowing that she loves shopping with me and my guilt for not having asked her to come join in the spree of the week.

"You missed brunch." She boldly stated.

The awe of guilt is two-fold. On one hand there is the knowledge that you forgot something important, while on the other hand is the fact of not minding that you've forgotten at all.

I grit and bared my teeth. "Yikes" I said softly.

"The girls were worried is all. Ivy needs to talk to you, she says to give her a call." She casually stated as she toyed with the dress I was holding. "I bet this would look killer with some black leather heels."

A smile stretched across my face, "Care to join me?" I offered.

"Is there something bothering you?"

The question of all questions….. Here for the second time that week, stood another person who knows me well, asking me something I couldn't put my finger on.

"I can't help feel like I'm missing something. Like the punch line hasn't come yet."

"Maybe you are just nervous about the party. No need to impatiently wait for the other shoe to drop."

Dana spent the rest of the afternoon with easing my mind with shopping bliss but as soon as we went our separate ways I found myself standing out front of Brent's office building.

I feel like I always end up there...absentmindedly standing on the sidewalk looking up to the world he lives in.

With my eye affixed towards the skyline, I wondered if he was in his office. Is it so hard to remove someone from our system?

The action-reaction part of our judgment doesn't often contemplate all the forward motions in advance before getting caught up in the moment.

I didn't think. I let my heart move my legs. Used my fingers to press the elevator button and eventually I found myself on an almost empty floor. The halls of Brent's office were practically lifeless. A light on here and there, but the only one that mattered was the one at the end of the hall...and that one was on.

Yes….I did….I found myself, standing on the opposite side of his office door. My heart, beating at a rapid pace in my chest somehow allowed a vacant courage to direct my hand to grip the door knob. Slowly I opened the door and found my Mr. New York busy and seated at his desk towards the end of his office.. It might have been my presences that startled him out of his seat, or maybe that was just my imagination.

"M, what are you doing here?" he asked, his voice slightly trembling.

At that precise moment I didn't know what to say. I didn't even know why I was there. I just knew I had to be near him.

"Are you okay?" he asked me when I didn't initially respond.

The smile came quickly. "I think." I answered honestly.

He took a few steps closer but I didn't move to meet his response.

"What do you mean, you think?"

The skyline caught my attention. The sun was setting and my heart was pounding. I felt whole. A completeness that I'd been missing since we were together. Everything inside me screamed that I needed to make this right.

"What's going to happen Brent; is this pull between us ever going to go away? I miss you. So much more than I should admit, but it hurts now. I can't change what happened but I love you too."

Brent closed the distance between us, and his being in front of me made sense. I finally let that wholeness sink in but something else sunk in....worry.

"I can't do this anymore, M. I'm marrying Megan on Saturday." his tone was clear but the way his eyes misted deceived him. And with that, my heart broke. He chose her after all.

Confused, I let out the breath I'd been holding and a tear I didn't know had even formed, fell.

"I'm sorry" he added softly, the heat of his breath reaching my face.

I looked up, through the tears that had finally begun to form, and noticed the full extent of pain in his expression.

"You don't want to marry her, Brent. You don't want to be tied to a heartless bitch for the rest of your life, so why are you doing this. Why are you making such a horrible mistake?" my asking came with a motion towards him.

"In my world, love isn't the easiest route, M. Business always comes before pleasure. She is business…."

"And I was pleasure." I shot back, the hurt becoming more apparent.

"No, you are my weakness, and they all know it. Do you think that Todd Jones is interest in you because of your pretty face and amazing personality?"

"What are you trying to say?"

He reached out and took hold of my arms. "You are my Achilles heel. What do you think happens to my blood when I see you talking to him, kissing him, or merely being around him?" he asked, his eyes peering into mine. "It boils, M. I can't think straight because it's always going to be you."

"Then Why can't it be ME that you marry on Saturday?" I sobbed, my face burying in his chest, my very core shivering with pain.

"There are things you just don't know, you shouldn't know. I'm protecting you from a world you never wanted to be a part of in the first place, and I finally understand why it's important to keep you out of it."

I let him hold me, but only because I couldn't imagine giving him up. For once I felt regret for having chosen someone else, running away from this love I've never stopped feeling for him.

"M, Look at me.' He asked, tilting my chin for our eyes to meet.

"You have my heart, and for now that is all that matters. I will always be here, whenever you need me."

"I need you with me, not in the shadows. Not married to a woman who loathes me." I shot back.

Brent's body reacted first. He pulled away from my hold and took a few steps back. As I reached out to him, he turned and faced the skyline.

"I made a deal long ago that can't be broken, Melissa."

"And there's never been a business man who's broken his word."

He swiftly turned around, "Not to a man like your father."

As a blade slices through flesh, his words opened a timeless wound......Daddy....

It all made sense. New York City has always been too small of a place to avoid such incredible odds. No matter how much I tried to ignore my birthright, it would always come back to bite me in the arse.

I nodded. It was all I needed. No longer plagued by the confusion that haunted my heart. Brent was a puppet, my father the master puppeteer.

Turning on my heels, I swore to myself I would never return to his office, never see the skyline that inspired my heart to beat. It was over. I'd lost the most important love.

The days that followed were **hollow**. I felt nothing, enjoyed nothing. Sunday morning I woke up sick to my stomach…Ivy insisted that nerves had gotten the better of me. She dropped off a calendar of events that she had booked for me, needing me to sign off that I would attend each and every one.

Funny how calendars force us to recall certain events. If you are a woman, the cycle is constant, ongoing….never ending until you reach middle age. An internal bodily clock ticking an endless tock, but in my case, it was this calendar that brought one stunning realization to light.....*I'm late...*

Sitting at the kitchen table with my coffee in hand, I stared at the weeks that have passed since I last had my period. So many things had happened in those weeks. On'rie, Brent, Jason, Todd....life happened in a world-wind of champagne and chaos.

The phone rang and sprang me from the daze. "Hello." I answered not even looking to see who it was.

"I'm sending a car to pick you up at 2. They should have you at the restaurant in time but if traffic is too backed up, let me know and I will stall the guest." Ivy informed, her tone all business.

"Thank you, I will be ready." Not that there was any doubt in that. Just as Ivy said, the car was downstairs at 2 o'clock sharp.

"Can we make a quick stop on the way, I need to pick something up at the drugstore. Would that be fine?"

"Yes, ma'am." The driver replied, opening the car door for me.

Fear. A stunning emotion we feel when we are unsure of ourselves. While capable of incapacitating us, the torture it holds over us comes from the fact that it does not kill us. We are forced to live through the surge of terror until we either bend to its grip or fight to free ourselves.

I bought a pregnancy test for the first time in my life and hid in the drugstore bathroom for the few minutes that it took me to pee on the stick. Fear forced me to hide said stick in my small purple Coach clutch and act as if it wasn't going to make me wonder all night long.

The moment my car reached the restaurant, I knew everything I had worked so hard for these past 6 months had finally come to fruition. On'rie opened the car door for me and was my escort into the party.

"Don't worry, just enjoy the moment. Everyone will want to talk to you, just smile and mingle."

Camera's snapped as I smiled and searched the room for one absent face. "Where is Ivy?" I asked, redirecting my attention to the host of my event.

"She is around. Here, have some champagne." He said, reaching over to one of the waiters and grabbed the sparkling bubbly for me. I took the flute but stared at it, contemplating if a sip would be appropriate.

He instantly noticed my hesitation. "What is it?"

"I um…" I paused, avoiding his glare. "I can't" I managed.

"Can't, or shouldn't?" he calmly questioned. His hand gently taking the flute out of mine and sipping from it as if it was only natural.

I watched as the clear glass touched his soft lips. "I shouldn't, On'rie."

Our eyes met and the unspoken conversation was more intense than ever.

"Melissa, Over here." Ivy called out.

Grateful for the distraction, I left Ben wondering, but I knew we would sort things out eventually.

It was half way through my night that I found myself in awe. I'd just finished reading a section from 'Love in the End' when I found a lone figure standing towards the back of the room.

"*Daddy*?" I whispered to myself.

Leaving the crowd, I made my way to where he stood.

"You shouldn't leave your party, Melissa." He scolded.

"You came. I didn't think I'd ever see you at one of my events."

"Yes, well, I had some business to attend to."

Never one to connect the dots, I let him continue.

"Have you decided on Mr. Jones' proposal?" he asked bluntly.

And there you have it....I was the business...

The huff and laugh came out involuntarily. "You're never going to change are you?" while it wasn't a question, I had opened up a moment for him to add to my opinion.

"I will always be your father, dear. It is my duty to protect you."

"Protect me?" I asked, insulted that he felt his behavior was to be considered noble.

"You are not protecting me, Daddy. You are trying to control me. First Brent, now Todd... I don't get what your end game is." the disgust I felt absolutely undeniable.

Dana must have seen the situation brewing with my father and came to where we stood.

"Sweetie, Ivy is gearing up for your next reading and your line is building up again."

"Thanks" I said to her, looking over only to see what she meant about my line, then directed my glare to the man I grew up idolizing. "I've had to give up everything because of your world. Stop trying to hurt me."

"It only hurts because you are fighting the truth."

"The truth, Daddy?" I asked, "The truth that you threatened the man I love so that you and your company could thrive in the perfect business deal. I am not a pawn for you to use whenever you see fit."

"If he loved you so much he wouldn't have married that gold digger." My father huffed.

I turned away from him and ignored his presence the entire evening.

I did notice the few minutes he had Todd's attention. While minimal as they were, I wondered if he was in on the bargain or not. Was it all a ploy to seal a deal that had nothing to do with his feelings towards me? Was his proposal to me just business as usual?

At the end of the evening On'rie stole a brief moment before I left.

"Should we talk before I leave for Paris?"

I smiled at his concern. "I will be fine. No matter what happens, I will be fine." I kissed his cheek and left him standing there alone.

Yes...he is a scum-bag, but at the base of his choices is a foundation of genuine wonder.

Amy, Ivy, and Dana decided to hop in the back of the limo with me.

"Did you think we wouldn't have some sort of after party?" Amy giggled, enthused by whatever plans they had in store for me.

"I'm telling you, Ivy really did you well tonight. There is no way you aren't the talk of the town tonight!" Dana mused.

"Yes, well, it was easy considering everyone was just as excited as we were." Ivy offered.

I couldn't focus on the buzz….my eyes were fixed to the small clutch I'd been gripping and the knowledge of what was inside.

"What's wrong, M?" Dana asked me as Ivy finished.

I met her glare, then looked to each of them. "I uh…"

"Melissa…" Amy started.

It was Ivy who I focused on. Her straight way of thinking would help me get through this. I unzipped the little purple Coach clutch and removed the white stick, making damn sure I didn't look at its results.

"Before the party, I had to make a stop."

"Oh my God…" Dana whispered first, loud enough for the four of us to take in a sharp breath.

"M…what does it say?" Amy asked nervously.

They say that in moments of truth we all show our true colors. Some prove how weak and frail their inner strength is, while others shock with the swift calm and coolness that overtakes us.

I squinted my eyes shut and lowered my head, knowing that the moment I opened them up, my life would forever be changed. Knowing, that nothing before this moment will ever be as important going forward.

Gripping that thought, I found the inner strength to open my eyes and see my future. Two little lines creating one very positive result, a moment in which my breath was literally taken from my lungs.

I'm pregnant.

Readers comment:

Anonymous November 12, 2013
WTF! I can't believe Brent married that BITCH but still tells you that you have his heart and he will always be there. I understand that your father is pulling strings on

him but come on, grow some balls! Stand up to him and give your heart to the one it belongs to...
AND, OMG! What??? Pregnant!!! Who's the "lucky" guy??? ;)
~ALF~

Anonymous <u>November 12, 2013</u>
I was only a matter of time.
Nancy

Anonymous <u>November 15, 2013</u>
Seriously!!!!! You ended it There?!?!?! Can't wait for next season to get here already!

SEASON 3

Tuesday, January 21, 2014
Changes Going Down
Season 3 Episode 1

Change is not always about actions or behaviors that become altered. Often it is a frame of mind that must take on new ideas and processes. If someone had told me four months ago that things would change for me, I wouldn't necessarily have argued with them. However, had they said I would be knocked up....Now that I would have questioned!

The limo ride home the night of my book launch event was only the beginning. Step by step, day by day that has passed since that incredible moment I withdrew a pregnancy test from my clutch has been eye opening. I went from living life selfishly, only thinking of myself, to spending every waking moment thinking about a life I would be bringing into the world.

A mother.

How am I supposed to be someone's mother when my life has been nothing but chaos for the past year?

Every choice I've made lead me to that moment of realizing I had completely screwed up.

And don't get me wrong....more so, don't confuse my words. I screwed up because even now, I have no clue who to thank for the bun in my oven. Doing the math, it could be On'rie, Brent, or even Jason.

The only positive that has come of the madness is my relationship with my parents. The moment I swallowed the news, I decided it was time to go home for a while. Marcus, while upset and disappointed I would be canceling my book tour for the foreseeable future, didn't ask too many questions when he heard my dad huffing in the back ground....

"When will you be back into the city?" he asked, his concern clear through the phone.

I will admit, the hardest part of the conversation were the tears I was biting back. "I'm not sure, not until after the New Year."

His sigh said so much more than anything he could have spoken to me. "Will you at least finish the book you're working on?"

"I promise. The next time you see me will be with a completed manuscript in hand."

"And Todd? What of his offer?"

It was my turn to sigh. "I can't right now. I just....I need to be around my family for the holidays."

Hanging up that call left my heart heavier than usual. Marcus has been so much more than a friend for the past few years. Since being in the city, I had all but stopped having contact with my family. Marcus and his wife became that family. Them, and the girls were all I needed to survive....or so I thought.

That instant, in the limo ride, we all realized there were 2 lines on that test, as opposed to 1, the girls went ballistic. Amy repeated,

'OMG' no less than 100 times. Dana stared at me while Ivy decided it was appropriate to scold me as to my promiscuous nature. I get it, I'm her client. She bitched and moaned about how it was going to be a scandal that the media would use to try to ruin me.

Eventually Dana yelled at her to shut up, but it was too late. Ivy had said enough to make up my mind. That night, when the girls finally left, I packed some bags and called my mom.

"Dear, how was your event. Your father said he popped in to show his support. Did he behave?" she sounded tired, half asleep even.

"I'm sorry if I woke you, Mom..."

"No, no dear, you didn't wake me. Tell me what's wrong. You sound like you've been crying."

Funny how mothers know their children, even after years of being apart. "Mom, I think I need to come home for a while. Do you think Daddy would be okay with that?"

"Oh, Sweetheart, you know your father would do just about anything for you. Of course you can come home for a while." She paused, "Actually, he is planning on driving back home in the morning. Give him a call and he'll have Joseph come pick you up before they head back this way."

"Thanks mom. I will see you soon."

"I love you, Darling."

Hanging up, I knew the next call would be the most difficult. My Tycoon father, the man who made a business deal to keep the man I loved away from me, was the only man I could put my trust in.

"I have to say, I'm surprised you are calling me after how we ended things tonight." He said, answering my call.

I mentally chanted my childhood mantra, 'I am my father's daughter, and I am my father's daughter...'

"I will never agree on how you conduct business, Daddy, Let's be clear on that," I started, the courage slowly building back up. "But as the head of our family, it is your responsibility to be the father we all deserve when one of us is dealing with something difficult."

"Where is this coming from, Melissa?" he said sharply.

"Daddy, promise me you will be here for me and you will not be a tyrant bastard." I ordered firmly.

"Melissa, what's going on?" His tone slower, darker.

"I need you to send Joseph to pick me up at my apartment before you leave to go back home."

After a brief pause, "We will be there at 8 sharp. Get some sleep."

I couldn't say another word as I heard the line click. He had hung up on me. It was the 'We' he had said that set me back. I hadn't expected him to make the trip into Manhattan to retrieve me.

The 5 hour drive upstate to Rochester was quiet. Daddy poured his attention into a file, while I decided that it was time to read all that I had written in the manuscript I was planning on finishing. By the time we had reached home, I knew exactly where I needed to go with the book.

It took a few weeks for me to get my bearings back about me. Mom was constantly asking me if I was okay, while I could see that Dad was waiting for me to admit to him why I had come home. By Thanksgiving I was puking my brains out. Mom put 2 and 2 together and helped me manage the pains. She promised she wouldn't tell my father until I was ready. That happened on Christmas morning.

After breakfast and gift exchange, Daddy was just sitting by the fireplace staring at the Christmas tree. He seemed so pensive, peaceful even. I sat across from him with a cup of hot chocolate in hand.

Somehow, I too got lost in the lights of the tree. I hadn't noticed him turn to stare at me until he spoke.

"So when are you going to trust me enough to open up to me?" he asked, his voice tender.

He waited, watched me play with my cup, and finally look up to him. "I'm pregnant."

The words caused his eyes to close and my center to quiver. The idea that I had disappointed him forced me to recall a moment 10 years prior when he had the same reaction to something I had done.

"And who shall your child be calling Daddy?" he asked finally. I didn't know how to reply. I think it's human nature to avoid the questions we find the most difficult to answer, but then again, this was my father. I couldn't reply because the consequences were so phenomenal that no one would completely comprehend.

"Melissa, answer the question." He demanded curtly.

"I can't Dad. I just can't."

He stood up and walked across the living room to where I was sitting. His height in front of me far more intimidating than the question itself.

"Tell me you know who the father is." He ordered his tone just a tad louder than before.

I stood up, my height matching his own. "I don't know who the father is." I stated plainly.

He shook his head and turned around. "Who may the possibilities be, then?"

"I had just broken up with On'rie, so it could be his, but…"

"But?" he interrupted, still not facing me.

"But I went out one night with the girls and think I might have slept with a friend of mine."

"So, it's either a friend's or a Frenchman man-whore ." He stated, turning to face me squarely.

"Not quite." I admitted sheepishly,

His eyes flared open and I knew it was now or never, "I also spent the night with Brent Bishop."

"WHAT!" he bellowed, his voice echoing throughout the house.

"That man will be the death of me!" he shouted, as he paced the room.

I sat back down at watched as his face turned 20 shades of red and he ranted for more than 30 minutes about how thoughtless I'd been.

Finally, he realized I was watching him and stopped. My mother had come downstairs to sit next to me.

"What do you plan on doing about this?"

What does one do at such a question….Me? I laughed and answered him rationally. "I will ask Jason and On'rie to provide a DNA sample being that I am on friendly terms with each of them. Once I reach 12 weeks, I will head back into the city and find out who's the father of my baby."

"And what if it turns out that Bishop is its father?"

"Like I said before, I don't agree with how you do your business daddy. For whatever reason, you have inadvertently caused me to lose the one and only true love of my life. Be that as it may, if this baby turns out to be Brent's, you can rest assure I have come to the decision that he will never know it as his."

"But Melissa…" my mother began, "Your child deserves to have a mother and a father."

"And it shall. I accepted Todd's proposal after I told him about my predicament. He said it didn't bother him. That he'd care for my child as much as he cares for me."

"What about love?"

What about it? No matter how hard I try to forget Brent, he's become a phantom that haunts my very existence.

Mother managed to accept my decision but only because Daddy asked her to. I knew he would agree with my decision because it meant he won. I would marry Todd and Brent would be shut out forever.

Funny thing about Forever in New York City….in a city of 8 million people forever is a blink away. My first stop back in the city was to see Marcus. Just as promised I carried with me a newly completed manuscript for his eyes only.

"So, how did it end?" he asked as I handed it to him as I walked into his office.

"It didn't end well, Marcus, not well at all." I replied, holding my arms out for a hug.

"It's so good to have you back." He whispered as he wrapped his arms around me.

As he pulled away, I caught his attention before he pulled too far away.

"I have a secret to tell you." I murmured.

"Oh?"

I smiled so he wouldn't worry about the truth I was about to confess. "I'm pregnant."

As odd as it was, his reaction mirrored my fathers.

"I didn't tell you for you to stress yourself out, Marcus. I actually need you to get a hold of Ben for me. I need him to come in to the city soon."

"Ben's the father?" he asked, his voice rather shrill.

The mask returned, a smile spread across my face but only because Marcus wouldn't approve of my behavior.

"Actually, I need him to take a DNA test. I need to find out who is the father."

"Melissa Anabeth Green!" he scolded.

Let's just say the next couple of weeks should be interesting with all the changes going down!

Readers comment:

> *Anonymous* January 21, 2014
> What a horrible decision. You should really think about what you are planning on doing here.
> Meredith

> *Anonymous* January 21, 2014
> I hope Brent is the father AND if he is, you need to tell him about the baby.
> ~ALF~

> *Anonymous* January 21, 2014
> Brent is a douche'

Anonymous January 21, 2014
and Ben is any better? what did her dad call him, a
Frenchman whore? She really needs to just be single until
this baby is born.
Callie   Kingston, Az

Anonymous   January 21, 2014
Brent is not a douche'! Todd asked her to marry him.
What is in it for him. It's definitely not LOVE! Brent
loves Melissa, not Megan. He needs to dump her and get
back to Melissa and HIS baby. ♥
~ALF~

DancingQueen January 21, 2014
If he loved her he would have already dumped Megan. I
think she is a strong enough woman to do this herself.
Forget boys! Just stock up on batteries and she'll be fine.

Anonymous   January 28, 2014
She doesn't need a man to raise the baby. Get rid of them
all, none of them are really ready for a commitment
anyway.

It is incredible how so many things could happen in just a matter of a few days. Marcus, while perturbed about my current state of being, was thrilled to have my manuscript. It literately took him less than 24 hours to get back to me with his initial take on the content. Boy was I blown away.

"Why….dear child, would you write something so heartbreaking?"

I had first asked myself that very question on Christmas Eve when I finished the last page. Contemplating the idea of tragedy was never my intention, but then again, I myself had been struggling with something intense.

"The story just happened, Marcus. I didn't mean for it to end the way that it did, but the character in question…." I didn't know how to explain it to him without it sounding like it was my flaws she was at fault for.

"The character in question what?" he asked as I trailed off.

All I could do was shrug my shoulders and crinkle my nose. "The story developed without my realizing it, and by the time I knew it, everything changed for her and there was no going back."

He of course nodded, staring down at the manuscript before him. "It moved me, my dear. Do you have an editor in mind to work on a few changes?"

It was funny he was bringing this up now. I was just thinking about working with someone to collaborate with. Readers never realize how much work it actually takes to have a book published. It's never just…oh looky let me go write a book, and Wham, I have a perfectly error-less novel ready in just a few short weeks. Usually, a book goes through several channels, and read by countless people before it ever hits the press stands.

"Not really sure, any suggestions?"

"Well, now that you mention it, I was referred to a guy and was thinking I might use him for what I'm working on now, but you can have first dibs on him. Yours will take less time than mine anyway."

Another guy - is this what I need in my life?? More testosterone?!?!?!

The visit ended with Marcus convincing me that the editor had positive marks coming out of his rear, he was very well connected and recommended; he would be a perfect fit.

All is well and good until a word is cut out of my manuscript for no apparent reason!

Being back in the city forced me to accept that the harsh cold weather, rude sidewalk walkers, and most of all the horrid cabby drivers were all terribly missed. My family's home upstate is great, calm, and relaxing but quite frankly I was starting to come out of my skin.

Okay, so now on to the Best and Worst part of my week....
Always best first. After months of only phone calls, emails, and text messages, I Finally had quality face to face time with my girls.

Our lunch took place at Ivy's house uptown....and no one would explain why it wasn't at the café. It wasn't until we (Dana, Amy, and myself) stepped off the elevator and into her living room that I realized it was a welcome back luncheon for me....Baby Themed no less!

"We figured it is never too soon to start planning and gifting!" Ivy cheered for herself as she scuffled her way over for a hug.

"My goodness, this is....wow." I sighed, just a tad bit overwhelmed.

Dana took my hand, "Sweetie, we just want you to know that we are here for you and you have our support."

The look in her eyes, all of their eyes as, I looked at each and every one of them brought tears to my eyes. Not of sadness but of utter joy.

"I was so scared that I'd be the oddball out, and everyone would just…" I started, then couldn't finish.

"Just forget you?"Amy interjected. "Becoming a mother doesn't mean we stop being friends, Melissa. It means we all become Aunties and your child has more family that loves it. That's just the way it is."

"She's right. You may not be able to party like it's, whatever, but you can still be a part of everything going on. I mean, you still have social obligations because of your relationship with Todd. We will just blend, and come up with an altered social calendar." Ivy added.

The girls bought me a beautiful rocking chair from Yoya, a Ralph Lauren diaper bag, and a gorgeous sleeper from Bonpoint .

"You 3 seriously think this baby is going to be a girl, dontcha?" I asked referring to the bright pink diaper bag.

"No, I don't." Dana answered firmly. "I got you that color because it's, 'Your' color. If you end up having a boy, at least the bag you carry will suggest that you are still in control of your style. Boy's shouldn't rob us of our femininity."

Her words left us clearly amused but utterly quiet. Lunch was interrupted by a rather confusing call. Marcus was insisting that I meet Ben for coffee, and that he needed to speak with me immediately.

I told the girls, and received the raised eyebrow and smirky smiles.

My response to the silent stares has been the same, "I am with Todd now. I'm not going to mess that up."

On'rie was already waiting for me when I got to the coffee shop. He seemed nervous, tired even. We exchanged pleasant greetings but I chose to sit across the table as opposed to next to him.

Something I'd never done before. I could see the effect immediately.

"Would you like some coffee?" he asked his accent as thick as I remembered.

"I'm good, thank you."

"Yes, that's right. Coffee is bad for the bebe."

Changing the subject to the point, "I'm glad you got into town as soon as you did. I'm sure the news Marcus broke to you wasn't a complete surprise, I understand how concerning it could be for you and your public persona."

"I could give a rat's arse what the press thinks, Mon Cheri'. It is our relationship I wish I hadn't ruined the way I did." he sighed, shook his head and went on, "What I wouldn't give to go back and do things differently. It could be you and I...and this baby." He admitted, his hand reaching out near mine but not coming close to touching it.

My eyes lowered to his hand and just watched....his wavering desire to reach out struck a chord.

"We all make choices, Ben. Our relationship isn't on the table for discussion, I'm with Todd now. All I'm asking is that you do your part involved in helping find out if this baby is yours. And above and beyond all else, making sure you keep this to yourself." It was cold, and for that I am truly sorry, but my heart....the one he danced on, can't pay a ticket to ride on the roller coaster he was talking about.

"Just tell me what I need to do."

Just as I thought I was gaining headway, the Bad brought along with it a cloud of questions needing answers.

A few days later, Dana stopped by suddenly just as I found myself staring at a blank Word document as Marcus insists that I try working on a new story. She came with distressing information.

"I'm not clear on what I just witnessed but honestly, M, it can't be good one way or another." She started.

"I was walking through the park in between meetings, trying to clear my head when I caught a glimpse of Todd and Megan sitting together on one of the benches. It took me by surprise and I had to make a quick turn so they wouldn't see me. By the time I found a safe place to turn around and look back at them, they had gotten up, and were hugging."

Internally, I have to admit….my raging Bitch was having a fit, but on the outside, I think I felt more ill than anything. Freddy Mercury's famous phrase, 'Another one bites the dust' came chiming in and made the whole situation more disgusting.

With a sigh and exhausting exhale, I tilted my head back and stared at my ceiling. "When is it ever going to be right?" I asked.

"What are you going to do?" Dana wondered but I couldn't answer something I too was asking myself.

I spent a few more days thinking about that one before it hit me that the least common denominator would have the most input. Daddy.

Luckily, it's Dad's policy to answer family calls first and foremost.

"Yes dear." His voice filled the line.

"Why would Todd and Megan be hugging in central park Daddy?" Straight and to the point.

"Wouldn't that be a question to direct to your fiancée my dear?"

It probably would… "It would if our relationship was something other than business, but you see Dad, I know you pushed Todd my way, so let me ask you this one more time. Why would Todd and Megan be hugging in the park?"

"Melissa, I honestly don't know but if I were you, I would just ask the man and then if you wouldn't mind getting back to me."

God help me but I believe my father really has no clue and the trouble with that….Todd can't use Business as an excuse when I ask him.

Why on Earth would my fiancée be anywhere near my ex-boyfriends new wife?

Might be about time to turn into what men despise the most……………….Curious!

Readers comment:

Anonymous January 28, 2014
sounds like you're getting a taste of your own medicine!

Anonymous January 29, 2014
That bag is fabulous! Thank you for linking to it!
Jennifer from Syracuse

Anonymous January 29, 2014
Yeah, I was just going to say the same thing. It's on sale too. Thanks for the linkage.

Molly -Jennifer's friend
Your blog is great, btw

Anonymous <u>January 29, 2014</u>
A business deal without a contract is easy to get out of, so a relationship is just as easy if you're not married.

Tuesday, February 4, 2014
Curiosity Killed the Cat
Season 3 Episode 3

Curiosity killed the cat…or so our mothers always use to tell us
growing up. Sometimes I wonder if the truth is really worth ruining
blissful ignorance. Ponder that for a few days and any inkling of
wanting and needing to know why something out of the ordinary
has happened will eat at the very edge of your reason.

For better or worse, I have always tried to avoid the pettiness
women are always finger pointed for being guilty of. Saying things
you don't mean, being all 'I'm okay' when in actuality you are
ready to poke someone's eye out, and lest not forget the current
state of things: Nosing around instead of outright asking.

"Why ask when you fear being lied to?" Amy insisted.

Oh, Yes…you bet I brought up what Dana saw to the other girls at
our weekly brunch. What's the point of having best friends if you
can't bounce your 1 mountainous concern off their heads to make
sense of it all?

"Todd seems so sensible. There is no way he would be doing
anything out of line. I mean, Megan is married to your Ex. You are
probably just missing something simple." Ivy added, munching
away at her toast.

My gaze met Dana's and it was the same worried look she carried
on her face the moment she walked into my place last week.

"What's the worst that could happen?" she sighed, rolling her eyes
up to the ceiling. "Get yourself a P.I. and see if there is anything to
it."

The Worst Thing…. I shake my head to that phrase every single
time.

So many things could be worse, and yet, they are not. So why push
the pendulum too hard.

"What came out of Ben's test?" Amy asked, lined with a curiosity of her own. I totally understand her standpoint on this subject.

Having Ben's test results back, either place her new relationship with Jason on troubled waters or more of those happy days.

"I should hear back sometime this week." I offered, somewhere along the line reaching out to comfort her with a hand squeeze.

"I'm fine, Melissa. We will work through this."

While her words were strong and sure, it was her eyes failing to meet mine which pushed me to believe how much stronger she was really being. Not knowing one way or another has forced my mind to focus on everything other than who really is my baby's daddy.

I tried avoiding baby talk for the remainder of our brunch, as a courtesy. Tried just sitting there, and being a part of everything, and yet not a part of anything. That was when I realized I was sitting at a table of people I adored and yet felt utterly alone. My eyes wandered towards the sunlight filled street through the window pane. People hustled from here to there, going about their lives. This great big world and everything so much larger than my silly little problems; a humbling moment indeed.

Later that day, I found myself looking for inspiration which has become a scarce commodity lately. Blue skies and an oddly warm winter day in the park lead to an hour of people watching. They meandered by in worlds of their own, but Nothing stuck as to what little bubbles they lived in.

It was a text message that caught me off guard and pushed me out of make believe.

Todd: That bench seems too big to be sitting there all alone.

My face darted up, and eyes focused to the bridge where his lone figure stood facing in my direction. He raised his palm, creating an equal reaction from my part.

Random?

It struck me then, that if there was ever going to be a moment I could have my heart to heart with Todd, it would be just then.

"What are you doing out here sitting all by your pretty little self?" he asked, kissing my cheek as he joined me.

"This is my favorite bench, didn't you know that?" I giggled shyly, staring out at that bridge thinking of how many memories it stirred.

"I would have joined you earlier, had I known you would be out here. This is such a lovely view." He turned to me again, "I enjoy visiting the park when I have a break from all my meetings."

The 'in' I had been waiting for.

"Speaking of which…." I started, reaching out to his hands. "I got a call from an acquaintance last week saying you'd been seen hugging Megan Moore right around here."

Where usually you would expect a thousand and one excuses or answers, Todd smiled and paused. His brilliant business mind was formulating his response….or was he just rethinking what his story would be.

Call my silly, or petty, or even untrustworthy…because I have a stellar past of honesty….but I know the reaction we feel when preparing a spectacular lie. Each word is like building a brick wall, layer upon layer of words and excuses go towards keeping that lie (wall) up and stable. If you are good at what you do, you end up believing the lies so much so, that they become a part of your life.

You've convinced yourself that the truth is what you keep repeating to those in your life. The problem with having said experience is being confronted with someone who could potentially be lying straight to your face.

I felt that concern. Every bit of my being struggled with what Dana had witnessed, and now, having him in front of me I just wanted him to tell me that it was nothing.

"I told you some time ago that I do business with the company Megan works for." He began.

I nodded because I do remember him mentioning that now.

~sigh~ I'm such an Idiot!

"We had a meeting run late and had a quick lunch together. There were actually a few of us that afternoon. We ended up talking about her parents, which I've known since I was a child, and she mentioned that her father has lung cancer. I gave her my apologies and told her our thoughts and prayers would be with her family."

Sinking slowly into the bench I felt the utter fool even having asked. He noticed by my lack of comment that I hadn't expected what he had admitted. He inched closer, the heat from his thigh warming my body, causing my eyes to meet his.

"You don't need to worry about Megan, M. She has and always will be just business."

The words, like a sharp blade, sliced into that inner temple of de ja vu. Those words, twice referred by men in my life, regarding this one pernicious snake, meant doom in my eyes. Brent made that statement, just before he told me he was marrying her….and now, now Todd says them in efforts to comfort me that nothing is between them. I wanted to scream.

I stood up from that bench, distanced myself without causing alarm. "I wish, for once, that this woman would be out of our lives. Out of our business." I turned to him at business, "I don't feel I should watch my every step because of her jealousy of me. She tried to ruin my literary career, and spread lies about me to the press."

"You need to find a way to deal with that without asking me to stop doing business with one of my clients, Melissa. Business and personal issues are always to stay separate in my world. While I appreciate that you and she have this major disagreement, I am not a person to choose sides."

"Sides?" I seethed, "I am going to be your wife, Todd. It's not about business….this is Very much personal. That is at least one thing I learned growing up my father's daughter. Family, your wife, children, and the people you love are always your side."

The features on his face neither changed nor faltered. He stood up and walked right up to me. The muscles on his upper arm flexing as he stepped closer.

"Then I will make arrangements to have someone else handle that account. I'm sorry if it caused you any undue stress." Reaching out and pulling my body close to his, he wrapped his arms around me in a protective cover.

It was the first time in 2 weeks that we had been close, emotionally as well as physically.

"I'm sorry too. Pregnancy hormones are a bitch!" I whispered in his ear.

He chuckled, "Don't worry about it; I'm still waiting on those cravings to really hit hard."

"Well," I stopped him, "If you really want to satisfy one of those, just bring me a peanut butter pickle sandwich and call it a day."

It was wide eyes and laughter all the way home. While I was still a little apprehensive about the Megan issue, I felt genuinely relieved that we had at least discussed it openly.

Final little tid-bit ☺, a morsel if you will…..Marcus had me talk to the new editor today. When I first heard about this Klive Morris, I cringed. I mean, seriously….why would your parents spell your name wrong?

(And don't give me this – originality crap) My worries boil down to 2 things…. A. That he doesn't tell me to cut something out, and B. He can't…CAN'T be handsome! Sadly, his voice created an image I was rather hoping not to have….brawny, intelligent – Clark Kent/Superman even.

We shall see, I have a meet and greet with him tomorrow. Joy to my little bubble.

Readers comment:

Anonymous February 04, 2014
I don't trust that Megan at all. Listen to your gut feeling and keep your eyes open!!!
~ALF~

Anonymous February 05, 2014
I agree! Listen, Todd seems like a smooth talker too, I'd keep my eyes open on him.
Chelsea

Anonymous February 08, 2014
Todd sounds like a car salesman waiting to make a sale. I wouldn't trust him as far as I could throw him.

Anonymous February 08, 2014
When are you going to realize that your karma is going to come bite you in the behind? If I were you, I would be waiting for everything to turn to shit. You just don't get it.
Nancy

Tuesday, February 11, 2014
Waiting for the Truth
Season 3 Episode 4

Two steps forward, ten steps back. Some changes are too little too late, especially when the truth happens to Slap you in the face.

Ben's paternity test results came back. He is not my baby's daddy....which leaves two other possibilities I had hoped not to worry about. He came by personally last week to open his envelope together. It was....prophetic to say the least. There was Relief in his eyes, while mine were filled with tears of hollowness.

I let Ben hold me, trying to comfort my aching heart. It felt right to have his warm sheltering arms wrap around my growing midsection.

"Mon Cheri, it will be fine. Your little one will be loved by many, no matter who turns out to be its maker." He whispered into my hair, the palm of his hands caressing my back.

I let the tears fall, let Ben be the one to calm me down. He owed me that much at least, even though I had forgiven him months ago.

Out of all the men in my life, he is who I would rather share my child with.

That night turned out to be the calm before the storm. Ben falling out of the Daddy running was the least of my problems. The instant Ben left, I realized I had to ask Jason to do a paternity test, which means Amy will be devastated.

Even if Jason turns out not to be my baby's father, the mere fact that I am putting Amy through the stress is enough to stain our friendship forever. If the choices now are Jason or Brent, to spare my best friend a lifetime of anguish, I would rather Brent be my peanut's father.

I stared at my cell phone for better part of 2 hours before I could call her. My inner strength stifled by the fear of losing her. Finally,

I dialed and she picked up, I asked her to come over, and the waiting game began.

Luckily, because of the time of night, Jason came with her. He wasn't surprised by what I had to say and ask. Amy, however, was taken back.

"And you are sure Ben's test came back negative?" she asked. "I mean, shouldn't you have him tested at a different facility?"

"The tests are standard, Amy." He countered quickly then looked over to me. "I will go tomorrow morning. The quicker we get this over with, the faster we can get on with our lives."

It was all well and good, but Amy hardly spoke to me at brunch the following day. Ivy monopolized the conversation discussing business….my business to be precise.

"While book sales and reviews are right on track, our lack of a tour is becoming a problem. I've had countless invitations for you to do a reading and a meet-and-greet. We can only avoid the press for so long before they figure out your condition one way or another." Dana interjected, "Ivy, she is pregnant for Christ sakes, not terminally ill."

"While I am thrilled to become an Aunty, I have to admit the Gigantic catastrophe this is going to cause your career. The scandal will reach the farthest ends of the literary universe and change your persona."

Her lack of confidence and high esteem for my ability to deal with this worries me. It left me with only one other option…..call my father. Ask his opinion and request his business counsel. It would also give me an opportunity to discuss the newest development involving Todd.

The call would be easy, what follows after would be where I would struggle.

I called Daddy on my way to Marcus'. I rescheduled our original meet and greet with my new editor only to feel forced into a meeting today, and while I wasn't in the mood, after hearing Ivy talk business all morning long, I would be lying if it wasn't guilt keeping this appointment.

He answered his cell, never letting my calls go into voicemail.

"Hi sweetheart, to what do I owe the pleasure of your voice this morning?" his political charm filled the line.

"I need your advice, once more." It's true...still is, even now, all these days later. My father, while an enigma all in his own, is the man I learned to judge men by. He is what he is.

His chuckles lead me to believe he was pleased, "What are fathers for if not to filter out learned wisdom."

"Am I ignorant in disbelieving that my pregnancy will ruin my literary career?"

"The world loves a baby bump Melissa. If you want to take control of the reaction you receive, then you should be the one to release the information to the media." He paused before asking, "What did you find out about Todd?"

There was a loaded question for ya. "When I asked him outright what his deal was with Megan, he admitted to it being all business. That was all well and good until the nagging feeling I had in my gut won and I found myself going through his cell phone."

When I stopped talking, Daddy's impatience filtered through the cell phone. "He's lying, isn't he?"

The crisp cool New York air ran a chill down my spine as I walked along the sidewalk, "Yes. He's lying about something, Daddy."

"Let me handle him, dear. I promise you he won't get away with whatever he is doing." He sharply stated.

Having my father take charge of my misfortunes was starting to become a habit….a Bad habit.

My mood going into that meeting was shot to hell, but that wasn't what I was going to truly struggle with. No, indeed the problem would be the man, I was meeting. Whose green eyes locked onto mine the moment I walked in.

The smile that spread across his face literally caught me off guard.

The Clark Kent version my imagination had created didn't do him justice, nor that twinkle in his eye as he shook my hand.

"It's a pleasure to meet you, finally." The thickness of his voice made mush of my resolve; I had to sit before I saw my entire manuscript at his disposal.

"Likewise, I'm sure." The words left my lips but my eyes were locked onto Marcus who could see I was a little captured.

"Would you like something to munch on, dear? You look a little pale." He laughed.

Heated cheeks were the least of my worries. There is this saying that my mother use to tell me growing up about a certain type of man. "He will come, like a hurricane, taking from you everything you never knew you had to give, until you are bare and exposed, and then he will take the very spark from your light."   Chalk it up to imagination or inspiration, but Klive brought this memory to bay.

"I'm fine; it's already been a long day." I returned the smile and reached into my bag to withdraw the manuscript; the reason we were all here.

Handing it to Klive, I noticed how his eyes only followed the stack of stark white paper in my grasp; the anticipation unnerving.

"It's not very thick is it?" his initial reaction amusing. It was how Marcus had responded to it at first as well.

"They are letters of sorts…"

"To Eliza?" he interrupted, looking up from the manuscript. The fascination something I hadn't expected.

Nodding again, I couldn't help the chuckle that left my throat. He wouldn't understand until he reads the whole story to know how dark it truly is.

"It doesn't have the type of ending you would expect, I'm afraid." I admitted, warning him, just in case he read my first novel.

His head tilted slightly, his smile vanishing and his expression completely changed. "Where did it come from, Melissa?"

A question I was sure I would have to answer at one point or another, and I knew the response I was supposed to say. Tell him that it came from life happening, and knowing happy endings don't always play out the way we expect them, but No…that's not what came out my mouth.

Klive waited, watching as I struggled with saying it.

"A broken heart……..where else do tragedies come from?"

From that point on, I felt exposed. The more we talked and tore apart my character, the more of me it felt like he was uncovering.

The story had been unleashed into the world and now someone new was playing in its words. It felt like nothing would ever be the same. Klive had become the hurricane my mother once warned of. By the time he left, I was out of sorts with where I stood in regards to this manuscript. Marcus must have sensed my discomfort.

"What is it?"

"Did I ever make you feel like your characters were disturbed?" in asking him, I was secretly begging to hear I'd never made him feel displaced.

"You had a lot to say, but it was mostly about my writing, not my characters." He started, "I'm sure Klive wasn't judging. He seemed to hit certain point's right on the money."

"Yes, but why do I feel like he was attacking me and not my manuscript?"

"Because like that child in your body, your books are like your children. You would fight tooth and nail to protect them."

"Maybe if I make Klive less a person, and more a character in my imagination, maybe he won't bother me so much. Does that sound stupid?"

Marcus started to shake his head, and sure, I know sometimes I'm a little kooky, but compartmentalizing people is always the best way to avoid disappointment. And let's face it....I've set myself up for a little pit fall here.

"Melissa, dear...you could give him another name, close your eyes and imagine him a different way, but he is still going to be Klive.

The man who is going to tear apart that manuscript and bring it to life."

Fine. So I will sit on the idea for now to change his name to something less.......Klive and pray I don't poke him in the eye with a sharp metaphor and what not.

Marcus ended up being right. The distraction lasted a few days; Klive didn't make any sort of contact, which worried me. What plans did he have for poor little Genevieve?

There was another person's lack of contact that worried me. Todd hadn't bothered to call for 2 days. Since I had spoken to Daddy. It made me wonder if I had made a mistake asking daddy for help. I picked up the phone and called Ben.

Why Ben? You might ask… My Frenchman has a knack for finding out information that is meant to stay in the shadows.

"I need you to do me an enormous favor." I began, thinking this would only go one way. "I need you to find out what Todd is hiding from me. I'm sick of being the innocent flower that everyone else is worried about. I know I'm stronger than that. Business nor not, there is no room in my life for another liar."

"Give me a few days; I will get someone right on it." He promised.

Readers comment:

Anonymous   February 12, 2014
Innocent is not a way I would describe you.

Anonymous   February 12, 2014
I say call him something else. Klive is not a good name for a sexy guy.
Meredith

Anonymous   February 12, 2014
Poor Amy! I am praying it isn't Jason's. You are a horrible friend.
Nancy

Growing up in a house with a father that expects perfection, a mother who denies affection, and a sibling that is always working on setting you up for a fall, you tend to have a thicker skin than most people. My childhood has a lot to do with why I have trust issues….Hell, Issues in general.

My request to On'rie was made in pure desperation. I wasn't completely sure if I could trust my father to keep me in the loop with what he had going on with Todd. I needed to uncover Todd's deep dark secret, the one he was sharing with Mrs. Megan Moore-Bishop.

As instructed, I waited a few days to hear back from On'rie…and a lot of life happened in consequence.

Ivy continued to firmly press her well placed thumb down on me to join a book tour and attend a young author's book conference but the more I looked at it from all directions, I found I was hiding behind an impressive brick wall.

The thick skin I had always prided myself on having was merely a protective cover, and it was now hiding everything I've created.

So what do you do when the epiphany that strikes you dissolves the fog that has been darkening all the wonderful possibilities in your life?

Well, you take a deep breath and leap into the life you are meant to live. I am meant to be something more than this fearful coward being bullied by a selfish jealous bitch. I'm not going to let her win. Of that I am certain!

As the clock tick tocked and I waited, I gave Ivy exactly what she wanted: A client willing to do anything to succeed.

"Book me into a tour; I'm ready when you are, let's just make it a light one." I caved in but it was freeing to give my best friend what she wanted.

"Are you sure, you've been on the fence about this for such a long time. I want to make sure this is what you want."

"Ivy, I'm sure. It's about time I go with the flow." The weight being lifted from my shoulders brought a smile to cheer up my face. The first of many for the span of the week.

"Well, great! I will work out the details and get back with you soon." she hesitated, "Have you thought about what you're planning on telling the press about your pregnancy?"

"Actually, I was hoping we could work on that together at brunch this week. I want the other girls in on it just in case they get prompted for an interview as an inside source."

It's only natural that some slimy reporter would try to skew the truth with mudding up what your closest friends say.

"Great, I will send you an email with prospective book tour ideas." Hanging up left me with my chin held a little higher, and confidence a little stronger.

That feeling of assurance boiled over as I found myself waiting for Klive at a local coffee shop, the next morning, to go over his thoughts about my manuscript. I'd held on to the idea of making him seem less a threat by merely imagining him as one of my characters....only problem with this pesky little plan is the fact that he keeps becoming a Clark Kent/Superman version of a man.

Maybe it's the handsome face concealed behind a set of thick rimmed opticals that makes it difficult to visualize him in any other manner. Being that he is new in my life, an individual who knows little to nothing about the thoughts behind certain glances here and there of his physique, I'm sure at least for a while I should be okay as far as avoiding genuine embarrassment.

He was business from the moment he plopped his figure in the metal seat in front of me.

"Did you manage to look over the notes I emailed you?" was his first case in point.

Ah, Yes... the notes. The pregnancy handbook I've been reading warns expectant mothers to avoid situations that will cause our blood pressure to rise.

"Indeed, I took your opinions into consideration and have decided that my character's immoral flaws are not to be questioned." I stated plainly, head tilting slightly and smirk firmly spread across my face.

Blank, emotionless Klive nodded once and scribbled almost angrily in his notebook. The reaction raising my curiosity level.

"I'm sorry but I don't understand why you think readers would believe that every female character is complete perfection."

His head snapped at the simple statement, "Not perfection, just not this vial thoughtless woman who is tremendously selfish."

There it went; he judged before trying to understand. "And you've never been selfish in your entire life?" I hissed, thwarted by his lack of depth.

He clearly, calmly took a deep breath. I'm sure he was mentally counting to ten as not to chew my head off. Is it bad that a tiny part in me was actually enjoying the banter? Could he be an innocent sparring partner that would challenge my intellectual self without any romantic entanglements?

One could only hope!

"You'd be surprised how revolted readers become from reading about a character whose remorse is limited to actions outside of their depth. I don't want to see your book fail because this character is boasting about her irrational decisions."

227

*Awww….how sweet….*but there is No Way in Hell I'm cutting her personality.

Characters develop for a reason. They become people and in changing them, we are changing the completeness of the story.

"Well, I'm not going to change her. Karma does its duty and life happens to her for a reason. So, Next."

The sigh of disappointment was followed by a book being planted next to my coffee cup. Somewhere in the back of my mind, hymnals and angels awed at a book my collection was lacking but now sitting only inches from my grasp. William Shakespeare Volume II of his collected works. I knew from recent searches that this copy contained the greatest tragedy of all time.

"What did Romeo and Juliet make you believe about love?" he asked; his eyes focused and clearly needing a more in-depth response.

"Why does it possibly matter?" thinking more of conserving my distraught ideas of what love does to an individual throughout the course of one's life.

"Tragedies, particularly the ones pertaining to the heart, always end in some form of grief but a lesson on love is clear and without a doubt learned by a reader."

I huffed, "I'm not Shakespeare, Klive." I stated plainly. But in that instant I didn't understand why I felt like I was being attacked more than receiving a suggestion.

"No, you're not… And your tragedy is missing a lesson. You need to decide what it is you want your readers to feel when they consume the last words. Sadness isn't enough, I don't feel complete and I don't think you do either."

"So what do you suggest?" I asked, without hesitating.

"Read the volume. Take it in. Every writer reacts differently to his work. In your case, I think it will be the best medicine you're given. Who knows, maybe even poor pitiful Genevieve will get a new layer added to her personality."

He chuckled, and I couldn't help but follow along. "Maybe you're right. Who knows, maybe she could be an inspired poet like he was." I mused innocently.

Klive placed his glasses back on and it hit me. The image fit. "Just so you know, so that you don't think I've gone utterly madd. I'm going to start calling you Clark Kent." I didn't directly face him, to admit the little tid bit.

"And why will you be doing this?" he asked, the smile so evident, one wouldn't need to be looking at him.

That was when it happened. My moment of the week.
I raised my eyelids, connected with his, and the baby moved in my belly.

"Oh!" I shouted. The distraction clearly a left field reaction.

"What it is" he stood up and rounded the table in nanoseconds. As an insane person would burst out laughing, my hands which now covered my midsection, followed by the giggling counter reaction.

"The baby just kicked me." I replied, astonished. I reached out, wanting to share the wonder with someone real, took his hand and placed it firmly on the spot the life beneath my skin was kicking.

It only took the time for my eyes to meet his for the tiny precious package in my being to replicate the ferocious kick for my new superman.

The swift kick from the inside produced a pearly white smile from Mr. Clark Kent.

"It's because you are my Superman. Even peanut can tell. He must know it's you by how fast my heart races when you're around."

He didn't say anything, and it was better that way. As usual, I'd said too much.

The usual brunch was sized down to just Ivy and I. Dana was out of town visiting her Aunt Marge, who was dying, and I'm sure Amy canceled because of Jason's results still not having come back yet. She has yet to return any of my 10 voicemails and texts. Space it is then.

Ivy wrangled me into a spotlight press release event for several of her clients. This was the opportunity Daddy had been talking about, for me to control how I released the news about my pregnancy. Ivy completely agreed.

"If they ask about Todd, just make sure you know exactly where your relationship status stands. We don't need to back pedal later."

'Yeah, Yeah, Yeah' I thought to myself.

Leaving the café left me with no other alternative to call Ben to see what his people came up with. It rang through to voicemail.

Desperate times call for desperate measures. Flipping my wrist to check the time on my watch, I made the firm decision ask the one man who would know why his wife was secretly meeting with my 'so called' boyfriend.

You can call it a mistake; I on the other hand will say it was bound to happen.

Fortunately, I didn't have to get on the elevator to speak to Brent Bishop.

As I walked up to the double glass doors, leading into the building, he was making his way out.

"Melissa." He whispered as he caught sight of me.

"We need to talk. If you have a moment that is?" I asked.

"Yeah, I was just going to grab something to eat."

I shook my head, praying he wasn't going to ask me to join him "this will only take a minute. I promise."

He reached out, taking my elbow in his grasp. "Let's go sit on a bench in the shade."

We both sat down and I struggled to gather my composure. Next to me sat the one man I'd been praying is not the father of my baby. A child he knew nothing about."

"So what is this about?" he asked, checking his wrist watch.

"Are Todd and Megan having an affair?" directly to the point. Reaction as expected, "What?" he shouted, his body shooting straight to his feet.

"Why would you ask that?"

"Um, because they have been text messaging each other for the better part of 3 weeks and secretly meeting in the park, exchanging God knows what." I retorted.

"Sheesus, M, that doesn't mean they are having an affair."

"Really. Funny how you have complete faith and trust in a woman who is just business." I stood up, already sick of the discussion. I couldn't even believe I thought speaking to him would help.

"Alright, I'm sorry." He stopped me from walking away. His hand reaching for my waist. The one place I knew I needed to keep him away from. My reaction was instantaneous. I jerked away, at precisely the same time my other arm crossed over my belly in a protective manner.

It created the reaction I wasn't prepared for.

"What's wrong?" he asked, his voice thick and deep.

"Nothing." I replied, too quickly for comfort.

"Really, because you've never been repulsed by my touch before."

"I know." Two words that said so much more than he deserved.

He inched towards me, and I actually feared looking in his eyes. If I couldn't tell him now, how was I going to address it to the press? The backlash would be so much worse.

When all was said and done, the courage found my conviction and I stood a little taller, (smile) spine a little straighter. "I'm pregnant."

I could hear the questions mounting in his brilliant mind, "There is a press release tonight in which I will address my growing midsection and lack of book tour for the time being."

His hands fell closely to the sides of his lean statuesque figure. His beautiful hazel eyes became darker, tormented even. And before he even opened his mouth to ask the single most devastating question, I could clearly note his flexing jaw muscle. He'd connected the dots and the anvil weighing on my shoulders for the past 4 months was finally lifted.

"Who is the father of your baby, M?"

But the only three words I could offer him today were nothing like the words I'd begged to hear leave his lips only months ago.

No….my three words were like a ghost positioning itself for a long and terrible haunting.

"I don't know."

Readers comment:

Anonymous   <u>February 19, 2014</u>
Oh My GOD!

Anonymous   <u>February 22, 2014</u>
The press is going to eat you alive. Well deserved of course.
Karma really is a bitch.
Nancy

Anonymous   <u>February 22, 2014</u>
I hope things between you and Amy get resolved. Jason was
just her 'friend' when the two of you had your questionable
night.
~ALF~

Tuesday, February 25, 2014
Tragic!
Season 3

Hi everyone, this is Ivy, one of Melissa's friends. I wish I had come across this blog under different circumstances and was able to contribute to it in a positive way. Unfortunately, something terrible happened yesterday to our dear friend, Melissa. She and Klive were on their way to meet Marcus when she was pushed onto the road and struck by a taxi cab.

Within hours, the article going around read:

Local author critically injured

Local socialite author, Melissa Green-Bergman was critically injured in a freak incident in front of Rockefeller Center, according to city police.

The accident occurred on Sixth Ave. and 49th Street around 2 in the afternoon, when she was struck by a taxi cab.

She was rushed to Bellevue Hospital but at this time, the condition of Ms. Green and her unborn child is unknown. The incident is still under police investigation.

Witnesses told police investigators she was thought to have been pushed into oncoming traffic by a male, while she was waiting to cross the street.

The suspect is said to have been approximately 5'10'' with brown hair and was wearing a black leather jacket.

If you have any information that may help the police department with this case, please contact Dt. Norris at the 144th precinct.

My beautiful and courageous friend had only two days ago publicly announced her pregnancy and addressed the lack of book tour for 'Love in the End' during the Young Author's Award ceremony for one of my other clients. She was glowing, and everyone noticed it.

Now, she lays unconscious in a hospital bed, unaware that everything has changed. Bumps and bruises fade, broken bones will heal, but the tiny precious life that had been growing inside of her is lost forever. The doctors barely saved Melissa's life, much less the tiny precious child inside of her.

Several theories have been whispered from the few of us close friends wandering the hospital halls of Belleveu as we wait for a change in her condition. Melissa's father, stern and cold stays at the window of her room, staring out as life continues on for everyone else in New York City. I overheard a brief phone conversation he had with Melissa's mother; apparently mom wasn't coming.

Things became interesting when Ben showed up. He had a brief exchange with Mr. Bergman, their harsh whispers peeked Marcus' interest but neither wanted to go into what the problem was at that time. The statement, 'they are going to pay' caused those in the room to raise eyebrows. On'rie retreated, softly kissing Melissa on the forehead and murmuring, I love you. I could see the tears in his eyes that he was trying to hide.

Melissa's new editor, Klive, stuck around as well. For the most part he stayed outside of her room, looking in through the hallway window. It was when we were coming back from getting something to eat that we found him sitting next to her. Dana stopped us from going in saying, "This has got to be hard on him. He was standing right next to her when it happened. He couldn't do anything to stop it. He watched as that cab..." I choked up as the strongest one of all of us couldn't even go on.

Looking back to Melissa, I caught sight of Klive lifting her hand to his mouth. His head lowering only signified 1 thing, he already has feelings for her, but it probably won't make any difference now.

The moment she wakes up, life will change. I've seen it before. Melissa's highs and lows are classic where men are involved. They've each pretty much represented chapters in her life. Some pages are brighter while some have been too dark to recall. I can only imagine where we go from here.

Amy came by, the news she brought with her caused Mr. Bergman to storm out of the room. Jason got his test results back, and while it was a mute point now, Melissa's baby had been fathered by Brent Bishop. We sat shocked, staring at our unconscious friend. At first I didn't understand why it was that her father had become so upset but then Ben showed up again. Being that Mr. Bergman was already out in the hall, he shared the new development with On'rie before he walked in. The shock on his face was classic.

Nosy little me, I flat out asked, "What's going on between you and her dad?"

He looked directly at me, questions clearly plastered in all of his features. "There is evidence that this was done deliberately."

Everyone in the hospital room gasped, myself included. Klive stood up, his height meeting Ben's.

"Why would someone want to kill her?" A question we were all asking.

Mr. Bergman walked back in the hospital room, and closed the door behind him.

"The police just put the two of them into custody." He directed at Ben. Then looked at Klive, "Since the moment she got into a relationship with Brent, she was a target on Megan Moore's radar. Melissa went to Ben asking for some information on Todd, but she had asked me, weeks ago, to find out what was going on between him and Megan."

It hit me then, I had been hounding Melissa for weeks about business while she was dealing with an extreme amount of personal bullshit.

"So what now?" Dana asked.

Her father walked around to the other side of Melissa's bed and took her hand. "It's simple. We let the police do their job and we focus on Melissa. She is going to be a mess when she wakes up, we all know that. She is going to push each and every one of us away from her. She's done it before. We just have to make sure we don't lose her."

Melissa's dad is right, on all accounts. So the waiting game begins, and the prayers continue.

I will try to keep you updated, via this blog, if Melissa doesn't wake up soon.

Thanks everyone for being a fan of my best friend.
Ivy

Readers comment:

Anonymous February 25, 2014
Thank you for telling us Ivy. I feel so sorry for Melissa. I hope they find out who is responsible for this horrific crime. I hope Amy can come to forgive her now that she knows Jason was not the dad. Melissa is going to need all her friends.
~ALF~

Anonymous February 26, 2014
Why on Earth would you have her loose her baby?
Jennifer

Anonymous February 27, 2014
It's because of nonsense like this that I wonder why I read this blog. Hit by a taxi cab? I see no reason why Melissa has even been a target on Megan Moore's radar. She got the guy, Melissa didn't. I sure hope you start providing answers to the many questions you are raising.
Nancy

Anonymous February 27, 2014
She is on Megan Moore's radar because Megan knows that "the guy" , as you put it, doesn't love her but is in fact still madly in love with Melissa. The only reason he is with Megan is because of Melissa's father. So, I do not know of what

nonsense you speak.
~ALF~

Anonymous <u>February 27, 2014</u>
I'm sorry but if Amy gets all 'Best friend' of Melissa at this point, I hope Melissa turns on her bitch face. Amy is Not a friend, and the weeks coming up to this point were proof!

Grief. A word I have often contemplated but never fully
comprehended. Being a person who has read a plethora of books, I
understand the emotions grief consists of, the stages I'm said to
transition through.

At the moment, denial. Nodding my head and agreeing with the
current state of things, I believe denial pretty much strikes the
bull's-eye.

'Every minute of every day', That statement is all I can focus on in
this present frame of mind.

When I woke up, I didn't process what I was being told. I felt like I
was trapped in a glass jar and everyone was talking at once. The
problem was that their words jumbled and strung together like a
buzzing moth in my ear.   Then reality came crashing in like a
torrent wave of darkness.

What I wouldn't give to feel the lulling notion of closing my eyes
once more. To have everything fade to black and that wave of
emptiness to strip this pain that doesn't seem to go away.

The damning words started making sense, even with their soothing
tones and gentle expressions; I saw the sorrow that lined their
hearts. Each and every one of them was there, like spectators to
watch my undoing.

The first admission, 'Melissa, dear, do you remember what
happened?" they asked me.

I didn't answer. I closed my eyes and fought the haze to make
sense of the images that flashed behind closed lids. The sounds that
echoed from the memories I'm not sure I will ever truly want to
recall.

Opening my eyes, I saw my father staring back at me, his eye misted with tears he was definitely fighting, I shook my head in submission.

"Sweetheart..." he started, his strong hands gently caressing mine, "you are in the hospital. You've been in a terrible accident."

Somehow, I knew that much but I let him continue. He told me about having been pushed into the street and being hit by a vehicle. That was when the haze of having woken up evaporated and I asked the only question that mattered.

"Daddy....is my baby okay?" five words that produced a response I hardly could explain to you in words.

I know he tried. Everyone in the room tried. But it will never be enough.

'Every minute of every day I'm broken...lost...devastated...empty'

I'm stuck in this hospital bed because of some sick jealousy an individual was consumed by. Every minute of every day that passes I am here, living....breathing, while my beautiful baby boy was stripped from me.

Never knowing the life filled with love he was set to have. What else is there but the loss?

Being of a rational mind, I can numb my emotions long enough to grasp at reality. I did that, that first night.

After the tears and chaos, I found myself building that wall, the one I had once torn down. My reality, once more a shell of what life is meant to be.

They will never understand, no one can understand. It's not the fact that I had a miscarriage, no, my precious little baby was murdered. They tried to murder me, but instead they took from me the only light that was keeping me in the sun. That is my reality now. Living, going on, knowing that 'what could have been' was suppose to be a child. My child. A child born of love, because for Fuck sake, Brent was his father....Yeah, they told me that too.

~Sigh~

After that first night, I let the numb consume all, allowed the denial phase to sink in deep. Daddy was the first to show up the following morning. I'm not exactly sure, but I suspect he snuck the security guard some cash to be allowed to come in before visiting hours started.

Him being there wasn't a nuisance, he's never really been much of a talker. After asking his usual few questions, he sat in the corner, took out his newspaper and entertained himself. The mere fact that he was with me was what worried me. Do they really believe what Ivy posted last week?

Marcus showed up, coffee for two in one hand and a bouquet of stone white roses in another.

"How do you feel today, my sweet?" he asked gently, as he planted a kiss on my forehead.

"I'm here. Doctor should be in shortly, the nurse said."
Using the rolling hospital table, he withdrew my coffee cup and handed it to me.

"Klive wanted me to let you know he would be by later. Poor guy has been beside himself."

Funny, Klive is beside himself. The empathy missing from its usual place in my mind had me wondering.

I didn't care. I don't care. Hmmmmm......

"You know, Marcus, I'm not really up for work right now..."I started. "I'm going to take some time off."

Dana saved me from his response. She walked in, seeing that I was awake and sitting up.

"I'm glad I didn't give in to the urge to sneak you a cup of coffee. Looks like someone already became the smuggler this morning."

"What can I say, I bring the best qualities out of those who love me." The sass in my voice filled the room, and while I thought it was funny, the serious expression on the three of their faces had me rolling my eyes.

"Anyway, are you heading to work?" I asked her, ignoring the stern stare daddy was giving me.

She sat in the seat next to me, "I was planning on staying a while, if that is okay with you?"

(Shame on Me!) I sighed, leaned my head back while still looking at her. "You don't have to stay. I'm not much for talking, or working, or anything. I really would just rather be left alone, to be honest." I didn't yell it, or sass it. It came out, calm, cool, and collect. It had been sitting there, the desire to be alone, since the moment my father walked through the hospital door.

"It's not about keeping you entertained. It's about you being surrounded by people who love you." My father scolded, getting to his feet and walking to the foot of my bed.

Yes, Love, there again, the word that rippled the wrong path for me.

My eyes lowered, more so because I wouldn't argue. I know my father wasn't going to leave. Of that I was sure. I can accept that I would have friendly faces popping in at any given moment during my stay in this God forsaken building. But secretly I paraded with the idea of running away, going away like I did when I left to Paris. The thought has merit, you can't tell me it doesn't.

Every question asked, soft tender caresses, added one secret notion to the steps forward in a direction away from any known reminisce of my present.

I will admit to the one moment of strange weakness since I woke. For starters, I can't walk without help, can't do much of anything, for that matter, without a nurse. I'd pressed the button and was waiting, impatiently I might add, to get some help to go to the bathroom. The moment my door opened, I felt relief and anguish all in the matter of 2 seconds flat. I thought it was the nurse, but turned out only to be Klive.

The disappointment smeared across my face must have been obvious, but by then I was already half way out of my bed. I couldn't hold it anymore. Determination is not to be confused with stubbornness in my case.

"Are you supposed to be getting out of bed by yourself?" he started, rounding my bed to meet me just as I placed my free leg on the cold floor.

"I can't wait anymore. I need to go to the bathroom." I sassed. I wasn't expecting his strong arms to wrap around my waist. "Just hold on to me." He ordered.

Slowly but surely, Klive helped me the short distance and saved me from an embarrassing situation.

Relief came quickly. Not just for the fact that I was able to function like a normal person, but also that I had him at the precise moment I needed him.

By the time the nurse arrived in my room, Klive was helping me back into bed. He made sure the nurse knew what had almost happened and she left- her face clearly 3 shades of red darker.

"And here I thought I would find a complete stranger." He stated plainly.

"What on Earth does that mean?" I sighed, ruffling my sheets back to normal.

His eyes thinned, questioning. Almost wavering as to the words he would choose. I huffed at his hesitation. He too thought me weak, and fragile.

"You know, you are not the only one that was there that day, Melissa." He started, the muscles in his jaw flexing.

That day. God damn him. That day we were walking together, life was filled with promise then.

"Yeah, I know." I countered softly.

"No," he shot back, his body sitting stiffer, straighter. "No, you don't."

"One minute we were laughing and talking, the next there was screaming and a deafening silence I will not soon forget. I understand clearly what you lost that afternoon, it's all I can think of, but don't sit there and think for one iota, that you were the only one there that day."

The pain he was feeling was written all over his face, in the tears that had started forming in his eyes but had not yet fallen.

"I'm sorry." Was all I could afford him.

"I'm sorry you lost your baby, Melissa, but I'm not sorry they saved your life."

He was the only person that could understand that day. Feel grief at the loss of innocence as I do. The strange weakness settled in, and I let him hold my hand a while. We sat there, saying nothing, doing nothing but staring at the way his skin laid quietly on mine.

It did not scorch, nor did it annoy. It was an easy simplicity that I'd never known before. It was then that I found myself doze off in a daydream of running away, with my Superman.

Readers comment:

Wednesday, March 12, 2014
A Little Truth, A Lot of Questions
Season 3 Episode 7

When did it all stop making sense? I swear I've listened to that
song a thousand times this past week. Obsessive. Yeah, I suppose
it is. At least some things haven't changed in this vast ocean I seem
to be drowning in.

 Time is standing still, but my tiny little world is spiraling out of
control. Just when I think I'm reaching out to solid ground, I slip
and find myself right back here, spiraling and in front of this laptop
wondering how it all got all jumbled up.

Right about there, the huff escapes my lips and I am filled with a
spite that couldn't be caught this week.

When we grieve, no matter what the cause, the pain finds a way to
attach itself to all the beautiful. Not only are you struck with
feeling a hurt that there is no end from, but you are also robbed of
the beauty from entering back in. That is, not until you've dealt
with emotions you tend to hide from.

Where did I get that mumbo jumbo from? A grief counselor the
hospital sent me to go see. Funny how I had to get someone to take
me, but the only person I could think of was the 1 person who
tends to hide from his emotions all together, Daddy.

I get it though, now, after decades of wondering why he is as solid
as a rock. I finally understand why he hides himself behind that
metaphoric brick wall. No one person could move forward from
this pain I'm feeling, unscathed. He built the wall to protect
himself from feeling wounds such as mine, and even then, I
wonder if what I'm going through has affected him in some way.

I caught him staring at me during the silent limo ride from my
place to the counselor's office. The usual questioning scowl was
lost behind the creases his brow was creating. He was curious,

concerned even, but was it fueled by how I was handling things, or wonder at how I hadn't managed to shatter into a million pieces.

I let him revel in his curiosity, neither giving the inch or the mile he would eventually expect. Once the door to that gate was opened, I fear daddy would never let it close. His, 'I told you so', quota is far from being met in my life, in this case, I would avoid hearing those four gruesome words for as long as possible.

But that's it though, isn't it. Daddy was itching to say something I completely agree with him on. He did tell me that Brent Bishop would do nothing but destroy my life, and look at the outcome. He was right, and I never understood why.

Dana would argue that none of this was Brent's faults, but I wouldn't know what Dana is saying these days. None of the girls in fact. I read what Ivy posted a couple weeks back, but this is not self proclamation. I am not shutting everyone out; on the contrary, I have all linked them to this blog. They will have, for the time being, what everyone else has. The same piece of me as those who read the inner brewing thoughts I give each week.

But, Dana would suggest that Brent is as innocent as I am (and that would seriously piss me off). Ivy would work on distracting me with anything quick and easy; work perhaps (and I'm not really in the mood). She knows all too well how specifically my ADD works and exactly what it is that easily sways my attention.

Amy....not that I've spoken to her in any capacity since before my accident, but Amy would suggest a stiff drink or two and a beautiful man. I can smile and admit that her proposition would be the one I'd go for right now.

No.... Daddy was always right about Brent Bishop; I just couldn't fully understand the capacity for his hatred until this week. The story, the rants of my being business, and always being kept at arm's length...it was because some skeletons were being rattled a tad too loudly.... But I will get to that in a moment.

247

By the time the limo had reached the building I was to spend the next hour in and be expected to release all the emotions that had been building up, I was ready to hear whatever daddy was building up for me.

At first, I thought that talking about the accident would be difficult, but in fact it's been much like telling a story. Recalling something that's been playing in my head over and over and just painting a picture with words for someone else to know about. I didn't cry when I told her about the walk up to the street corner.

She asked me if I could remember what Klive and I were discussing before I was pushed....and I do. Klive was nagging me about Genevieve, the main character in my book. He had made a comment about not liking her, that she bothers him. I laughed, and then.......that's it. I don't remember anything after that, other than waking up to everyone in my room. That's when life changed.

The grief counselor asked questions but all I could focus on was remembering waking up. The anguish on everyone's faces, the tears they were trying so hard to hold back. They weren't tears of relief...Thinking about it now, I wonder if any of them thought it best I didn't wake up. I mean, I would never have to hurt.

I didn't tell the grief counselor that.....I know my friends wanted me to wake up.

~Sigh~

The can of worms she opened up was something I hadn't expected.

She asked if I had spoken to the father of the baby I'd lost. I know my face flushed several hot shades of red as I could feel the heat rising from my center.

Anger. Resentment. Blame. Those are the three words that form every time I make the connection between Brent and my baby.

I was nice to the lady; God knows she isn't to blame for anything that I'm going through. My lack of desire to answer the question prompted the remainder of my week.

"It will be hard to talk to him, of that you can be sure, but you should think of finding closure so that moving on will happen smoothly. Otherwise, the healing process will take so much longer."

I nodded, agreeing only because I was itching to leave. The idea of being back in a limo with Daddy seemed so much more appealing than sitting across from a person who merely wanted to pry every deep dark emotion from the parking spot it had placed itself in my soul.

It wasn't until the flood gates with my father opened that I wished I was back in the counselor's quiet office.

"How was your session?" he asked curiously.

"It was fine."

That was when he made the first sarcastic huff. "Everything is Fine with you, isn't it?"

My reaction was smug. I stared out the tinted windows begging for my street to come quickly.

"Did you even talk to her?"

Sighing, I could do nothing more than to give him the play by play.

He said nothing until Brent's name was brought up.

"Why does she want you to talk to him? Doesn't she know that he is the reason you are in this mess to begin with?" he lashed out.

"Jesus Dad, I can't read her mind."

"Don't you even think for one second that talking to him will change anything. He is a bastard for what he's done to you."

"Wait," I paused him. "What he's done to me? Is there something I'm missing here?" I couldn't help but question my father. He always knows more than he is ever willing to share. His, I know what's best for you, ideals always chiming in with handing out information.

"That man comes from a long line of bastards, Melissa. He is just like his father, playing with women's emotions, ignoring what's right to satisfy the ambitious need to be better than everyone else."

I had to digest what he confessed before I could ask to know what he meant by it. Truthfully, Daddy sounded a lot like a scorned man than an upset one. For a moment, maybe I believed it was just my imagination but the way he was sitting in his seat suggested that every muscle in his body was tense. What he was holding on to internally was eating him alive.

"What did Brent's father do to you, Daddy?" A simple question that got me a scowl.

"It doesn't matter now. You are better off without Brent in your life…"

I had to interrupt. That is how it always goes, the 'Trust Me' mentality that says nothing other than: Do what I'm telling you to do.

"No, I think after what I've been through, I deserve to know why the father of my dead baby is Off limits."

He turned to me, his whole body shifting. Face square to mine, "His father had an affair with your mother when we were young. She left me just after you were born. Right around the same time my company fell short and we lost a major business deal. Turns out, Bishop engineered the whole situation to weaken me, distract me, and take my eye off the ball. When your mother came to realize she had been used…." He hesitated, coming out of the memory. He looked at me, questioning himself, "She was pregnant, with Bishop's child."

My hands shot straight up to cover my mouth. Shock. No wonder there was so much bad blood.

"What happened to that baby?" I asked, cautiously of course.

"Melissa, that family, All of them are bad news. Forget the man; he will only hurt you in the end."

Realizing he hadn't answered my question, only skirted around it, had me understanding it was something he was unwilling to talk about. "You're right, you know." I admitted, realizing that we had finally reached my street.

"And Daddy, he has already hurt me. Not much more to it than that." I kissed his cheek and left the limo. My awkward walk to my place was short, but not without wonder.

Sitting on my doorstep was a face I wasn't expecting, but didn't mind seeing.

Klive sat there, reading a novel, waiting for me. The smile my presence produced was interesting. Am I still capable of doing that? Making a man happy I've arrived.

"Marcus said you were going to be back around now. I had a few questions for you but the email I started was confusing so I figured we could just work it out in person. Is that okay?"

Hmmmm....Pretty wordy for a simple, We have work to do, statement.

"Yeah, if you do something for me." I stated boldly.

"Anything." He shot it out a little too quickly, which in turn had him laughing that nervous laugh he does.

Unlocking my door, I asked the favor to end all favors, "Be by my side as I talk to Brent."

Readers comment:

Anonymous   <u>March 13, 2014</u>
I understand your father being angry and upset with Brent's father but it really has nothing to do with Brent himself. Go talk with him and clear the air. I'm glad you went to talk to someone. It may help you with the grieving process.
~ALF~

Anonymous   <u>March 13, 2014</u>
Oh Come On! Are you telling me you are actually contemplating going to see that man after everything. Just leave well enough alone.
OrioleCal

Anonymous   <u>March 14, 2014</u>
For a minute there I thought you gave up blogging, but damned enough here it is.

Anonymous   <u>March 14, 2014</u>
Call Me!
-Amy

Anonymous   <u>M arch 15, 2014</u>
Yeah, go ahead and blame the guy, but honey, it ain't his fault you got in over your head. You need to grow up! You lost your baby because you do nothing but make bad choice after bad choice. Going to see Brent is a BAD choice! Leave him be already.
Nancy

The first thought that passes through a person's mind when confronted with a serious question, is whether or not they take the time to answer reasonably. There are, on occasion, moments where words rattle out creating the illusion of a response, but the truth remains that those moments are irrelevant.

At least they should be considered neither here nor there.

God knows I've tried to be rational, let my emotions go on the way side while speaking to certain people, but sometimes I fail, and miserably at that.

Last week Klive agreed to accompany me to speak with Brent. This was all well and good until I read some of the comments in response to that blog.

The anonymous comments caused my head to tilt in thought.

It boiled down to: 'do I', or 'don't I?'

*Do I call Amy as she asked?

*Do I just leave Brent be?

*Do I make it a point to find out the whole truth about my mother?

It is with all the time in the world that I find myself confined to a chair in front of my laptop with nothing to say. I feared, for a brief moment, that my muse had been suffocated, my curiosity stifled, and my wonder would never visit me again.

Fear itself is a crippling disease, a sickness of the mind that could easily overpower the body. Sadly, there is no mental antidote to cure fear. Willpower is generally the only method to conquer it, and yet, I've hardly been known to contain enough of it on my own.

I read on someone's twitter feed, When all else fails, go back to the beginning and retrace your steps.

So I did that.

I went back to April 8th, 2013. Just shy of a year ago, when I started writing this blog. Back when it was a weekly ritual to attend fashionable events that Ivy or Amy would get us VIP passes for. There was no concern of word count, or content. I wasn't constantly battling with a publishing company as to when my next book would be released nor an editor about my character's obvious flaws. I hadn't lost anything, and the possibilities were endless. I hadn't been scarred by sadness or loss and my wholeness was still intact.

Does it really matter how we get to where we are? Every step of the way, reality formed into a form of chaos that I'd never thought to be a part of.

~shakes head~

That chaos ends today. The thicker skin set in, and I stretched into it and found a formidable woman, the one I've become because of all the scars this past year has created.

Why the change of heart?   Two words….. I'm tired.

It's exhausting being depressed and angry. In the past 9 days I have gone through a sequence of phases that everyone thinks of as a normal progression of loss, but to me, there is nothing normal about it.

I grieved a future as a mother by rejecting everyone I cared about, became angry at a man who betrayed me, blamed myself for not seeing the signs of Megan's hatred, almost lost my muse due to a dark sadness I'd never experienced before and finally……Finally, I accepted what was never going to be.

It's taxing on the soul to fight grief. So I let it be, found the strength to transition, and here I am, on the other side, looking back and feeling a terrible weight having lifted from my heart.

What helped?

I let Klive take me to see Brent. It was the best thing that could have happened. Thinking back, the encounter rippled into all the other stages...

"Are you sure you want to do this?" Klive asked, his hand firmly gripping the taxi cab inner door handle.

It makes me wonder if men realize how obvious they are when they feel concern for another person. Their eyebrows, while not intentionally creasing together, form worry lines between them.

With Klive, I knew what he felt before he opened his mouth.

"With you by my side, I could do anything." I admitted willfully.

Do I mean it? – That remains to be seen.

Accepting my response, he opened the door and let us out of the taxi that sat directly in front of Mr. NY's office building.

How many times had I come to this very building, looked up and felt courage and conviction? My, my, how time changes us. I felt ....numb. I knew why I was there but had to look up to remember what it once felt like.

"Everything is different now." I whispered quietly, not sure if my words would travel in the afternoon breeze.

"And in time, this too will seem easier." Klive added.

I dared not look to him then, he took my hand and tugged me along to the doors and into the elevator.

Funny how I once wrote about that elevator, and how they made me feel....in <u>Love in the End</u>, she found herself staring at her reflection in an elevator. Her imagination got the better of her and she saw a face other than her own staring back at her.

"Klive, do you think Cain reminded you of Brent or On'rie?"

"Why do you ask?"

"Curious, I suppose. You have so many opinions where my characters are concerned."

A chuckle escaped him and he turned to face me, "Not all of them, only the ones that don't seem real." He replied, his amusement clear.

"She is real enough to me."

He shook his head at me and the elevator arrived at its destination.

"It's now or never."

"Indeed it is." He added, taking my hand in his own once more and leading the way to Brent's secretary.

She recognized me immediately, rounding her desk and reaching out to offer her condolences.

"My dear, I am so sorry for what you have been through."

I'd gotten a lot of that lately, having come out of the shadows and back into the real world.

"Is he in?" my voice cracked and weak.

She looked from me to Klive, "Well, he is in, but I'm not sure if he will take you both."

"Would you ask if we could come in? I'd rather not intrude today." I offered.

As she walked back around her desk, I noticed how Klive was focused on the windows behind me.

We waited, but it didn't take long for her to come back to tell us to go on back to his office. It never occurred to me to worry if he would see me or not, a part of me just knew he wouldn't say no.

Just before we reached the door, Klive let go of my hand and whispered, "I will be right behind you the whole time."

I entered the room first, and saw Brent sitting at the edge of his desk waiting for me. He was always waiting.

"I am surprised, to say the least." He began. "When you didn't return any of my calls, I just assumed the silence was my answer, that you aren't interested in forgiving me."

Shame on him for assuming.

"No, you are right to believe that sentiment, Brent. I will never forgive you for what Megan did." I retorted, my spine straightening slightly.

"M, you have to believe that I never, in a million years, imagined she would take things to where she did." He tried to argue.

My hand lifted, "Just stop. I'm not here to listen to your ignorance, Brent."

"Ignorance!" he shouted back, his body leaving the desk and taking a step closer to us.

"Yes, that is exactly what you've been. You were naive to think that she, a business deal, would accept any entanglements we might share. "

"You are the naïve one, Melissa. You lied to me for months and now you are blaming me for what happened to you." He countered, throwing his hands in the air and turning back to his desk.

With his reaction I felt myself turning to see Klive standing behind me. He was a statue, my pillar of strength, the one I trusted to bring me here. His lips pursed together and he slightly tilted his head, as if saying, 'tell him the truth'.

I nodded, knowing what would come next.

The moment my eyes locked back on to Brent, I felt the anger inside ready to be released.

"Our baby is dead, Brent, and we will never get him back. That future, the one filled with dreams and happiness is gone. Stop calling me. Stop asking for forgiveness. You chose her, and ultimately, in doing so, you lost every right to feel anything for me. Don't grieve this baby, it may have shared your blood but damn it Brent, it would still be thriving had you not chosen her. "

"So that's it then. You are going to punish me. Push me away, and what? Move on to someone like the man who's behind you? What is he, your new boyfriend?"

That was right about the time I felt the freedom. How the blood in my system boiled, not with anger or resentment, but with the conviction I'd not felt since before the accident.

I didn't answer Brent's question as to who Klive was. In fact, I turned around and made my way out of the office. Klive followed behind me, neither saying a word nor slowing my step when I began to hear the crashing of glass from Brent's office.

The whole way back to my place, in the cab, he stared at me. Probably in awe. I know, in some small way I too was in awe of myself.

"Would you like company?" he asked as we reached my house.

"You know, I have some phone calls to make. Appointments to schedule. I have been in seclusion longer than I should have." I started, "Come by in the morning, bring me some coffee." I smiled, reaching out and squeezing his hand.

"Tomorrow it is then."

I called Amy and made amends with her. Don't be angry with her, she isn't the sort to handle emotional situations well. My predicament forced her to realize how much she cared about the man she chose to be in love with.

Marcus and Ivy were thrilled I was coming out of the shadows, and have Big plans ahead.

There is one thing I have yet to deal with....and am not sure which way to go with it. My book, the one that is coming out in a couple months.

Klive is worried about my character, Genevieve. He seems unable to accept her flaws, her immoral sense of living, but sheesh, she is just a character.

I've been going in circles and it all boils down to one question:

What is he really worried about?

Readers comment:

Anonymous   March 21, 2014
First, I'm happy that you are beginning to "live" again. I'm also happy that you made amends with Amy and went to see Brent for some type of closure. That will help the healing process a little bit. I know you've had some harsh comments but don't listen to the "HATERS". They will always "hate". Especially, don't listen to the idiot that said you lost your baby because it was your fault. IT WAS NOT YOUR FAULT!!! (just wanted to make sure everyone heard that) The jealous and hateful little bitch, Megan, is the reason you lost your baby. You may have made some bad choices but haven't we all? My last words of advice to you is to take time to heal and look forward to the future...
~ALF~

Tuesday, April 1, 2014
Possibilities
Season 3 Episode 9

Wanting to know something is completely different from Needing to know.

At around 6 or 7 years old, in school, we are taught the differences between needs and wants. The fact that people in general have difficulties with mastering that little concept all throughout their lives is a little mystery no one really worries about.

We struggle our entire lives never understanding the difference between what is necessary compared to indulgences we feel are uber important.

I know you get what I'm saying; we have all faced this in our lives.

My current desire is slowing becoming an obsession – a Needing to know something that was once based on just a wanting to know.

I found myself unable to write anything this past week because of the need that has consumed all my thoughts.

Daddy's little confession regarding my mother having had an illegitimate child by my father's 'arch nemesis', Mr. Charles Bishop – Brent's father, was not only a shocker but turns out to be a real thought provoker.

Looking back at my childhood, the manner in which she mothered us, and even the times she disregarded us, a lot of it now makes little sense. I'd always believe she just had her moments, and sometimes didn't care, but the truth could be far more complicated.

My father turned out to be of little help, and it may have been just his way of trying to seal off a can of worms he now realizes he'd opened.

"Melissa, don't go down this road." He started, his nerves clearly aggravated. I could tell by the way his forehead forced worry lines to show.

"Daddy, you can't just tell me something like that and honestly believe I'm not going to ask you questions. I mean, Shit. It really is rather unbelievable that no one has ever said anything, that the tabloids didn't get wind of it."

"Look here young lady, our family name has taken a lot of heat because of you. Don't be like your mother and smear the empire I've built because of your selfish need to know something that has been locked away for a lifetime. It's none of your business."

"Selfish need, are you flipping kidding me. I am your daughter, for Christ sakes. I'm a part of this family, and if mom had another kid, I have the right to know about that person."

"That person, Melissa, is Not your family. Get that through your pretty little head. Accept it and move on. I'm warning you. This is off limits." His tone was clear, I was not to go meddling.

But Daddy knows me better than that. It was concern in his voice that slowed me down.
I brought the subject up to Marcus later on after my discussion with my father. His take was completely different.

"There is a story there for sure my dear. Even if you don't look into it, you will find yourself creating a scenario to replace the answers you're not getting."

"So you think I should look into it?" I inquired cautiously.

He raised his wine glass, smile and replied, "I think you should do what your conscience will be able to live with."

A chuckle erupted from my chest, and without realizing it, I was laughing at the idea that I would listen to my conscience.

"Indeed a humorous idea my dear, but be cautious which road you find yourself going down." His words, stopped me cold. "I don't mean it to alarm you, but a man like your father is not one to trifle with. You may be his daughter, but as he referred to it, his empire has been his life's work. For the sake of his company, I feel your father is the type of man to sell his soul to the devil to keep it from crumbling to ash."

The warning was simple, and yet, the longer I stared at Marcus going on about it as if the statement was one of a light hearted conversation forced me to realize I was too naïve to see my father as anything other than just Daddy.

"He wouldn't hurt me, though." I found myself saying out loud after a while of silence.

His movements stopped and he looked up from my manuscript, "That is the bigger question, isn't it. Do you trust in him so much that you would defy his orders?"

It is in those involuntary moments in our lives that we pause momentarily, the movements in which curiosity pushes us towards and treat said situation like a wicked chessboard.

Later on, a few days in fact, I found myself having coffee with Klive in a coffee shop on the outskirts of Central Park. At first I thought he would be a fabulous distraction, that is, until we started talking about possible storylines for my next manuscript. From what I've been told, my lack of desire to complete the current piece is a typical writer flaw. So, on we go to create what will come next.

Funny little thing about that is, Klive is still caught up on Dear Eliza, and thinks I should find retribution with the next story.

"Truth is Melissa, you are going to have a bit of backlash when this Eliza one comes out." He said, shaking his head the way he does when he wants to argue a fact. "They are going to want more, but with a better ending."

"It won't take too long to get the next one up and at'em, I just need the right inspiration."

The statement caught his attention rather quickly, "what do you mean by that?"

"You know, I mean, with the first I had Paris and On'rie. This last one is an obvious reaction to my turbulent relationship with Brent and with loss in general." My eyes fell to the mocha color of my coffee and how tiny my hands seemed holding the warm mug.

"Paris is a beautiful place in the spring." He commented off hand, a smile creeping across his gorgeous face.

"Yes, well the summer was seductive enough for one lifetime."

His eyebrow raised and we both laughed at my silliness. "I suppose a trip wouldn't be scandalous. Not like this, I mean. We could go and see where the inspiration leads us."

"Us?" he asked, catching on to my play on words.

"Well, I mean, it would be much easier if you edited While I wrote. The manuscript would be just about ready by the time I get to, The End."

"So you are asking me to go on a trip with you?" he said as he crossed his arms across his chest, his voice much more seductive than I could have ever imagined.

"Klive, it's a business trip." I lied to myself with those 4 words. It was much more than business, we both knew it.

He nodded, looked away for a flash of a second then back; his eyes met mine.

"Yes." He stated plainly.

Eyebrows burrowing together, "Yes, what?" I asked.

"Yes I will run away with you." The words came out followed by a grin that said more than the words.

"But we are not…" I tried to clarify.

"Shhhh…." He cut me off, his fingers gently reaching out and softly touching my lips.

"Let your imagination take you to a place you've never been. Tell a story capable of stealing my breath." He whispered so close to me I could feel the heat radiating from his body.

Could it be that Klive is my new muse? That all I really need is to have the right sort of man to fill the shoes of my sexual inspiration?

The moment I got back home, sat down at my laptop, I knew what the story was that I had to write.

Yes, I perceive that eventually I will be asking questions my father would rather I not ask. I can't ignore the greater need to learn the truth about the woman I call mother, and a sibling I knew nothing about.

A trip with Klive isn't my idea of running away from anything. In fact, I can't compare this trip to the one I took to Paris at all. I'm not pinning over a man who broke my heart. I'm not even running from my emotions at having lost my child. I've dealt with both losses, grown from them, but I refuse to allow the growth to scare away a muse I've grown rather fond of.

Tuesday, April 8, 2014
Simply Said
Season 3 Episode 10

Simply put, there are several things you should Never do when trying to put yourself back together...in my case, build a repertoire of condemnable qualities...but let's focus on the 'shoulds'...

First off, eat lunch. No matter what the reason may be, if you are single in Manhattan, Lunch is the difference between lightweight and shoulder weight. (Drinks were on Amy! I took advantage)

Next up, Think before you speak, step, and slap. (Blushes on the last) A lady shouldn't have a foul mouth, being tipsy is no reason to stumble in heels, and well... There are no excuses for bitch slapping someone we loathe. (I ran into Brent while under said champagne spell)

Of all thing, laugh at the little things. And I don't mean, echem...'little things' (wink, wink). I'm simply saying that when someone, anyone, wants to argue about an idea, or process, let them say what they want and move on. So for example, when Klive compared me to the main character in Dear Eliza, stating that he finally understands where I draw the chaos she creates....it would have been easier to laugh at him. ~Did I though...not a chance. No, I took off my high heel, shook it at him and chased him in the rain for about 5 minutes before I found myself laughing at the drunken nonsense!

Also, when you get a wakeup call from your friend, say thank you...calling her 5 letter words first thing in the morning causes for a thousand apologies later...(when the coffee has had time to jog your memory). Dana is getting married. Her single status is permanently no longer in service! Congrats to her!

Finally...and yes, this week is short and simple. Always ask the right questions. Don't worry about the right or wrong, easy or difficult ones....ALWAYS ask the question that will produce the precise response you need. Liquid courage does a lot of things, many bad but the one good it did me was ask 2 people similar questions.

1. My mother...I asked her to tell me about the child she had with Charles Bishop. Her response, while shocking was genuine. She only knows that it was a girl and that Charles took her.

2. Was to Brent (before I slapped him of course) I asked him if he knew of our parents having had an affair. His response, callous and cruel pinned my emotions against the wall, "My father and your mother paid the same price we did at your fathers expense." The slap came out of nowhere....

Maybe it was his voice that just angered me...or just maybe I knew what his response would be.

He took a hold of my wrist and smashed my body to his, "M, the truth will destroy 2 empires. Leave this be."

As a viper would look at its prey before striking, my words danced in front of him. "The truth will set us free. And so it shall be."

Simply said, the answer has always been right in front of me. Why hide a secret in the darkness when no one will look in plain sight.

The secrets that we keep.....are never really secrets that we can hide.

Readers comment:

   Anonymous   April 08, 2014
   I don't get why Brent blames your father for your messed up relationship. Didn't you leave Brent to begin with? How is that Bergman's fault?
   Meredith

DancingQueen <u>April 08, 2014</u>
OMG! What if Brent was the love child!

Anonymous <u>April 09, 2014</u>
Who is Dana marrying? I missed this!
OrioleCal

Tuesday, April 15, 2014
Her eyes gave it away
Season 3 Episode 10

Last week I made my blog short and sweet. Mostly because I've been so overwhelmed with life that the little things became tedious.

I will admit, plainly, that finding out I had another sibling out there in the span of the world, threw me for a loop. Everything I had ever thought in life, all the conclusions about my parents' relationship I'd made, have been shattered; turned to dust in this quest for the truth.

But now, the truth itself is rather unbelievable. Shit, I have a great imagination; can spin a tale like the best of them, cliffhangers and all, but the pieces that I'm unfolding don't add up.

Brent blames Daddy- Of course. Swears that his father is a good man. On the contrary, my father points to Charles and deems him the devil incarnate. My mother shakes her head, waves her hand as though my questions will vanish into the air we breathe.

I will assure you, I am not giving up. I am in fact, my father's daughter.

Being a Bergman meant something once, a long time ago. The little girl I use to be...bright eyed and in awe of the power my father wielded. He would take me into his office, in the tallest building in New York City and I would just watch him order people around. I never wondered or worried about a thing, he was always one step ahead of the game. Even knew what people would ask before the words left their mouth. His response ready to fire.

This might be why he has only had one response for me in the past 2 weeks. 'Let this go, Melissa!'

While the firmness has increased with every one of the 4 words, I'm sure his resolve is teetering at a rupture point. I mean, how much more can one person take?

I will say, the moment Brent expressed his disdain for my desire to know the truth I found myself wanting to know so much more. The magnification of this need had me sitting back early last week after my blog.

I mean, really? I know the truth is insane, but his statement was, 'Bring down 2 empires'….My face scrunches every time I think about it.

Klive, while still annoyed by my drunken immaturity, was willing to work peacefully on the final revisions of 'Dear Eliza' at Marcus' place.

"I think that's it. We should be good to send it to print." He paused dramatically. "Luckily, the distractions didn't get in the way."

"I'm not distracted, Klive. I'm A.D.D. I must have 5 different tasks going on at once for any one of those to see a completion."

"So this sibling hunt is a task then?"

What could I do but stare at him.

No. I don't see it as a task. Nor a treasure hunt, as my brother threw at me earlier this week.

"I need to know."

"Yes, I get that. But you need to look at the bigger picture Melissa. Your loved ones are insisting that you leave this be. Warning you that uncovering the truth will bring nothing but a colossal mess."

"Hold on a second, Brent is not a loved one." I shot back at him.

"Thou dost protest too much!" he sarcastically countered. The grin slowly stretching across his face.

Inwardly I was all, 'yeah, yeah, yeah' but in truth, finishing Dear Eliza has me accepting certain truths of my own.

My silence made things awkward.

"I thought…" he started.

"I know." I stopped him. "I'm sorry Klive. I suppose I would equate him to being my Henry."

"and what, you're Genevieve?" he said, pausing before adding, "I can't accept that Melissa. Everything is a game to him, or as he puts it…Business."

"As much as I hate to admit this, he is my polar north."

"You are not a Magnet, Melissa!" Klive got up from the sofa across from me and paced the length of Marcus' living room.

"He won't even tell you who your sibling is. What type of love hides things?"

"I don't need him to tell me who my sibling is, Klive." I admitted without thinking the statement through.

His movements stopped and I felt the heat of is questioning glare upon my being before he even said a word.

"What was that?"

My eyes lifted to meet him, his face shifting from annoyed to questioning to even a spark of concern. The truth is, my imagination did the math the moment Daddy told me about said Love Child. As I said last week, the easiest place to hide any secret is in the open daylight. Why question the unquestionable. A tale being thread through a golden spindle would never be torn apart. Charles Bishop sits at the tip of a golden empire. His children have always been the center of his universe, the obvious was to look to his own children.

"Brent's little sister has my eyes."

Readers comment:

Anonymous   April 30, 2014

That man is so in love with you it's crazy. And I don't mean Brent! You need to think long and hard about what you want out of your future, because the love that lasts forever is with the man who knows who you are, the good and the bad.
Meredith

Anonymous   April 30, 2014

Don't listen to anyone. Go with your heart this time instead of your head. But tell him he needs to start divorce proceedings with Megan before you get back together. Klive may love you but you don't love him so he needs to know that now. He will get over it soon enough. Be honest with Brent, let him know that you and Klive spoke and there is no romantic relationship between you two.
~ ALF~

Anonymous   May 01, 2014

Just don't run off to Paris with Klive.
OrioleCal

Tuesday May 13, 2014
And So It Goes
Season 3 Finale

Little much of anything can surprise me anymore. I say this because I am never in the loop of what I suspect is the whole picture, therefore, I am forever waiting on the rest of the story.

I will admit to you a little secret I hadn't planned on telling anyone, at least not for a while at least.

All this time, since the moment I met Brent, I thought I had met my soul mate. Trial and tribulations are meant to test us, and with all of that, my heart still aches for him.

Now, does this mean I will have my happily ever after with him?

Even now, I can't say for sure, but I can say, I learned a little something from my own writing.

The afternoon, before my book release event, I had to go see Klive. Dressed in my Chanel, heels to the brim, and courage gripped firmly in my palms.

I was taking him my new manuscript. He'd asked what I would be working on next....little did he know I had already started on the next chapter in my life.

"What is this?" he asked as I handed it to him, standing in the center of his living room.

"It is insurance." I tried not to smile, but I sensed he caught the flicker the corners of my mouth took in an upward movement.

"I don't understand."

Of course he didn't, most men don't.

"You are amazing at what you do. I find myself at a crossroads with which direction I want to take with my life. Literary wise as well as personal." I shook my head, looking around, finding the right words to express this next part without leaving questions floating between us.

"You are an important force in my life, and I cherish your place in it. You've become a sort of conscience I never thought I could have, but with that being said, there is a wall that prevents me from making those emotions flourish into anything more than they are."

"Brent….Brent is that wall." He stated.

"I love him. I always have. I can't make myself un-love him."

Klive sighed, slid his fingers through his hair and stared at me.

"That feeling you carry around for him, the magnet that attracts you to him…I have that too, but for you."

"Klive…" I started.

"No, don't." he put his hand up, his body inching closer to mine.

"That day I held you in my arms, your body almost lifeless, was one of the most life altering moments in my life. It hit me in those moments that I had never told you how amazing you are, and how incredibly talented you are. I'd never had the courage to take you into my arms and show you how much I've always wanted you, to show you how much you mean to me."

I could feel the heat from his body, and his gorgeous eyes lulling me into a trance. His hand gently caressed my upper arm as he continued to inch forward.

"Courage is a tricky little thing." I whispered softly.

"Indeed it is." He murmured just before his lips touched mine.

There have been times, I will admit, that my choices have created loud sirens to go off in my pretty little head. Those are usually the moments I know I shouldn't be doing something in particular.

God help me, but the more I kissed Klive back, the more I waited for those sirens to go off, and they never did. I stood there, staring at him, and wondered to myself, 'What now?'

Klive drove me through what seemed like endless traffic to the book release. The two of us on opposite ends of his car in silence. The whole way, I found myself absentmindedly touching my lips.

The awkwardness didn't end once we arrived either. In fact, Klive escorted me into the building as if we were an item. His hand on the small of my back, photographers snapping from every corner.

Marcus met us at the door, and Ivy was ready for the festivities with her clipboard in hand. She had reporters from the papers waiting for comments and a snip-it from the book.

After the initial world wind entrance, I noticed Ben at the bar and found my way to say hi to him. He turned to see me just as I reached him.

"Mon Cheri, you are a sight for sore eyes." He greeted, per his charming self.

"I'm so glad you could come."

"and I, honored you wanted me here." He responded quickly.

"Are you kidding me, without you, none of this would have ever happened. No matter what."

"You give me too much credit, but I adore you for it."

He pulled me into a hug and I felt myself wanting to cry. Felt myself wanting to run away again.

The tears filled my eyes and I hid my face in his chest.

"What's wrong?" he hushed into my ear.

All I could do was shake my head.

"Everything is all wrong. Nothing turned out the way it was suppose to, Ben."

"Come, Come now. You're just emotional with all the hoopla tonight."

My head snapped up at him, but I couldn't say anything. My eyes were filled with tears and I was basically surrounded by hundreds of people I didn't know.

He took out a handkerchief and blotted under my eyes.

"Don't mess up your makeup. Ivy will have a fit if the pictures aren't perfect." He chuckled.

His smile creating the reaction I expect he was working for, because I giggled in response.

We were interrupted by a New York Times reporter and the night started with questions about the book.

Dear Eliza was an instant hit. A woman's book, a realistic tale of what a woman goes through as she falls in love.

At some point in the night, I read to the crowd about love not being easy. Explained how, even if we find love, the perfection behind it is an illusion. Talked about perception being 99% of the problem.

At one point, I looked out into the crowd and saw three faces staring at me. Brent, my father, and Klive. The three men in my life that are currently making it hard for me to understand love.

Brent, says he loves me, but hasn't made an attempt to divorce his wife who tried to have me murdered. Preaches his undying devotion for our love but there is doubt that shrouds my acceptance of it.

My father, says he loves me, but lied to me my whole life about a sibling. While a part of me understand the situation, I don't know how to get past the fact that he could have, at one point told me the truth.

Klive, has never uttered the words, but God help me, I believe him. 100%.

I paused and read a poem from the novel....

'Fairytales have, 'the end' while reality has tomorrow.
Stories have laughter and life is filled with sorrows.
With every smile, a tear is equally shed,
But love is not woven with endless moments of perfection.
The forever kind is flawed and scarred like a colorful thread.'

I could see that the three of them understood the meaning behind the words. Reality creates fiction, which creates reality. My truth stands firm. Love has never been easy for me, most of the time it's the hardest emotion for me to understand, but knowing who you can love with least effort chimes a clear picture at the end of the day. Patience, endurance, trust, faith....I feel all of those emotions surging through my system every time I think of Klive. My heart swayed to the most unlikely character and I realized that while love is difficult, it is also what makes us who we are.

When the night was over, the crowd dispersed and I sat at the bar drinking a stiff scotch. I knew Klive was still roaming around with Marcus, and would find him soon enough and tell him how I felt.

Brent walked over to where I sat staring at my crystal glass.

"Great night." he mused.

"Yeah, among all things, I came to a conclusion you've been waiting for." My eyes stayed on the sweating glass.

I heard him sigh and felt as his body shifted his weight from one side to the other.

"Timing has never been on our side, has it?"

That was when my head turned and I looked at him....I really saw him. "It has never been about timing, Brent." I sighed.

"We are complicated. Plain and simple. Love is many things, but nothing like what we have."

My words silenced him, and I found myself watching him head for the door and leave into the night.

I was not surprised however when Daddy came to sit next to me.

"I'll have what she is having." He ordered the bartender.

"Not the night you expected?" he asked, his demeanor somewhat curious.

"Tell me, Daddy…" I started, taking a sip before I laid it all out on the line.

"Did you orchestrate my relationship with Todd knowing he was having an affair with Brent's wife?"

I didn't have to look at my father's face to know he was shocked I was being so blunt.

I did anyway to gauge the truth behind his response. Sadly it was his pause which gave him away.

"Melissa…" he tried.

"No, Daddy, don't. I can only imagine how much your guilt has been eating away at you."

April Gutierrez

There was shame, guilt, and sadness I saw in the shadow clouding his demeanor. He was no longer that tyrant that I was afraid of, but someone I now understood.

"So much so I have done something I thought I never would." He said as he drank his scotch in one gulp.

"Turn around Melissa." He ordered, looking at me as the loving father I grew up with usually did.

Why was I afraid? .....deep down I knew what he had done, the only thing that would ever repair my relationship with him.

She stood behind me, the sister I never had the chance to know.

Samantha Bishop, smiling at me with tears in her eyes.

"I didn't believe him at first, but looking at you, I know he isn't lying. You are my sister." She smiled.

Reaching out, I pulled her into a hug and instantly felt the connection.

Tomorrow is not promised, but today and how we choose to live it, is what makes life worth living.

Thank you for this past year,
Melissa Green